SOUTHERNMOST

Southernmost

———

A NOVEL

SILAS HOUSE

ALGONQUIN BOOKS OF CHAPEL HILL 2018

Published by
ALGONQUIN BOOKS OF CHAPEL HILL
Post Office Box 2225
Chapel Hill, North Carolina 27515-2225

a division of
WORKMAN PUBLISHING
225 Varick Street
New York, New York 10014

LIBRARY OF CONGRESS CATALOGING-IN-PUBLICATION DATA
Names: House, Silas, 1971– author.
Title: Southernmost / a novel by Silas House.
Description: First edition. | Chapel Hill, North Carolina :
Algonquin Books of Chapel Hill, 2018. | "Published simultaneously
in Canada by Thomas Allen & Son Limited."
Identifiers: LCCN 2017047856 (print) | LCCN 2017050189 (ebook) |
ISBN 9781616208295 (ebook) | ISBN 9781616206253 (hardcover : alk. paper)
Subjects: LCSH: Clergy—Fiction. | Fathers and sons—Fiction. | Gay men—Family
relationships—Fiction. | Parental kidnapping—Fiction. | Tennessee—Fiction.
Classification: LCC PS3558.O8659 (ebook) |
LCC PS3558.O8659 S68 2018 (print) | DDC 813/.6—dc23
LC record available at https://lccn.loc.gov/2017047856

10 9 8 7 6 5 4 3 2 1
First Edition

For
Jason Kyle Howard

Try to walk this earth an honest man
but evil waves at me its ugly hand.
The radar watches me from above, shoutin' down:
"I hope you make it on this earth."
Sometimes this world will leave you, Lord,
kickin' and a-screamin', wonderin' if
you'll see the next day through.
But as for me I do believe
that good luck comes from tryin',
so until I get mine
I'll work the whole day through.

—JIM JAMES, "Honest Man"

The river is within us, the sea is all about us.

—T. S. ELIOT, *The Dry Salvages*

SOUTHERNMOST

PART ONE

This Is to Mother You

1.

The rain had been falling with a pounding meanness, without ceasing for two days, and then the water rose all at once in the middle of the night, a brutal rush so fast Asher thought at first a dam might have broken somewhere upstream. The ground had simply become so saturated it could not hold any more water. All the creeks were conspiring down the ridges until they washed out into the Cumberland. There was no use in anyone going to bed because they all knew what was going to happen. They only had to wait.

The day dawned without any sign of sun—a sky that groaned open from a black night to a dull, purpling gray of morning—and

Asher went out to walk the ridge and get a full eye on the situation. The news wasn't telling them anything worthwhile. He could hear the flood before he reached the top of the ridge. There he saw the massively swollen river supping at the edges of the lower fields, ten feet above its own banks, a foamy broth climbing so steadily he could actually see its ascent, and then he knew he had to go get Zelda.

They had all thought the last flood was as bad as things could get but the water hadn't risen half this quickly. He maneuvered his Jeep across two bridges whose undersides were being caressed by the river and by the time he got to her house the water was nipping at her porch. He had to park on the rise at the top of her driveway and wade into waist-deep water that took his breath with its iciness. Zelda stood on the porch like a statue of an old woman, clutching a stack of picture albums. That was all she had grabbed.

"Come on!" Asher hollered. The river raged so loudly he wasn't sure if she could hear him and she made no motion to acknowledge she had.

But then Zelda took a step forward and froze; he could see she was terrified. Zelda had been on this very porch the first time he ever met her. She had risen from her chair to embrace him, holding him the way his own mother never had. Another memory, too: they had gone wading in the Cumberland on the hottest day of the year. "You're like a son to me," she had said, gathering her yellow dress tail in one hand so it wouldn't get wet, and he had realized then that had been one of the main reasons he had married Lydia: to have a mother, to have arms around him to let him know he mattered.

The muck sucked at Asher's legs as he offered his hand to help Zelda off the porch. He fought with his feet to keep from going any deeper. Finally she reached out, resigned to silence because of the swollen river's roar. He pulled her toward him and latched his arm around her waist as they made their way back up to the rise where he had left the Jeep. Her body was hot and doughy to his touch. She sank in the mud and he had to pull her along and then carry her in some places. Butterscotch-colored water frothed around their legs, filled with tree limbs and garbage and all manner of debris they had to dodge. He helped her up into the vehicle and her fingers trembled in his grip.

Still the rain was falling in a torrent, washing across his windshield in a violence of nature he had never before witnessed. He had never seen it rain so hard, ever, and certainly not for this long.

Asher knew he shouldn't drive through the water overtaking the first bridge, but they made it. The vehicle coughed up the hill, the engine choked with river but managed to recover just before it sputtered out. By the time they reached the second bridge it had disappeared beneath a pasture that had become a lake. Asher knew the land well so he switched back around and pulled onto the railroad tracks where they racketed along—the Jeep shaking like it might fall apart, Zelda letting out little yelps every once in a while—until they had reached the road to his house. The whole valley was under water. From where they drove along the ridgeline they could look down and see it all spread out before them like the end of time had come to Cumberland Valley.

They watched a trailer home being swept away, the roof of a house, a pickup truck. Cows struggling to stay afloat. "Oh no!

Asher!" Zelda said at that, as if he might be able to dive in and help the cattle to find higher ground, but they both knew there was nothing to be done. So many trees, all with the lush full leaves of late June. Chickens sitting in a calm line down the length of a white church steeple. It must have been swept from far up the river as it wasn't familiar to him; he knew by heart the looks of every church nearby.

Asher saw the brick walls of a house collapse and then the roof was swept down the widening Cumberland while two men stood on the hill, watching. He knew the house had only recently been built by a songwriter from Nashville. He hadn't lived in there more than a couple months and now the house was altogether gone. Asher kept driving. He had to get back to make sure their house was still high above the water line, to see that Justin was alright.

And there he was, waiting right on the porch for them. Justin leaned against the banister with his arms crossed. Still miffed because Asher had not let him go along, not knowing how dangerous the roads would be. He was eight, but small for his age, and more like an old man in his bearing and thinking. Just as they pulled in, Lydia stepped out of the front door as if she had been watching at the window, and went to put her arm around Justin's neck but he scrambled away from her, running out to greet his granny.

THEIRS WAS ONE of the lucky houses, situated on the ridge where the water couldn't reach them, although the river was far too close to put Asher at ease. The last flood had destroyed so much, but it had not threatened them. This one was licking awfully close and if the rain kept falling the Cumberland would have no choice but to keep rising until the water was seeping into their home. His church had been built on the highest point in those parts more than a hundred years before. But many in his congregation would be homeless. Some of them had only recently rebuilt from the last flood. He had no idea how he would handle all the care they would need.

Throughout the day Zelda and Lydia watched the useless television news while Asher and Justin watched the river rise, watched the rain fall. Justin would not leave his side.

"Are we gonna be okay?" he asked, his green eyes latched on to Asher's green eyes.

"Yes, buddy," Asher said, his hand capped over his son's head. "Don't you worry."

But Asher *was* worried.

Even worse than the rising water, even worse than the fact that he had not heard one siren or seen one helicopter or any sign of help from the government (they were alone out here, then, he realized, until the storm was over; help from the law always came *after* it was needed), even worse than when the electricity blinked out of being, even worse than Lydia doing nothing but praying in the shadowy cave of her room—was that they couldn't find Roscoe anywhere.

Asher stood in the doorway until Lydia said her quiet "Amen" then told her he was going out to look for the dog again. Although it was early afternoon her room was very dark; she hadn't opened the curtains. He could barely see her as she knelt beside the bed. Just when he was about to say that he was leaving he could make out that she had extended her hand toward him. "Won't you come here and pray with me?" she said.

He stepped into the shadows with hesitation; he wanted to tell

her that faith without works is dead, that God doesn't hear those
kinds of prayers. He knelt beside her at the bed and felt foolish
in doing so. She had already bowed her head but now she lay her
hand palm-up atop the bedspread. When he didn't respond right
away she turned to look at him.

"What is it?" she whispered.

He intertwined his fingers with hers and bowed his head. She
followed suit, the words trembling quietly on her lips: "Lord, we
come to you to ask that you help our little dog . . ." In their
tradition he was expected to say his own prayer aloud as well,
their words mingling into a sort of woven chant. But he didn't
pray aloud. He kept his head bowed and felt her sweaty hand in
his own and all while she pleaded with God he could think only
Please please please. That was the only kind of invocation he possessed now.

He imagined the worst possibilities: Roscoe being swept away
in the flood, his little front legs paddling furiously to stay afloat;
even worse, Roscoe washed ashore somewhere, drowned, no more.
This was one reason prayer was so hard for him these days—
stillness was a danger for him, causing his mind to conjure the
worst scenarios and dreads.

He listened to her—"We know you can do all things, Heav-
enly Father, we believe that you know all and see all"—and wanted
to believe that this might have some impact on them finding the
dog, but he didn't think it would. Not anymore. The way they
thought of God and prayer and worship was so different now
that it might as well have been a wide river between them, further
widened by floodwaters. Asher remained patient throughout her

long prayer but as soon as she finished he let go of her hand and bolted from the room and went outside.

He roamed back and forth beneath the cover of the porch, hands cupped around his mouth, hollering the little dog's name again and again. He kept expecting Roscoe to race into the yard—zigzagging around the three dogwoods in his showing-off way—and then skip up the steps and wend his wet body between Asher's legs, jumping up to lick Justin on the mouth. But he did not come.

"He probably got turned around because of the water being over his path," Asher said to Justin when he came out. They both knew of Roscoe's love for wading in the shoals in the mornings, rain or not. Asher found himself lying to his son again, something he had promised himself he would never do. "He's smart. He'll find his way back."

Justin turned his attention back to the sopping yard. He squinted his eyes to see through the spears of rain, watching for his dog.

THE HOUSE HAD grown hot. They opened all of the windows but this did little more for the heat than to add dampness. Zelda and Lydia cooked supper on the gas stove. They used what they could from the freezer since it would all thaw out and be ruined anyway. The adults picked at the pork chops and fried corn, nudging the food around their plates with forks, picking up their slices of bread only to sit them back down, uneaten. Only Justin was able to eat.

After supper Asher stood at the window and watched the rain

lash at the glass as greenish-gray clouds loomed overhead. Lydia came up behind him without warning and put her hand on the soft meat of his upper arm, causing him to draw away in a startled flinch.

"Why couldn't you pray aloud with me?" she asked, quietly. "For Roscoe."

"I said my own kind of prayer, Lydia."

"But you couldn't pray with *me*," she said. "Y'all everyone cut me out. Push me away. You, my own little boy, my own mother." Her brow was knitted with grief. "Feels like I'm all alone in this world."

"I'm sorry it feels that way," he said, and after a time she stepped away into the shadows.

ASHER WENT BACK out to help the closest neighbors but there was nothing to do except watch their lives float away or pray that their houses would be spared. *This was too much*, they said. *This one felt like a judgment.* They stood on the ridges together as the night gathered in, black and thick. The electricity was off as far as they could see, a total darkness unlike any Asher had ever known. He wondered about the two men he had seen earlier, and felt guilty that he had not offered them a ride while some of the roads were still navigable. Nobody would be going anywhere now.

Back home they all sat in the living room without saying much. There was little to be said. Justin slept off and on, leaned against Asher on the couch, but he awoke at the slightest sound and sometimes at his own dreams.

Around midnight the rain fell only in thin lines for a time and then it finally stopped, just like that, like someone had snapped their fingers, the night's stillness somehow more threatening than the showers had been. Now they could hear the roaring river, churning with trees and houses and animals. They might have heard the cries of calves or the terrified whinnies of horses right through the walls of the house itself but all the other debris was too loud for that, a cacophony of loss. They didn't know it yet but the flood had killed more than forty people and soon, once the floodwaters began to drop, corpses would be revealed in the treetops, trapped in houses, or washed up on the banks of the Cumberland River.

Now that night had capped itself down around the world, Justin had grown more upset and was unable to go back to sleep after being awakened by a low, Rapture-like thunder.

"I can't stand it," Justin said. There were tears in his eyes and he was struggling to not shed them. "He's lost out there."

Sometimes Asher worried the boy might always be able to get along better with animals than other people. Other times he thought that might not be such a bad fate. If there was anything he had learned so far in life it was that dogs often made better friends than folks did.

"It's alright, little buddy," Asher whispered against his son's forehead, patting his small back. "He'll make it home." As long as he kept telling Justin everything was okay everything *would* be okay. He felt his own assurances might be the only thing holding the entire world together at this moment.

"Hush crying, now, honey," Lydia said, her voice sudden and

stark in the darkness of the living room. Her face was lit with the glow from the candles. "Boys don't cry and go on like that."

Asher set his eyes on her in a way to warn her against saying more. Why shouldn't the boy be able to grieve over his dog?

Zelda looked from Asher to her daughter, letting them both know that this was no night to argue.

Lydia made her voice tender, quieter: "If he doesn't toughen up I'm afraid the world'll eat him alive."

Asher rose and took his son with him out to the porch.

They stood listening to the moan and groan of the impregnated river. No lights anywhere. The threatening convulsions of lightning, way off in the distance back toward Nashville. Asher looked up. The clouds had drifted away and with all electricity gone there were more stars than he had ever seen in his life, stars strewn out in such a mass that they looked like shimmery silver clouds.

"Look, Justin," he said. "Look at all the stars."

"God," Justin whispered.

And then: he was gone.

2

sher ran to the ridge first. Justin's favorite place. He hoped that's where he had gone instead of down to the boiling river that had spilled over into the lower yard. He knew that Justin was trying to find Roscoe.

Asher raced behind the house and past the toolshed, one corner being devoured by the saturated ground, past their ruined garden—his bushy tomato plants beaten down into the rich black dirt by the rain, full ditches between each destroyed row—and onto the path that led up the ridge. Here the earth was so wet it sucked at his shoes. Up ahead were the thick woods crowding the ridge behind their house. Asher stopped at the mouth of the path to allow his eyes to adjust.

The woods were all blackness, the full trees of high summer blocking out any starlight that might have guided his way. But he knew these woods so well he could walk through them with his eyes closed. The noise down at the river seemed larger now, a wall of grinding and moaning. Trees and cars rubbing up against refrigerators and the roofs of houses. Still Asher was sure he had heard Roscoe barking. Perhaps Justin had heard this, too, and was following the deceptive sound. Hearing has a way of fooling itself to believe what it wants.

The night smelled like a rotten log, the kind that mushed under his foot on their evening walks together. Asher had taught his son the names of trees and how to identify them. The feel of the bark, the shapes of the leaves. The hickory trees were scaly-barked, the tulip poplars possessed greenish-yellow flowers in the early summer. Sometimes Asher would stop and put his hand out to rest against Justin's upper chest. "Hush, listen," Asher would say dramatically, trying to drill into Justin's head the importance of this world up on the ridge. Then he'd tell Justin that *birdie birdie birdie* call was a redbird's. "Remember that song, now," he'd say, and the little boy would eat it all up, big-eyed and openhearted. Those days wouldn't last forever. He thought of the way Justin carefully tucked feathers or bits of quartz or buckeyes into his nature collection when they found them and then hid them in his Prince Albert cigar box when they returned home.

Asher hollered his name, over and over.

He couldn't see much except the black silhouettes of the trees closest to him. Once Asher had found Justin and Roscoe in a grassy bald back in the woods, asleep. Roscoe's head rested on Justin's arm like a pillow, his wet black nose touching Justin's neck.

Asher had come to the boundary fence and he was sure Justin wouldn't have gone past that, so he took off at a jog until he had come back out into the starlit yard behind their house.

He looked under the porch, in the toolshed (where he grabbed a great hank of thick rope, just in case, wrapping it around his torso from shoulder to hip), even in the doghouse. He cupped his hands and hollered his son's name but his voice was lost on the wall of noise. He ran back into the house and told Lydia and Zelda to come help him look.

"Vanished?" Lydia said.

He had seen the lightning earlier and knew that it was most likely raining again to the east. More water back there could drive this flood up in seconds. Or Justin could just stumble into the water trying to save Roscoe. He was out there and they had to find him immediately. "We've got to look."

All three of them roamed the yard, calling Justin's name. Lydia prayed aloud that he would be found. Asher felt sick to his stomach; they had lost him. He was *gone*. Just like Roscoe.

"I'm going down to the river," Asher called.

"Asher, wait!" Zelda hollered, one hand out in front of her as if she were about to catch a ball being thrown to her. But Asher did not wait and didn't realize for a moment that Lydia was right at his heels even though it would have made more sense for them to look in different directions to cover more ground.

They had no other choice but to go to the flood. Here the tree cover was not so thick; the starlight managed to shine through the willows. Asher could see the flood growing before his eyes as if a tidal wave was sweeping toward them. He could see only the very tops of the concrete railings of the bridge and even they were disappearing as the water heightened.

Then: the great screeching grind of the house pirouetting as it was swept down the Cumberland toward them, the surge of water unfolding itself across the valley, the three figures hollering as they ran toward them, the screaming of a child.

3

Asher didn't know the two men running with Justin down the water's edge, yelling and pointing to the floating house as if Asher and Lydia hadn't seen it, hadn't heard the people screaming from inside it. Asher didn't know how he had the foresight to run to the nearest willow that wasn't already submerged and tie the rope there. The men with Justin were shouting to him but he could not hear over the groaning of the floodwaters. He could see that the house was going to slam into the bridge and when that happened, the people inside might be forced into the water. He could make out two: a man, he thought, holding a child in his arms as he thrust his body out of a window that was crowded with tree limbs. The man was screaming and the child was crying and both were little more than silhouettes about to die.

The larger of the two men with Justin saw what Asher was doing and ran to him. Asher thrust the rope into the man's hands and hoped he would be able to hold it taut. Already the man had looped and tied the rope around his waist.

Asher watched as the man disappeared into the water.

They could no longer see the concrete bridge but it was clear to them when the house crashed into it. The lumber splintered and cried out. Trees and a car and cow corpses had been bobbing behind the house in the surge and now they all plowed into the side of it, the nose of the car bursting through a wall. The man and child were still in the window, the man folded over the windowsill like a towel, the child still holding on to him, still crying out. Now Asher could see only glimpses of them behind the building debris, but they were there. He did not think to pray and later he would remember this with guilt.

The roped man had disappeared. Then, there was a jolt on the rope, like a monstrous catfish at the end of a fishing line, and the man was crawling along the top of the overturned car, hurrying but also careful in where he stepped across the underbelly of the vehicle. The child was screaming more loudly now, then pounded on the man's shoulder to rouse him.

The rope was burning Asher's hands, cutting into his fingers and across the meat of his palm.

Then, even though Asher had not prayed (perhaps someone else had, perhaps all of them had except him), the house turned in

one ninety-degree angle so that the people in the window neared
the bank. The rescuer wrested them out of the house and then
pulled them across a few feet of the frothing water.

When the roped man handed off the little girl—Asher could
see her now—over his shoulder, the father in the window instinc-
tively reached out for her as if the flood was carrying her away. He
leaned out so far that he nearly fell from his precarious perch in
the window. The rescuer pushed through the water—going under
once, the child along with him, causing all of them on the bank to
cry out and step forward.

The father pushed himself out of the window and was swallowed by the river.

The girl lay on the ground near Asher's feet, Lydia and Zelda
descending upon her as she coughed up floodwater and clutched
at her throat as if being strangled. Only then did Asher see that
most of her clothes had been ripped off and he looked away because she was older than he had thought, a teenager. He pulled
his soaked tee shirt over his head and handed it to Lydia so she
could cover the girl's small breasts. The man with the rope turned
to go back but then he collapsed, spewing forth a green spray of
the river that had gulped down his throat.

Asher let go of the rope and ran to the edge of the thrashing
water, where the father had made it to a shallow spot where he
could lie with the top half of his body out of the flood. He wasn't
able to pull himself forward any farther but he reached for his
child, his hands out to her even as he fought to find air instead of
river in his lungs.

Asher waded in, hooked his arms under the man's armpits

and pulled him out of the water. He stood over him, suddenly aware that he was out of breath himself. He bent, his hands on his knees as he tried to gather himself. When he turned his head he saw them. The other two men farther down the slope. The one with the rope cutting into his waist lay gasping for breath. The other squatted on the ground, leaning over him, and then kissed the rescuer's face (forehead, under each eye, even on the mouth), begging him to be alright.

4

Of course they knew them once they were able to see their faces clearly: Caleb Carey, one of the deacons at Asher's church, and his daughter, Rosalee, just five years older than Justin. Their house had been washed nearly two miles down the river. Asher and the stranger helped Caleb walk up the ridge to the house. The other man carried Rosalee in his arms. They had not gone far before Caleb vomited up floodwater. Only a trickle, but he heaved violently as if there was more that never came. He ate at great gulps of breath.

"He's having a panic attack," Lydia said.

"No, I think he's in shock," Asher said. He'd been a lifeguard at Montgomery Bell one summer and had not realized until now that he had retained some of his first-aid training. Caleb collapsed under their arms. They carried his deadweight up to the house and laid him down on the couch, stacking two pillows beneath his feet.

Caleb's skin was grayish, his eyes very narrow. "She's drowned," he mumbled. "She's drowned, Asher."

"No, no, Rosalee is right here with us. She's fine."

"No. She." He couldn't say more, but his eyes had become large, unfocused.

Of course, Asher thought. Not Rosalee. Caleb's wife. She was nowhere to be found.

By candlelight the others put Rosalee in the guest bedroom where Zelda would tend to her.

"Is he dead?" Justin asked, suddenly next to Asher.

"No, he's just exhausted, and in shock," Asher said. "But he'll be okay, buddy. There's no getting him out to a hospital tonight."

"I thought I heard Roscoe," Justin said. "That's why I ran off. I thought he was down there, barking."

"He ran right into me," said the man, who had tied the rope about his waist, and when Asher got a good look at him he saw that he was the songwriter who lived down the road. He had that look of country music singers who never become stars nowadays, but always used to: square-jawed, handsome, but with too much worry on his face, too much living through the hard times. These days those men were the songwriters but not the singers.

"Thank you for bringing him back," Asher said.

The other one laughed in a good-natured way. He was black-headed, black-eyed. "He brought *us*," the dark one said.

"I'm sure glad he did," Asher said. "I could have never gotten them out by myself."

"I'm ashamed," the smaller one said, "that I froze down there. I couldn't make my legs move. I just couldn't move."

No one said anything. It seemed that if they did his shame would bloom larger.

For a brief time they watched Caleb breathe, gulping at air, then breathing so shallowly they could barely see his chest rising. Then the songwriter said his name was Jimmy and his partner was Stephen and they had only recently built the house down the road, the one Zelda and Asher had watched collapse earlier. Since Asher knew a songwriter owned the place, at first he thought Jimmy meant Stephen was his *songwriting* partner. But the way Jimmy said the word let Asher know he was searching for a reaction. Then he remembered Jimmy kissing Stephen down there by the water. He had not imagined it.

Asher said "Oh," nodded. He had never met a gay couple in his life—that he knew of, anyway. More than one of his congregants today had blamed this new flood on the Supreme Court's ruling. No coincidence that the rain had started the same day as the marriages started happening over in Nashville, they said. Asher had said nothing because how could he argue with people who had just watched their lives carried away on the river?

"We lost our house today," Stephen said. "We'd been following the water's edge for the last couple hours, and then this little feller showed up."

"I told them they could stay with us, Dad," Justin said.

"You're that preacher, right?" Stephen said. There was some amount of suspicion in his voice.

Asher told him he was and saw the men's eyes meet.

Justin's head came to rest against Asher's arm.

"Poor little feller," Jimmy said. "He's a sight, now, ain't he?"

"He sure is," Asher said, and situated Justin on the seat so that his neck wouldn't be cricked.

"We didn't know what else to do," Jimmy said, "but to keep walking until we found somewhere—"

Then Asher realized how tired they must be, standing in that rain since early this morning, wading along the muddy edges of the water, saving Caleb and his daughter, clad in soaking wet jeans that must have been rubbing their skin raw. And then it dawned on Asher that he was sitting there in muddied clothes, too. And that the skin had peeled away from his hands in a half-inch stripe where the rope had burned through. They all needed food. They needed to rest.

Asher took them into the house and then into his and Lydia's bedroom and gave them pants and shirts, left them alone to change. Candlelight stuttered against the walls of Justin's room as Asher passed and he could hear Zelda in there talking softly to Rosalee about her mother. Rosalee had seen her go under. "I had a hold of her hand," Rosalee said, then could say no more. He eavesdropped long enough to hear that.

The house seemed completely different with nothing more than candlelight. The ceilings higher, the rooms larger. All was shadows around Lydia as she stood in the middle of the living room.

"Will he be alright?" she said, her eyes on Caleb, who was trembling in a kind of sleep.

"I think so. His breathing is calmed down. I can't find any wounds on him anywhere. He got bruised up a little, but that's all."

"Did those men leave?"

"No," Asher said. "They're putting on some dry clothes."

"We can't have them in here, Asher," she said quietly.

"They don't have anywhere else to go," Asher whispered. "We're the lucky ones."

"What would the congregation say? It's not right—"

"Not right to help people in trouble?"

"I *know* who they are," she said. "They're—you know what they *are*, Asher. We can't have them in here around Justin."

"So you wouldn't want Justin around my own brother?"

"That's not the same."

"But you wouldn't," he said.

She kept her eyes on his, unyielding.

"They've lost everything they have," Asher said.

"I feel bad for them, but I don't know what we're supposed to do," she said.

"We give them a place to stay. That's what. We be kind to them."

"Asher, you know as well as—"

"Hebrews says to entertain strangers," Asher said, thinking the Bible might have some sway on her.

"Asher." Lydia's face was golden but hard-edged in the candlelight. "We can't let them share a bed in this house."

Only then did Asher realize the men were standing in the hallway.

"If you could direct us to the next closest place that didn't flood, we'd appreciate it," Jimmy said, his face lost to the shadows.

"We've got plenty of room right here," Asher said.

Lydia started to speak, then put a hand to her mouth.

"We won't trouble you," Jimmy said in his even way.

"We don't go where we're not wanted," Stephen added.

They were all frozen there with silence between them: Jimmy's hand on the doorknob, Stephen in the shadows, Lydia tucked behind Asher as if he were a shield, Asher in the middle of the room, feeling like a fool.

"We appreciate the clothes," Jimmy said.

Stephen moved toward the door. "We'll get them back to you."

Asher wanted to beg them to stay but he didn't want to shame them any further.

"At least let me get you something to eat," Asher offered.

"I can make you up a plate," Lydia said, then, too late.

They slipped out the door and Asher followed but they were down the steps and enveloped in darkness before he even got to the porch steps. He hollered and told them to follow the ridgeline north on up to their neighbor Kathi's; she'd be good to them. He didn't know then that the Cumberland had risen so high it had taken her home, too.

"I'm sorry!" Asher called out above the roar of the flood.

Asher looked up at all those stars again. It wasn't right for such a sky to be shining above them when so many people had lost so much. But the sky doesn't pay a bit of attention to the things that happen to us, the joys or sorrows either one.

5

When the water receded later that week, Asher took Caleb and Rosalee to Caleb's sister in Nashville. Then he drove Zelda to her house, which had miraculously survived with nothing more than the front porch washed away. He made his way back in silence, weaving through Cumberland Valley to check on the members of his congregation and his neighbors. Most of the bridges had washed out, replaced with piles of brush and twisted guardrails, stoves, recliners, chunks of Sheetrock that had once been the walls of homes. The county roads had buckled under the weight of the water, and were now undulating strips of blacktop that occasionally broke

away, as if the sides of the road had been bitten off. The bot-
tomland along the river had morphed into ponds pocked with
johnboats carrying people trying to find their belongings. Down
near Greene's Branch two men in a wobbly rowboat nearly tipped
over as they pulled a body onboard. They were out in the middle
of a cornfield and did not seem real until Asher caught sight of the
corpse, a man whose clothes had been ripped away by the water,
his side gashed open.

He tried to pray but could not find it in himself to do so.

Asher watched as his neighbors trod the soaked ground or
waded the water, picking among the debris to see if there was
anything that held some semblance of Before the Flood, picture
albums whose photographs had miraculously not been destroyed,
a stuffed animal, a pistol still in its lockbox.

At the water's edge, he found Roscoe.

The dog's coat was so matted with mud and dirt that Asher
didn't know him at first—but when Asher put his hand on Roscoe's
head and felt the familiar shape of his skull, he knew.

"Oh, buddy," Asher said, squatting down. Roscoe's red collar
had been ripped off, but it was certainly him, their good boy who
had watched over Justin his whole life. Asher was overcome by a
kind of grief he had never felt before, a feeling more like injustice.
He carried Roscoe over to a patch of pinewoods and buried him
with the shovel he had been using to dig out his neighbor's belongings and he cried over the dog, over all the loss of today and before.

But again he could not pray and felt no sense of that kind of
prayer anywhere in him. He had spent his life finding words to
make himself and others feel comforted. Always before the words

were right there, without having to think much about them. Perhaps that had been the problem all along.

So Asher kneeled and put his hand on the wet ground. "Roscoe, you were the best old boy that ever was," he said. "Thank you, thank you, thank you."

That was a kind of prayer, he supposed. There were different kinds of prayer and different kinds of belief and he might be able to figure all that out someday, but not yet.

ASHER ROAMED FROM one neighbor to the next, most of them members of his church. He embraced the ones who needed that, shook the hands of the ones who weren't ready to be embraced. He helped them search for their belongings or push their vehicles out of the mud or stretch tarpaulins to sleep under. Anything to be near their house-seats. But he did not offer to pray with any of them.

Asher walked up toward Kathi Hoskins's house, situated on a shelf overlooking the Cumberland. In the aftermath of the last flood she had housed several of her homeless neighbors in her home high above the flood-line, and it was to her that Asher had sent the newly homeless men. But as he came up the ridge he saw Kathi's house was gone. There was only the concrete foundation. A toilet and shower stall stood on it along with half a wall of crumbling Sheetrock. All else had been washed away. He found her sitting on the ridge with her three dogs crowded close, two of them curled against her and sleeping tired sleeps, one with his ears alert as if the house might come floating back and reassemble itself if he kept good watch.

Asher sat down beside her, the two sleeping dogs stirring just long enough to make sure he was someone they knew and trusted. She did not speak but after a time she laid her head on his shoulder. Her eyes were fixed on the spot where her house had stood. Her flannel shirt was damp. He had never seen her without eyeglasses and wondered if she had somehow lost them in the race to get out of the house before the flood swallowed it whole. He sat with her and felt more at home here with the silence and his childhood friend and her dogs sitting in the pasture with the wet ground beneath them than he did back at his house.

HE REACHED HOME just as the sky was purpling into night. The dimming of the day yawned itself out over the troubled land as he stood looking at his house. He had to go in; Justin was in there.

Just as his hand reached the knob, the front door swung open and Lydia stood large there. "Lord, Asher, you're covered in mud. Won't you undress here on the porch? I'll get you a towel."

I have been on the road to Damascus, he wanted to say.

He strode past her and Justin came bounding across the room, arms out to wrap around Asher's waist. He knew the boy would be muddied and Lydia would have a fit, but he didn't care. After what he had gone through today. The corpse. The dead cattle, eyes milky and bulbous. The people walking like ghosts. Roscoe. After all of that, he didn't care about anything but this one moment of his little boy running to him.

"Did you find him? Did you find Roscoe?"

Asher told him that maybe Roscoe had gotten carried downstream and someone was taking care of him now and he was just fine and happy and was thinking of them but couldn't get back. Asher told him that Roscoe dreamt of them when he slept. "I bet his new owner laughs at him for running and wagging his tail in his sleep," he said.

Lydia sat down on the ottoman with Justin and rubbed his back, round and round in a circle.

"I bet they don't know he's thinking about playing with you," Asher added.

"I want him back, though," Justin said.

"The main thing is he's alright," Asher said. "Any day now he might come running through the woods and right up on the porch. If he can ever find his way back, he will."

6

That night, Asher dreamt of his brother.

Luke was caught in the dark, rocking waters, struggling to stay afloat among all the debris. Asher was standing on the ridge and he could see Luke out there, screaming, his face pleading with Asher to help him, to do anything. *I'm drowning*, he cried out. *I'm dying*. Yet Asher did not move. He wanted to, but his legs and arms would not cooperate. And then, the river swallowed Luke and he was gone.

Asher shuddered awake, found himself slumped on the couch where exhaustion had overcome him. He remembered now, the weariness easing down over his body the way a midday cloud shadow can be seen, moving over a pasture. The tiredness, rock-heavy, from the top of his head to the soles of his feet. Justin had gone to sleep there with him, his legs stretched across Asher's lap, mouth thrown open in complete rest, a soft little snore revving in his nostrils. Lydia had thrown an afghan over them.

The house ticked with the kind of silence that happens only in the middle of the night.

The dream had left him with a grief he could not shed. He slipped outside and sat on the top step of the porch, looking up at the night sky. No stars now, as clouds had moved back in. The valley was still and black; he could not even see the trees just past the porch.

Ever since the men had come to the house he had been thinking of Luke.

Ten years without his brother. He thought of their mother sitting at the yellow kitchen table while Luke danced across the red linoleum. Asher was laughing and clapping—only twelve, Luke four years older. Their mother's mouth clenched into a wrinkled line, like a pink drawstring purse. "I Don't Want to Know" on the radio—all those drums and that steering guitar and the hands clapping and the voices of Fleetwood Mac—and Luke was moving every part of himself, twisting, shaking, laughing with his head thrown back. Asher didn't know what had come over his brother; he only ever danced like this when it was just the two of them. But the music had been too good and so he had jumped up to dance.

Their mother darted up quick as a spider, snapped off the radio in one sharp click of her wrist.

The word she had said to Luke then.

(*faggot*)

Luke ran from the room, from the house, down to the willow-shadowy banks of the Cumberland, where Asher found him later, watching the river.

He remembered Luke's whitish-blue eyes, the way a column of gnats had been churning above the Cumberland. The lush dark green of the trees, Luke's clenched jaw, his refusal to cry. Up on the ridge a congregation of starlings arose in a great humming movement of blackness from the hickories, hundreds of birds becoming one undulating mass. A sign, he had thought back then. A wonder.

The second time their mother had used the word was when Luke told her the truth.

"It's how I'm made," Luke had said, his words even and calm, as if he were saying a blessing over supper.

Their mother had run into her room and returned with their dead father's pistol. She'd pressed the barrel against Luke's forehead and Asher had been frozen in place as a strange calm overtook Luke's face.

"I'd rather see you dead than like *this*," she said, her words cramped and close together like bad cursive. The pistol did not tremble in her hand. "Eat up with AIDS. An abomination. You'd be better off dead. You hear me?"

"I'm alive," Luke had said, and there had been no malice in his voice, only a statement of fact. "I'm here."

When she took the pistol away from his forehead a small red circle remained.

Luke stood before her, his eyes trained on hers.

"I was just trying to scare you," she said. "Wasn't even loaded."

"You're the one who's scared," he said, and then he left. That was the last time Luke had ever spoken to their mother and he was long gone and unreachable by the time she died. Asher hadn't seen him in ten years.

He thought again of the two men, somewhere out there in the darkness, looking for a dry place to sleep. He could hardly stand the thought of it. He thought of Lydia, sleeping soundly back there in their bedroom, numbed by the church.

Asher took note of how silent the night stood. Usually by this time of summer there would be a symphony of crickets, katydids, tree frogs, perhaps even early cicadas. But there was nothing except the black night and a complete quiet.

He moved to a rocking chair and stayed there until the sky bloomed into dawn, a spell of stillness broken only when Lydia stepped out onto the porch.

"Couldn't you sleep?" she asked, very quietly, and sat in one of the rockers.

He didn't look at her. Across the Cumberland a jagged breath of mist was gliding along the ridge spine so he watched that instead. "I can't do this anymore," he said.

"What are you talking about?" There was a little laugh in her throat at the last word.

He turned to look at her then. She had closed her eyes and leaned her head against the back of the rocker. Her face was bathed in the pink golden light of the rising sun.

There was a night he remembered, when they had first started courting. They had gone for a walk in the woods after church. Cedars breathing out their musk.

"We don't see eye-to-eye anymore," Asher said, suddenly so tired, so weary.

"We've got a partnership, Asher," she said. She sprang up and went into the house, but he followed. In the kitchen she was scooping coffee into the filter with her back to him.

He had been a sensation back when they first met, the preacher who was burning through all of the churches round these parts with his Holy Ghost revivals. He had visited her church and she had set her sights on him. After church they had stood at the door talking long after the last car left the parking lot, then he'd asked her to go to the Dairy Dart for milkshakes. She'd worn a dress decorated with little yellow Easter flowers. He liked the way she brought her fingers up to her mouth when she laughed, the determined way she had strolled into the restaurant, her shoulders back as if she owned the place. The next week they had walked through the woods and down to the Cumberland. She slipped her arm into the crook of his. Her laugh was big and full. The prettiest girl he had ever known, full of life and a desire to be of service through the church. The perfect pastor's wife. They had only dated a couple of months before he asked her to marry him and they had run off to Nashville without telling anyone. She used to take hold of his hand and make him feel safe. She used to touch him and he had wanted that so much, to have someone reach out and put their hand on the back of his neck, to put their head on his shoulder.

"I can't get over the way you turned those men away," he said. She sat down at the kitchen table. She was still so lovely, her long neck, chestnut curls on her forehead, those big brown eyes. She had the coloring of a whip-poor-will and was as small-boned as one, too. The most lonesome of birds. She had been a good wife to him in many ways. But this was too much. This thing he could not overlook. "Just sent them back out into the flood."

"Asher, you're—" She struggled to collect her words and latched her eyes to her hands. "You're blowing that up into something—"

"That could have been my brother you turned away like that," he said.

"We have to stand up for what's right, Asher."

Now he saw that her hands were trembling. That evening in the cedar woods her hand had felt so small in his. That little moment in time when they thought they could build a real life together.

The room was filled with the dark scent of brewed coffee but neither of them moved to get a cup.

"I've studied on it a lot, Lydia. You know I don't believe that way anymore. All my life I've thought I've understood everything in that Bible, but now I know that none of us can know the mind of God. He's too big for that."

"I won't change my beliefs," she said, "just because you have. A person can't go their whole life believing that one plus one equals two, then have someone tell them it equals three and just—" she snapped her fingers "—start believing that. It don't work that way."

She was a preacher's daughter and then had gone straight to being a preacher's wife. This was her life's work. But for the first time he realized he heard fear in her voice. She had grown afraid of everything. Once she had been open to the whole world—her head thrown back in laughter with the scent of those cedars all around them—and now her rigidity and fear had turned into something bordering on meanness.

"And my job is to keep my child from seeing two men together like that. And to make sure my husband stays on the right path. If I lay down my beliefs, I'm betraying you and Justin."

"Lydia, listen to me. You've gotten belief confused with judgment. We're not to judge. You've let all this judgment from the church take you over. It's taken the joy out of you."

"There's no joy in this world like the kind I feel at church."

"Well, it doesn't have to be that way. And this fear in you. This hatred. You're afraid of anybody who's different. Of anything that's not your way."

"I'm at fault because I've stayed the same and you've changed?"

He thought for a moment. "I reckon so."

"All a person has is what they believe in, Asher. Haven't you been preaching that very thing your whole life?"

"They're our neighbors," he said.

"I love you, Asher," she said, her voice pleading now, low, careful. "I've always loved you."

He couldn't say the same to her, and he was surprised by this. But there it was, clear as the new morning.

7

School started back right on time in early August even though the buses still couldn't run to most places because of the construction to rebuild the roads and bridges. A month of broiling summer had done little more than dry out the mud. School had been back in session only a week when Asher received the call that Justin had been hurt in a fight.

In the principal's office Asher saw that Justin's mouth was busted and swollen, a straight cut—crisscrossed now with three tiny bandages—ran along the cheekbone beneath his right eye, which was already turning a greenish blue. Blood was caked in his nostrils. Asher could see how ashamed Justin was, the way he was trying to hold it together and put on a brave face and act like this was not a big deal.

Asher tried to not react. He ran his hand down the back of Justin's head, cupping his fingers around his son's small neck as he sat beside him. Justin's dazed eyes were fixed on the principal.

Mrs. Jackson was from way down in Mississippi and spoke in an elegant drawl, the way people did in movies when they were trying to sound Southern.

"Justin, darlin, do you want to tell your daddy what happened with me in the room, or do you want me to leave?" Mrs. Jackson leaned forward and the scratchy fabric of her pink blazer scritched loudly in the silent office.

"It won't make any difference." Justin's voice was very small and he spoke his words to the floor.

"Why do you say that, now, honey?" Mrs. Jackson spoke with a soothing firmness. "I need to talk to whoever did this to you. You don't want them doing it to anybody else, do you?"

"No, ma'am," he whispered. Asher saw that Justin's hands were clenched together in his lap. He could hardly stand to see his son in this shape. He wanted to knock the hell out of somebody himself.

Beyond the office the school had grown very quiet. By the time Asher had arrived all the schoolchildren had been unleashed upon the world, bursting outside in a great chattering herd. Now they had gone on home and Asher could hear the ticking of the plain round clock that hung on the cinder block wall behind Mrs. Jackson's head. Beyond that was the chilling wind of the air conditioner.

"The therapy has been really good for Justin, so I'd encourage y'all to talk to her about what happened today."

"Therapy?" Asher said.

Mrs. Jackson let out a nervous breath. She lit her eyes on Asher's face with apology. "If he tells you anything and is willing to share it with me, please let me know. I won't allow bullying to go on in my school." Now she looked to Justin, softening her gaze. "Darlin, you just let me know and I *will* make this stop. Do you understand, sugar?"

"Yes, ma'am," Justin answered.

On the way out Justin seemed even smaller than usual.

They rode along in silence for a time and then Justin asked if he could play some music. When Asher said he could Justin plugged in his phone and sang along with the singer's high voice: *Wonderful, wonderful, wonderful the way I feel.* Lately he had been playing this song constantly. The windows were down and the warm air smoothed against their faces, ruffling their hair. Justin let his hand float up and down on the rushing wind.

The world still smelled like the flood, the scent of rotting cattle and grainy mud and the twisted yellow insides of trees. They passed a whole row of foundations where there had once been houses. A line of white FEMA trucks, an old van perched in the crooked limbs of a magnolia tree whose leaves had been stripped away by the floodwaters.

"Justin, tell me who did that to you," Asher said finally.

"It's not a big deal," Justin said, sitting back against the seat now.

"Tell me, I said."

"This boy pushed me off the slide."

"Why?"

Justin shrugged. He picked at an old scab on the back of his hand, lifting its edges with his fingernail. "Because he hates me. Always has."

"Why would anybody hate you?"

Justin watched the pastures pass by, kept his eyes on the glint of the river between the trees.

"What's this about going to see a therapist, buddy?"

"Mom takes me, on Wednesdays. In Nashville."

"Why didn't you tell me about this?"

"She told me not to. She said it'd worry you."

At the house, Asher turned off the engine but did not get out of the Jeep. The motor clicked and they both kept their eyes on the muddy river.

"If I tell you something, will you promise to not be mad at me?" Justin asked.

"Depends on what it is," Asher said.

"I believe in God, but I don't believe in church." Justin turned to face him. "I said that at recess today, because this girl was praying that the Titans would win. And when she told the others they said I was going to hell. And one of 'em pushed me off the slide."

Asher didn't know what to say. He had not realized until now that he might feel the same way.

"Do you think I will?" Justin asked.

"Will what?"

"Go to hell."

"No," Asher said instantly, forcibly. He knew that preachers just like him were the very ones who had put thoughts like this into his son's mind, into the minds of all those children on the playground. He sat for a time, trying to gather more to say, but he was at a loss.

Asher opened his door. He put his hand on Justin's back as they walked up to the house. "We ought to go walking up on the ridge after supper," Asher said. "The foxgloves should be blooming by now." These days the woods felt more and more like the only kind of church he wanted to be a part of.

8

When Stephen and Jimmy started coming to their church on Sunday mornings, three different members of the church's board asked Asher what he was going to do about it.

"I'm going to welcome them in," Asher said. He didn't say how badly he wished he could go back to the day he turned his brother away and make that right. He wanted to, though.

Then more of the congregation called him, and some showed up at his house saying, *We can't have that kind of thing going on in our church* or *I can't let my children be around such as that* and *You know what they are* or *You have to do something, Pastor Sharp.*

Caleb Carey was the loudest voice against them. He demanded they be told to not come back.

"I can't do that, Caleb," Asher said. "I won't tell anyone they're not welcome here."

"There's churches in Nashville that accept their kind," Caleb said. "Let 'em go there."

"I told you, I won't turn anybody away from worshipping."

"I'll call a special meeting of the other deacons if I have to," Caleb said. He had once been a man of such humility and now there was anger tight in his shoulders, an aggression in the cords of his neck. He had lost nearly everything in the waters twice now and it had taken more than his wife and house. "If you don't run them queers off, then I will."

"Nobody's running anyone off from this church, now, Caleb." He rose then. He couldn't sit still when he was so angry. "One of those men saved you, Caleb. Saved Rosalee."

"That doesn't make it right, what they are. We can't condone that, Asher." Caleb wiped sweat from his brow and looked away. Then his anger gathered again. "Next they'll be wanting you to preach their wedding. What will you do then?"

"Caleb, I know you're mad. And I don't blame you. You lost so much." Asher stopped, struggling for the right words. "But treating them bad won't make you feel any better."

"I'm not going to be like everybody else in this country and give up my beliefs to be polite."

"Don't let this turn you mean."

Caleb shook his head. "What's happened to you, Asher Sharp?" He left Asher's office door wide open.

"WHAT ARE YOU *thinking*, Asher?" Lydia said after she took her first drink of coffee. "You want to lose your church?"

"What are *you* thinking?"

She snorted. "What are you talking about?"

"I know you've been taking Justin to a therapist. Why would you do that, then tell him to not tell me?"

"I thought it would help things," she said, her face suddenly red. "If he wasn't so wrought up all the time."

"Justin's not the problem," Asher said, keeping his words small and even. "This world is. Nobody can just let a person *be*."

Lydia fell silent.

"I want to talk to this therapist," he said, thinking of the pills doctors gave to boys like Justin. He would not have the shine rubbed out of his son.

"It's not normal, to be so tenderhearted," she said, standing now, the sun shining so brightly through the kitchen window behind her that her face was lost to him. "How can a person get through their day when they worry about every little thing in the world? He can't walk across the yard without worrying about hurting an ant, Asher! He's got to quit *feeling* so much."

"Why should he?" Asher thundered.

Lydia dashed the last of her coffee out into the sink and washed the mug with her back to him.

"I know you think you're protecting him," he said. "But I want him left alone."

AS THEY DROVE to Nashville Lydia flicked on the radio and tuned the knob to a gospel station out of the eastern mountains.

They listened only for an excruciating moment to a preacher screaming about how the Christian flag would be banned next before Asher snapped it off. Lydia sighed and pulled a CD mix of gospel songs from the console and slid it into the player.

Justin nudged white earbuds into his ears.

"What do you listen to on there all the time?" she asked, turning in her seat.

"My Morning Jacket, mostly."

"What's that?"

Justin tugged at the white cord, popping out one of the earbuds. "Just a band," he said.

"What kind of band?"

"My favorite band. Jim James is the lead singer and he—"

"They better not be cussing and going on," she said, eyeing him.

"They're not like that," Asher said.

"Why do you like them?" Now she spoke toward the windshield.

"I just like the way they sound. Listening to them makes me feel the way you feel when you're at church."

To Asher's surprise she laughed. "I doubt that," she said.

Justin put the earbuds back in and turned his music up, leaning his head back on the seat.

And then there was Nashville spread out in front of them with its stadium and the Batman Building and the kind of white haze that always stood between it and the rest of the world once warm weather set in. But they weren't going downtown. One exit, then one street and another and then they were in a brick box of a building. A young pretty girl who talked like a baby showed them into a room that looked like somewhere to sit and watch TV instead of talk to a doctor. Except there was no TV. Just a couch and two chairs and a coffee table with nothing but a grayish-pink box of Kleenex. The window looked out over the parking lot. Asher could see their car down there, baking in the summertime. There was a plastic ivy plant on the windowsill, in the sun, which troubled him. A fake plant sitting in the light. Asher imagined the leaves were very warm.

Asher hated all of this. The featureless room and the silence and the sickening scent of a vanilla deodorizer plugged into an outlet.

The therapist came in and leaned over to shake Justin's hand like they were partners in crime. Then she said hello to Lydia as if they were old friends and turned to Asher as if only now realizing he was there, saying he should call her Leslie. Her teeth were very, very white. Leslie sat and crossed her legs, her stockings scratching together, then balanced a notepad atop her leg.

"Now Justin, we're going to talk for just a minute with your mama and daddy here and then you and I will speak alone. Will that be okay?"

"Yeah, but I don't call her 'Mama,'" Justin said, as if he had explained this before and was exhausted by repeating it. "I call her 'Mom.'"

"Oh, that's okay." Leslie laughed like there was some reason that wouldn't be okay and wrote something down on the notepad. To Asher she seemed like a blank piece of paper and he had to chastise himself to keep from disliking her just because he had been left out of all of this by Lydia.

Lydia began to talk, saying lots of things about Justin as if he wasn't sitting right there: "He's such a good boy, we're very proud of him but he still gets real upset if somebody or something is hurt even though I tell him that's part of life, that's just the way it is, and he can't stand it if somebody is crying or upset. And I know you all talked about it but he still just has to touch everything."

Justin was feeling the warm leaves of the fake plant in the window and seemed to not hear a word of this. Asher was surprised that this kind of conversation would happen in front of the boy. Leslie was scrawling across her notepad and looked up at Lydia as if enthralled.

"He stays sick all the time because of it, always a runny nose or a cough or stomach virus," Lydia continued. Asher thought she'd never hush. "And there's a boy who's been picking on him at school. Today we just want to bring his daddy into the conversation."

Leslie stood and motioned Justin into another room for his private therapy. "I'll call y'all in before too long!" she said, as if all of this was meant to be great fun.

He stared at Lydia and he hoped that she could read his mind because he was thinking how he wasn't sure if he could ever get over her doing this behind his back.

THE THERAPIST SAID Justin had an anxiety disorder. "G-A-D, I'm thinking, or Anxiety Disorder N-O-S," she said, looking them in the eye, acting like everybody living in this world ought to know what all those initials stood for. "Since this is our third time together I think I'm going to refer him to a psychiatrist and I'm betting they'll start him on an anxiolytic med, or an S-S-R-I—"

"Wait a minute now," Asher told her, holding up his hand. "What if he's just good to the bone? Maybe he's just a good little boy."

The woman leaned forward and tented her fingers. "You are extremely fortunate to have been blessed with this good little soul," she said, and Asher knew she was believing every word she was about to say. "Really. I've seen children like this before, and they are wonderful. But you have to remember that it makes a hard life for him, carrying all these burdens on his little shoulders. I have no desire to change who Justin is, and neither will Dr. Conley. But I think he will agree with me that we can make his life a little more manageable."

"But he's not *un*manageable," Asher said.

"Asher, just let her explain," Lydia said, and put her hand on his thigh.

"Mr. Sharp, I don't think you're aware of how stressful everyday life is for Justin. He worries about *every*thing. He worries about being different from other kids. He worries that his grandmother might die in the night because she's old. He worries about the dog that was lost in the flood—"

"All those things sound like reasonable things to worry about to me, things any kid might—"

"Yes," Leslie said, smiling as if she was interrupting a child who was delighting her. "Of course. But the difference is that these things have such a tremendous impact on Justin that I'm afraid he might develop ulcers or other physical manifestations. We have to treat him properly."

"There's no way you're putting my boy on pills," he said, and stood.

"Well, that's not up to me anyway, Asher. That'll be up to the psychiatrist," Leslie said, and he felt like demanding that she not call him by his first name. He hated how familiar perfect strangers were these days. But he remained silent.

And so here was another reason to stay: to not uproot everything his son had ever known, to protect Justin.

9

The next Sunday, the two men came to church again and everyone turned in the creaky pews to watch them walk down the aisle. The men sat about halfway back and when they did the family sitting on the other end of the pew made a big commotion of getting up and moving to the front row. Jimmy nodded his head in greeting but only a couple people acknowledged him. Stephen kept his eyes on the floor.

Surely the men knew how these people felt about them. But maybe, Asher thought, that was *why* they came. Maybe they wanted to test this place and see what would happen.

Asher couldn't blame them for that.

He had a sermon prepared on the rocks of the Israelites but now another idea came to him. It was easy to discount people when you didn't know them or couldn't see them. But here these men were, right in front of them, their faces full of expectation. Maybe they weren't trying to test anyone; maybe they wanted to worship with a congregation. He remembered the tender way Jimmy had kissed Stephen's eyelids during the flood. His forehead. His mouth. Asher realized that he was standing there in silence, watching them while everyone else watched him. He had to say something.

So he turned to Hebrews 13:2–3: *Be not forgetful to entertain strangers: for thereby some have entertained angels unawares. Remember them that are in bonds, as bound with them; and them which suffer adversity, as being yourselves also in the body.* Then he quoted Matthew 25:35: *For I was hungered, and ye gave me meat: I was thirsty, and ye gave me drink: I was a stranger, and ye took me in.* He flipped to Romans 12:13, and read: *Distributing to the necessity of saints; given to hospitality.*

"This is what we have to do: be good to each other. If someone is different from you, get to know them instead of turning your back on them. For years I've preached to you that you should judge others, and lead them to change their ways. But I've changed my way of thinking. What I'm telling you right now is that the only one who can judge any of us is God above." Electricity ran up the backs of his arms, causing him to shiver as if he were about to speak in tongues.

He waited for someone to join in. This was a congregation that liked to participate, shouting "Amen!" or "Hallelujah!" to punctuate the rhythm of the sermon, but today they all sat silent.

Asher caught sight of Justin, who was leaning in close to Zelda. He was doing this for him, to show him that church didn't have to dim the God in people, that it could do the opposite.

Lydia sat on the other side of Justin, nearby yet apart. Her arms were folded and she shook her head just enough for Asher to notice, trying to protect him.

"All my life I've been told to love the sinner and hate the sin. But I'm telling you it's not my place to say that other people who aren't hurting anyone are committing a sin. I'm telling you what John said to us in the Scripture: 'Thou doest faithfully whatsoever thou doest to the brethren, and to strangers.' Do you know what this verse is saying to us?"

He took a deep breath as he waited for a response from the congregation. There was none. He saw all their faces like snapshots being thrown down on a table in front of him.

"It means you're pleasing God when you are good to strangers. That's our charge." He paused, hearing the quiet. Since no one else would say it, he offered a quiet "Amen."

The choir hesitated before rising. Asher turned to them and threw his arms wide. "Sing 'This Little Light of Mine' for us, will you?"

Asher sang along with the choir, who were doing a pretty feeble job although they usually had the Power all over them. The congregation always stood and sang along, too, but they didn't today. Asher scanned their faces. He didn't care if he had their approval and didn't want to appear as if he did.

As the choir finished he walked to the back of the church where the double doors led outside, just as he always did.

"Lord," he said at the door, "help us to love one another as you have loved us, without question, without judgment, without persecution. Amen."

All at once everyone was on their feet and shuffling out as if carrying heavy loads. At the door some of them shook his hand, but others filed past. They already knew what they were going to do and they would offer him no Judas kiss.

Some who paused to shake Asher's hand goodbye looked sad. He had hurt them. He hadn't wanted to. Others looked troubled because they knew what would happen. They all knew this would be the last of his preaching here, for defying the church. Only Kathi Hoskins hugged him. "Thank you," she said.

Lydia and Zelda slid past but Justin broke through, pushing past the legs of folks until he reached his father.

Jimmy and Stephen had waited to be last.

Jimmy shook Asher's hand, holding on to it tightly. "We didn't want to cause you any trouble," he said. "We just thought that it might be safe to come here because we could tell you were a good man, even if your wife didn't want us about. And so we thought—"

"I'm ashamed of how they acted," Asher said.

"Hey there," Jimmy said, looking down. "Here's the little man that led us out of the wilderness."

"Hidy," Justin said, then scrambled down the steps to the car.

"That was a brave thing you just did," Jimmy said. "We should've never moved out here and thought it would be any different. We've been living in a motor home, trying to rebuild."

"We're not about to let anybody run us off," Stephen said.

Jimmy looked so tired, like he had been fighting all his life.

The grief had cut his face with deep furrows around his mouth and across his forehead, but his eyes shone out from the hurt. Asher thought of Luke and wondered if the troubles of his last few years showed on his face like this, too, knowing he had put some of those marks on his brother's skin.

"I wish things were different," Asher said.

Jimmy nodded. He glanced at Stephen. "I know this is asking a lot, Pastor Sharp. But we wondered if—not right now, but sometime in the future—you'd consider marrying us. Maybe next year, once we get our house built." Jimmy was twisting a baseball cap between both hands. "It'd mean a lot to me, personally, to have a preacher do it, and you're the only one I ever knew of to stand up for us, to really put it on the line like that."

Asher had always heard about people breaking into cold sweats and now he knew it was true. Suddenly his body felt drenched.

"We'd want it out at our house," Jimmy added. "Not here at the church. Just us."

He saw the faces of his congregation, of Lydia, of Caleb Carey. He was beyond caring what any of them thought. But still, years and years of believing one way was hard to let go of completely.

"I don't know, to tell you the truth," Asher said, and he heard his voice trembling, "I'd have to think about it."

"Never mind," Stephen said. "Let's go, Jimmy."

"Wait, now." Jimmy caught Stephen by the wrist. "Just be patient a minute."

Stephen turned and shoved his hands into his pants pockets. "We've been patient our whole lives."

"I always said I'd never get married until I could in my own state. Where I was born and raised," Jimmy said, evenly and calmly, as if he had been waiting to say these things. "Now that it's finally legal here, I just thought you might be—"

"I'm sorry," Asher said. "I just can't say for certain right now."

Jimmy shook Asher's hand. "We appreciate how you've stood up for us."

"But we're as good as any other couple," Stephen said. "We ought to be treated just the same."

"I know you should," Asher stammered. "I agree—"

Stephen stood before him, waiting for him to find the rest of his words. But the man already knew Asher was a coward. Stephen turned and shuffled down the steps.

"You take care," Jimmy said, polite despite the disappointment in his voice. He stepped past Asher, out into the blinding white light.

Asher stood on the stoop and watched their car pull away and go over the ridge until it was completely out of sight.

"Come on, Asher!" Lydia hollered from the car, where she and Zelda sat fanning themselves, Lydia with the church program and Zelda with her purse. "We're burning up."

10

The last time Asher had heard from Luke was shortly before the flood. Like the times before that, it was only an unsigned postcard.

On the front was a photograph of a bird on a beach with an impossibly blue ocean beyond. The bird's wings were an orange-edged brown, each one perfect and lovely. Its beak was long and black, as were its knobby legs, jutting out of a soft white down. There was something sorrowful about the way the round brown eye was gazing off into the distance.

On the back of the card there was Asher's name and address, an American flag stamp, and a postmark from Key West, Florida, on the right, but this, best of all, on the left: the words *the roaring alongside he takes for granted* printed out in neat block letters. The handwriting was the same as on the previous two cards he had received over the last couple of years. Each had contained a fragment quote like this.

The first card he had received almost two years ago. On its front, an aerial view of the island of Key West. On the back, this message: *Everything That Is, Is Holy.*

Asher had only to type the quotes into a search engine on the internet to find out where they came from. The first card had led him to Thomas Merton. He had ordered a couple of his books and discovered ways of thinking about religion that he had never thought about: acceptance, identity, freedom. In Merton he found that the key to knowing God better was to know himself better. Reading Merton's books made him feel there was the possibility of his feeling like a good person again.

Luke used to read and talk about going to the island all the time. It had been his dream to live there. He could see Luke before him now, his eyes alight with the thought of escape: "Down there, people can be who they want to be," he'd say. Luke had always recommended music and books to Asher as a child and teenager but had stopped once Asher started preaching and became closed off from anyone who didn't go to his church. Now Luke was sending his quiet recommendations once again.

On the second card there had been a view of the sea in all its glory, a water that begged to be jumped into, the vast green-blue-white ocean fading off toward a purpling sky. On the back: *Sometimes the hurt is so deep deep deep,* and that led him to Patty

Griffin. For years now he had not listened to anything besides gospel music. The way she sang—so full of sadness and trouble, yet always hope—sounded like Luke.

So now here, this third one. He read the quote again and then took note of the little explanatory paragraph at the top of the card:

The <u>*sandpiper*</u> *is a wading shorebird often seen on the beaches of the eastern seaboard. Unlike most birds, the* <u>*sandpiper*</u> *is more agile on the ground than in the air.*

The underlines stood in the same blue ink as the quote.

At his laptop Asher typed in the quote and the word *sandpiper* and sure enough there was a poem with that title. He read it through several times, trying to understand what his brother might be saying to him. Asher printed out a copy, folded it into a neat square and slid it into his wallet so he could reread it some more.

He went out onto the front porch. A thin rain was falling, causing breaths of mist to ease out of the ridge cleft across the river.

He had not changed as much as he had convinced himself. When put to the test, he had failed. It was like he had failed his brother once again.

Asher pulled his phone from his back pocket and called Caleb Carey.

"I've made up my mind. If any of you try to keep those men from this church, I'll leave with them."

"They chose their way of life," Caleb said. "So now they have to stick with their own kind."

"Caleb, you're the one making a choice here. Not those men."

"What choice?"

"The choice to be mean-hearted." He said, and clicked off the call.

He sat there for a long while as the rain changed over to a fine mist. All the little live things in the trees and grasses clicked and sang.

When Lydia came out he figured she was calling him into supper—he had smelled the chicken frying in the kitchen. "Caleb has called in all of the deacons," she said. "To ask them to have a church vote on keeping you or not."

"I hope they don't," he said. "I'm done."

"You can't just give up," she said. "We don't get to just sit down when we're weary."

He stood and went to the porch railing, looking out at the valley. She stayed behind him.

"I know you want to do what you think is the right thing," she said. "But you have to do what's right for *us*. For Justin, especially."

A breeze rose up from the river.

"Everybody in this world has to make compromises," she continued. "Every day of our lives—"

Asher watched the wind in the dark-green trees. Asher remembered Zelda telling him once that her Cherokee granny had always said God lived in the trees, way up in the top branches.

Lydia swept the porch now, her eyes intent on her work. He watched her move along the floorboards with the straw broom. Her arms were a golden-brown, as they always were in summertime. He had always liked to watch her work, especially outside: in the garden, around the yard. She knew how to can, how to

raise plants and flowers. She could do anything she took the notion to learn. Ever since she was a young woman she had known
exactly what she believed and if she had ever doubted it she had
never articulated that to him. She had always believed that if
she worked and prayed everything else would fall into place. He
wished he could be more like that and not always full of all these
questions.

And he wished he could tell her about the postcards, but
she had been glad when Luke disappeared. She had never said as
much, but he knew just the same.

"You're not talking to me," she said, bringing the broom back
in a wide arc so she could send all the debris scattering from the
top step and out onto the yard. She turned to face him and tucked
the broom handle against her shoulder. He could see the young
woman he had married so clearly: that clean-scrubbed face of
youth, mesmerized in the second pew while he preached a fiery
sermon.

"How could you give up everything for two strangers?" she
said now. "You know what those men do is wrong."

"Those men are no different than my own brother."

"But they're not Luke."

"It's the same difference, Lydia. You turned them away because of who they are."

She sat in one of the rockers and looked out at the river, the
muscle in her jaw tensing. "I don't know how to get through to you."

He looked down at his hands.

"I should've offered for them to stay," she said, with hesitation. "But I didn't know how to do that. I didn't know how to say

to them, 'Y'all can stay here as long as you don't sleep together.' I couldn't have that, around Justin. So it was easier to just not invite them."

"The world's not the same as it was when we were growing up, Lydia."

"So I should accept just any old way?" She scoffed, a sound in the back of her throat. "I should agree with the world because it's changed?"

"There's no use denying to Justin that different kinds of people exist. He'll live in this world with them. He'll know them. And those kids at school might be backward now but that whole generation—they think about this differently than we were taught to."

"That don't make it right." Her lovely brown eyes could become hard so quickly. "And my job is to let him know what's right and what's wrong."

"It's more important to show him how to be good to people than how to judge them."

She arose as if she was going to go inside, but she reconsidered and eased back down into the rocker again.

After a time she spoke. "When I was a real little girl my daddy told me that the world would try to change me. And to not let that happen. I don't want to judge them. I want to love the sinner and hate the sin. But that don't mean I'm going to let it come into my own home."

Asher stepped off the porch—

"Where are you *going*?" she called after him, agitated now. "You used to believe this way, too."

—and went to the grove of willow trees down by the Cumberland River, the trees where he and Luke had spent so many afternoons as boys. He lay down beneath the trees and watched the summer breeze shake their long branches. He thought about a God who had made the trees, and the river, and himself, and Lydia. Where was that God, these days? So far up in the trees Asher couldn't feel Him anymore? Or just completely gone?

After a time he went into the house to pack his things.

11

He stayed a couple nights in the River Inn out near Ashland City. The room smelled of stagnant air conditioner water and the carpet was threadbare in places but the sheets and tub were clean enough. There was a massive old television perched on a banged-up dresser and he kept it on to fight the silence: game show hosts with bright white teeth, the local news anchors talking perkily about the flood recovery and county court clerks who wouldn't give marriage licenses to gay couples, the depressing infomercials late at night. He spoke to Justin a couple times a day and only once did the boy ask what was going to happen.

"Everything'll be okay, buddy," Asher said, and once again he found himself telling his son something that might or might not be true.

He hadn't packed much more than a shaving kit and a few books. He couldn't concentrate enough to read. Sometimes he stood by the window and watched the parking lot where he saw cars come and go, people smoking as they gazed up at the moon, a couple who couldn't help stopping to kiss passionately before they went on to the office to check in.

He found a trailer for rent out on Cheatham Lake and called to ask if he could see it. An old woman who leaned on a cane unlocked the door for him. "You'll need to call and get the juice and gas switched out of the last renter's name," the landlady said, and listed all the things she didn't allow her tenants to do. She was the most humorless person he had ever met. There was no furniture and it had not been lived in for a while but it was in good enough shape and its large windows looked out on the water where a white boat was pulling a water-skier, its sound a comforting hum in the distance. Even though he was very far out in the country there was still a strong cell signal so he could talk to Justin anytime he wanted. He went back out to the house to get a few more of his things and Lydia met him at the door.

"Justin's still at school," she said.

"I know it. I just need to get some clothes," he said. He moved to go into the house but she stood in the middle of the open door.

"You really intend to do this? To leave?"

"I don't see any other way around it."

"But I don't believe in divorce. I can't do that."

"Let me get my clothes, Lydia."

"Asher," she said. He could hear the hurt in her voice, could see it on her face.

"I want out of this," he said. "All of it."

"What are you talking about?"

"It's over, Lydia. There's no use pretending—"

Lydia shook her head as if she couldn't wrap her mind around what he was saying. But she refused to cry. She steeled herself, her face becoming squarer with determination, then stepped aside so he could pass.

He threw some clothes into a duffel bag and filled a couple Walmart bags with shoes. He took a small framed photograph of Justin holding up the first fish he'd ever caught, the Robert Frost book where he kept the postcards hidden. He was surprised by the strange sense of freedom he felt as he gathered his things. She was still standing in the door when he came back with the bags, the book tucked under his arm.

"I'm going to take this little picture with me," he said, holding it out.

"We can't just throw our family away," she said. He could see how afraid she was. He left her there on the porch, where she was still standing as he pulled away.

HE DROVE ON over to Zelda's to tell her the news.

"I hate this. I do. But I can't live with her, either," Zelda said. "You know I love her better than anything. But she's too hard on folks," Zelda said. Asher suspected she had seen it coming even longer than he had. "I never was a good enough Christian for her liking."

"Nobody ever was except her daddy," Asher said, and they laughed a bit at that.

"That's the truth," Zelda said. "I'll say this for her, she sticks to what she believes. But a person can believe something so hard they lose sight of everything else."

"You know it'll be a big scandal. A Pentecostal preacher getting a divorce," he said, feeling loopy with relief. Perhaps this is what people meant when they said sometimes you had to laugh to keep from crying. "But after what I said Sunday they'll run me off anyway."

She asked him to stay for supper and he did. Lydia had always accused her mother of siding with him on everything. Zelda fried green tomatoes and corn bread while he sliced cucumbers and cleaned green onions she had bought at Kathi Hoskins's grocery. The floodwaters had carried her garden away. They ate on the porch and drank a pitcher of sweet tea. They watched the hickory-nut green water of the river and sat chatting for a while, then they both fell silent. That was one thing he loved about Zelda: she let a person be. She knew how to be quiet. Most folks couldn't do that.

"I sure do love the cool of the day," Zelda said, finally, and popped a slice of fried green tomato into her mouth, chewing it with vigor. She always referred to the evening time this way, and Asher sometimes found himself repeating it aloud.

Asher helped her with the dishes and the thin kitchen curtains breathed in and out at the windows. A sprawling willow tree stood near the kitchen and every time a breeze stirred the willow leaves made a small quiet music against the screens.

"The best part about open windows at night is when I wake

up in the morning, I can hear the birds praying in the trees," Zelda said, her hands in the soapy water. She had said this to him many times before, too, but Asher loved hearing her say it each time.

When he told her goodbye she finally got choked up and put her hands over her face. "You'll always be family," she said. "Nothing'll change that."

He stopped at the Dollar General on his way back out to the lake trailer and bought an air mattress to sleep on, a set of sheets, a couple of pillows, a little lamp. He'd worry about everything else later. He wished he had gotten a quilt for the weight on his body but he could make it for a couple nights. He switched off the chilling air conditioner and opened the windows, filling the house with insect song arising from the lake bank. The mattress squeaked beneath him as he tried to get situated. He read the Elizabeth Bishop poem again as his eyes grew heavy. He thought of the sandpipers on the Key West beaches, of his brother living there in that place so different from home.

JUSTIN WAS IN awe of the panoramic view of the lake from the trailer windows and didn't seem to notice that there was hardly any furniture. Anticipating Justin's visit Asher had bought a sunken old couch from the Goodwill and cleaned it with a shampooer he rented from the hardware store. He had bought another air mattress for Justin to sleep on—"It's just like we're camping," he told his son, although Justin seemed unconcerned—but other than that the trailer was bare.

"Can we go swimming?" Justin asked, peering out the uncurtained window.

"I don't see why not," Asher said. "That's why I made you bring your trunks."

They changed and followed the winding path down to the water and spent a long while there splashing and swimming. How different things were going to be. Already he felt like one of those divorced fathers on television who always just buy their kids pizza and let them do whatever fun thing they want. He knew things couldn't stay that way. And he also knew that missing him would only get worse.

The day before, he had received the call from Caleb Carey he had been expecting: the deacons had met and had called a church-wide meeting to vote if he should be kept on as their pastor or not. Lydia had said she would pick up Justin after the meeting, no emotion whatsoever in her voice, as if she was already treating the shared parentage of their son like a business deal.

That afternoon Zelda cooked early on account of the church meeting and after their swim Asher hurried Justin to get ready so they could be there on time. They loaded their plates with chicken, mashed potatoes, fresh green beans, a slice of tomato so red Asher's mouth watered.

Once they were settled at the table Asher said the blessing and while he still had ahold of Zelda and Justin's hands he turned to his son. "Whatever happens between me and your mother, we're a family. You remember that, alright?" Justin looked back at him blank-faced. "There's all different kind of families. Alright, now?"

Justin nodded and scooped potatoes into his mouth.

After supper Asher strolled down to the river to study on what he would say to the church when they voted him out. He knew they would. Zelda's and Kathi's votes would likely be the only ones in his favor. And if they didn't, he would resign. He watched the river and listened to the mockingbirds singing in the willows. Heat was rising from the lush hills around him, moving in over the valley and causing a thin white haze to swim over the ridges in the distance. After a time he stood and made his way back to Zelda's. Through the kitchen window he heard Zelda: "Your parents wouldn't want me to tell you this but I want you to be prepared, alright?"

"Yes, ma'am."

"You're older than they think you are," she said. "Your daddy's fixing to lose his job at the church. I want you to know what's going on. But you can't tell them I told you."

"I won't." Justin sounded like he was just fine with the notion of Asher losing his job. Maybe he hoped that Asher would so he wouldn't have to go to church every time the door was cracked.

"I've spent my whole life listening to everybody else," she said. She had always talked to Justin like he was an adult. "First my daddy, and then your granddaddy, and then your mother. But inside, I only listen to myself. Does that make sense?"

"I guess."

"What the church is doing to your daddy—it's not right. They're going to fire him because he wouldn't turn people away. And if there's one thing I know for sure it's that you never shun somebody because you don't agree with them. We're ever one of us children of God. You remember that. Alright?"

"Yes, ma'am," Justin said again.

Asher came up the porch steps and opened the screen door. "Y'all ready?"

12

The windows were open, only letting in heat and loud birdsong. Church programs from last Sunday had been turned into fans, and women dotted their foreheads with Kleenex. The air conditioner had stopped again and the church was packed because they all wanted to hear what Asher would have to say. Jimmy and Stephen were not there.

The congregation had been assembled, given slips of paper, and cast their votes. Caleb Carey and a couple of the other deacons had made a big show of going into the church office to count the votes and a hum had arisen over the whispering crowd while they waited. Asher stood by the door at the back of the church, looking out the glass doors onto the parking lot and didn't move until Caleb stood in the pulpit. "The vote is final: five to stay and forty-one to terminate," Caleb read in his monotone way. "The deacons will start a new pastor search. That concludes our meeting today."

"I want to say something," Asher said, striding up the aisle. A few people had stood up but now they sat back down.

Caleb had his right hand up, waving it. "The church bylaws don't specify that the outgoing pastor be allowed a response."

"I've pastored this church for ten years and served it a lot longer than that," Asher said, and Caleb threw his hands up. He sat down heavily in the front pew, shaking his head.

Asher faced the congregation. "I've served it all this time and you've voted me out because I welcomed two men to our congregation. Because I refused to turn them away."

Flap flap flap went the church programs as they fanned.

"My brother and I had it pretty rough when we were boys. Our mother was a hard woman and she lived a hard life. Some of you helped us when she was so sick, and I thank you for that. But it's easy to help somebody you agree with. If you had known Luke was like Jimmy and Stephen I wonder if you would've helped us at all."

A breeze slithered through the windows. A girl was holding up her phone to take a picture of Asher. Far off down the road he could hear a car passing, playing a rap song, the bass *thump th-thump thumping* until the ridge came between the car and the church.

"Ten years ago Luke came and told me about his struggle

and asked me for my support. I reacted the way I'd been raised to: I called him an abomination. Being afraid of somebody who's different'll make an awful meanness come over you. I said a lot of things I'm ashamed of now."

He felt tears on his face but didn't wipe them away.

"We've got to quit this judgment!" he implored, louder than he intended, the last word caught in the height of his beseeching cry. He was surprised by the sound of himself, the release of a grief that had been living within him for years now. As instantly as the words had burst forth he saw how startled some of them were, drawing back in disbelief. He put his hand out to steady himself against the pulpit.

He dropped his head to gather himself and again caught sight of the teenaged girl holding up her phone. She was filming, he realized. Well, let her.

"All he wanted was for me to love him for who he was, and I couldn't give it to him." He drew in a ragged breath. "I never knew of my brother to lie. But when he told me he was born that way, I accused him of lying. I told him he had been turned over to a reprobate mind. Because I had been taught that. And I lost my brother. Not because of a choice he made, but because I chose to turn my back on him."

He plucked his Bible up from the pulpit and held it in the air.

"You can use the Word to judge and condemn people or you can use it to love them. The day I turned Luke away, I felt that doubt pulsing inside me. Sometimes I wonder if that doubt isn't God, giving us a little nudge."

A couple stood up and shuffled out with their children. Caleb

Carey arose, one hand up before him, signaling that Asher had said enough.

"When those two men came into this church to be part of a congregation," Asher continued, "after a flood took everything they had, you refused to speak to them. All their lives, people have told them they're no good, that they're abominations, that they don't deserve God's love. They came here seeking it. But you couldn't find the decency in yourself to be good to them. So I don't want to be your pastor. You had your meeting and you fired me, but I'm here to tell you I had already quit *you*."

Zelda let out a heaving sob. No one else flinched.

Caleb took a step forward. "That's enough, now, Asher—"

"I've been with you when your people died, when they were sick. I've visited you in the hospital. I barely slept for three days after the flood so I could tend to each one of you who lost a home. And I'm afraid that you are going to let this hatred take you over."

Asher stood before them, scanning the congregation, touching eyes with each one of them who had the decency to look at him. The teenaged girl—he had baptized her himself, in the Cumberland, on a day heavy with bruised, stormy skies, but in this moment he couldn't think of her name—was still filming him.

Some were struggling to not break down now. Asher knew of at least one couple that had turned their backs on their son. There were undoubtedly others.

"All I ask of you is to search your hearts." He was pleading with them. "Don't make the mistakes I've made."

That was all he had to say. He wiped his face with the back of his hand and walked down the aisle, pausing at the pew where

Lydia sat with Zelda and Justin, waiting for them to join him. Zelda struggled to get up, and Justin scrambled past, sliding over the legs of others until he reached his father. He took Asher's hand. Lydia set her eyes on his, but didn't budge.

They walked out, Asher and his boy and his wife's mother who was like his mother. When he reached the door and looked back on the congregation he could see that several women had surrounded Lydia, praying with their hands on her head, speaking in tongues now, the strange words curling through the air.

13

They sat there in the car, the engine and air conditioner running, while everyone else left. Asher kept his eyes on the dashboard. "Kathi's waving at you," Zelda said, quietly, but he didn't look up. "The Turners looked this way," she said after a minute. Justin sat in the back seat listening to music on his earbuds, looking out on the green pastures.

Then there was a startling rap on Asher's window and he jumped, looking up to see Lydia leaned in close to the glass. "Bring Justin back to the house," she said, and turned to her own car, her shoes crunching on the gravel.

"I should have rode with her," Zelda said. "She'll say I was choosing sides for staying in here with you."

"I don't know why I'm so upset," he said. "I was going to quit them anyway, so I shouldn't be mad they fired me."

"Well, nobody wants to be turned away," Zelda said, patting him on the shoulder.

"It's the why that burns me up."

They rode the rest of the way in silence, the radio playing country songs low between them. Asher was struck by what a perfect summer day lay out before them. The trees were a lush, dark green and the river shone alongside the road. Cumberland Valley was about the prettiest place he'd ever seen. Everything looked new to him.

At the house Zelda said for him to go on in. "We'll go down here to the riverbank and skip us some rocks."

Lydia sat on the couch, tucked in as close to the arm as she could get, her legs and arms crossed. "You just destroyed everything we've worked for our whole lives. Building a congregation. A church that mattered."

"I can't go on doing it, Lydia. I've told you."

"You could've just walked away. But you had to ruin it for me, too. How am I supposed to show my face in there?"

"I had to stand up for what I believed in."

Only now did she look up at him and her face was crumbling with sorrow. "I'm so afraid, Asher. The way you acted in there. I don't know you at all."

She rose from the couch, left him standing there in the living room, and disappeared down the hallway. He stood there and took in everything he had known over the last dozen years. This room. The scent of it (cinnamon), the way the light slanted through the picture window in a perfect rectangle this time of day in summertime. The three little dogwoods he could see from the picture window, the glint of river beyond them, and farther still, the ridge. The clicking of the old mantle clock's pendulum. The remotes lined up on the coffee table. The recliner with the worn patches on its arms.

Lydia came back with two black garbage bags weighed down with clothes. She sat them down by the front door and fumbled for the knob, opening it wide. He could see how powerful she felt in this moment. "This is what you've wanted all this time," she said. "Go."

He had not realized it, but some part of him had always thought that she might change, that she might see his way of thinking and try to come round to it. He knew now that wasn't going to happen. He could see this on her face, but also in the set of her shoulders, by the tense of the muscle in her arm as she held on to the doorknob, her eyes hard on him. "Go on," she said.

"Don't keep my boy away from me," he said, knowing she would try.

"We're going to be laughingstocks now."

"That church doesn't make up this whole place," he said, "this whole country."

"Go on." She swiped her hand through the air, pointing to the door.

Zelda and Justin were coming up the hill from the river as he stepped from the porch. Justin dared his granny to race him and she tried for only a second to keep up with him before she stopped, laughing, hands on her knees. Then Justin ran into Asher's leg and caught hold of it, out of breath.

"I'll see you in a couple days, buddy," Asher said.

"I want to go back out to the lake, with you."

"No, now, Justin," Lydia said, trying to steady her voice, "you've got school."

"Not till Monday."

Asher put his hand on the boy's back. "I'll bring him back tomorrow evening. Let him go with me for tonight."

"You've given up your family because of this," Lydia said. She took hold of Justin's shoulder and he pulled away from her. "No judge in this state will even let you have joint custody after the stunt you just pulled."

Asher thought of the way he had lost control of his temper, the way he had yelled and cried. Folks in the audience recoiling. And the girl, filming every bit of it.

"Just go, Asher," Zelda said, finally drawing near. "For now."

He drove away. At the curve in the road at the bottom of the hill he stopped his Jeep and looked back. There was the home he was leaving. But already gone inside were the people he had known and loved so well.

14

For a time Lydia agreed to let Asher take Justin every other weekend and one night a week. Asher cooked him grilled cheeses and fried baloney sandwiches. As long as it was warm enough they swam in the green, still waters of Cheatham Lake. There was an abundance of treasures for Justin's nature collection on the lake's shore: tiny white mollusk shells, cardinal flowers he dried between the pages of book, a small gray trilobite. Often Asher sat on the bank and watched Justin's determined reverence as he studied leaves or rocks, wondering what this divorce would do to his little boy.

Then he received the notice by registered mail: Lydia had gone to court with the video of him in church.

Asher didn't know any lawyers so he chose the first one he found online and drove to her office on the square in Choctaw. In the waiting room he sat looking out the window at the tall war memorial topped with a Confederate soldier. The receptionist apologized that the attorney was late for their appointment; twice he caught her staring at him from behind the screen of her computer. She was playing music there—a string of country songs that all sounded like the same young man singing about fishing, and his truck, and his girl. The receptionist looked too young for this job—like she had just graduated from high school—and spoke with a babyish voice, her eyelashes spidery with clumped mascara. The lawyer hustled in, wiping her hands on a paper towel and still chewing the remnants of her lunch.

She shook Asher's hand. "I'm Jane Fisher, but you can call me Fisher," she said, then belched quietly into the cup of her palm. "Let's go on into my office."

She settled herself behind her desk and offered no small talk. "So tell me what's going on, Mr. Sharp."

"I'm terrified I'm going to lose my son," he said.

"Why would that happen?"

He told her all about Jimmy and Stephen, being fired from the church, the video. She kept her eyes on him and listened silently until he was finished, then perched her reading glasses on her nose and tapped at her laptop's keyboard, hunting and pecking. She watched the screen for a moment before speaking.

"Well, they're going to say the video proves you had a nervous breakdown—"

"But it's just tears in my eyes, just a plea to the congre—"

"—and that you're unstable. And honestly, Mr. Sharp, you're demanding that your church welcome a gay couple to their congregation. In a county where the court clerk is refusing to give marriage licenses to gay couples. In a state that believes traditional religion is under attack." Fisher seemed amused by the whole situation. She stifled her laugh and pulled at the lapels of her blazer and leaned forward on her desk. "I'm not laughing at you, Mr. Sharp, but at how ridiculous all of that is. *And* remember that we're in a county where both the family court judges ran on"— she thrust both hands into the air to make air quotes—"'family values' campaigns and used Bible verses on their posters. Not to mention that there are actually people around here who honestly believe the flood was God's response to the Supreme Court decision." The attorney let out a big breath and ran a hand over her face. Asher noticed that she didn't wear a single ring. Her nails had been painted with a clear polish that caught the light from the window. "I mean—good Lord. Sometimes you have to laugh to keep from crying, you know?" She shook her head. "You *have* seen the video, haven't you?"

Asher shook his head, no.

"Well, everybody else has," Fisher said, turning the screen toward him. "It's gone viral."

There he was, face contorted, tears in his eyes. The lawyer had the video muted but Asher could read his own lips when he yelled out "We've got to quit this judgement!" Even without the sound he could see how bad it would look in court, out of context. Then Fisher tapped her finger on the bottom right corner of the screen. "Look at that. It's gone from fifty-some thousand this morning to a million views. In less than five hours. That's not good for our case."

"Why would it go up so much in one day?"

"Some celebrity probably tweeted the link," Fisher said, shrugging. "Who knows? I don't even try to understand how the world works today."

Asher put his face in his hands for only a second, then locked his eyes on the lawyer's. "I can't lose my little boy." He searched for the right words and could land only on a cliché. "He's my whole world."

"Well, it's my job to make sure that doesn't happen." Fisher swung the laptop back around to face herself. There was a kind of determination in every move she made, an announcement that she didn't put up with any BS from anyone. She kept her eyes on the video as she scrolled through the comments. She paused to dig in her desk drawer and withdrew an orange, which she peeled in silence as she read her screen. The mouthwatering smell bloomed between them. At last Fisher drew the membranes of orange apart and held a couple out on her palm. "Want one? I just washed my hands."

"No," Asher said with more exasperation than he intended to reveal.

"But I need you to know right now that you'll never get equal custody, Mr. Sharp," she said, the chewed orange flashing on her tongue. "It doesn't work that way. Even under normal circumstances a man rarely gets that unless the mother has been proven to be on drugs or to be abusive. And mostly with good reason." She took the glasses from her face and looked at Asher. "The deadbeat dads make it bad for the occasional good ones. Unfortunately, there are plenty of those."

On the other side of the door the receptionist had turned up her country music.

"She's petitioning to be sole custodian—"

"What does that mean, exactly?" Asher asked.

"Well, if she gains that she won't have to consult you to choose medical treatment or to make decisions about school, religion. She would even have to give special approval for you to see his grades. It pretty much gives her complete control." Asher could see that the attorney was in her element now, lining all of this out. "So, what we want is joint custody, which would give you these same rights, and more time with your boy. But there's no way you'll get him equal time, alright? I want to be clear about that. Not unless the two of you come to a mutual decision about that. And maybe she'll come around to that someday. People calm down eventually. Time works wonders in a divorce case."

Asher felt disappointment running over him.

"The good news is that most of these comments are calling you a folk hero." Fisher shut the laptop and pushed it to the side of his desk. "The bad news is that it looks like those comments aren't coming from people 'round here."

"So you'll take the case? You'll help me?"

Fisher didn't crack a smile. "Hell yes I'll take it. I'd be crazy not to."

"Why do you say that?"

Fisher laughed as if Asher had said something foolish. "Because this has the potential to be a high-publicity case, to tell you the truth. The way those views are going up on that video. The fact that this happened so close to the Supreme Court decision on marriage equality. I mean, it's perfect timing." Fisher put another orange slice into her mouth. "But also, not all of us here disagree with what you said in that video."

Fisher spent some time studying the order in detail. "I'm sorry to say that there's more." Lydia's lawyer was insisting on supervised visits. "She says the video proves you're not in your right mind and prone to 'outbursts of temper.'"

"But she knows I'm a good father," Asher said. "She *knows* I'm not crazy."

"Maybe she's just being vindictive. People lose their minds during divorces. I see it happen all the time. Men and women. It happened to me *and* my ex in our divorce. Now we're good friends." Fisher pushed the papers away from her and put her arms behind her head, leaning back in her chair. "And maybe it's just a smart move on her lawyer's part. It establishes there's a problem so they can deny you joint custody later."

"Her mother will testify for me. Zelda Crosby. We've always been real close. She's as close to me as she is to Lydia, her own daughter."

"But Lydia *is* her daughter, Mr. Sharp. And that's what it'll come down to, in the end. I would bet you cash money on that."

ASHER'S VISITS WITH Justin took place in the basement of the Choctaw courthouse on Saturdays. The supervisor was a woman who sat in the corner playing games on her cell phone while he and Justin talked or played rummy. The supervisor always wore a gray pantsuit and pulled her hair back in a tight ponytail that made her look like her head was being yanked back.

"How are you, buddy?" Asher asked Justin. "How are things going?"

"Just going to school," Justin said, kicking his heels against the chair legs. "Mom's going to church all the time and makes me go most of the time. The other night this big group of women came and prayed over me until Granny made them quit."

"She did?"

Justin nodded. "They were speaking in tongues and she told them they were scaring me and took me outside. We sat on the porch until church was over. Mom stayed in there forever. Every time we go she stays after and everybody prays for her like she's dying."

"It'll get better soon," Asher said.

"I want you to come home," Justin said, tiny globes of tears teetering on his eyelashes.

"Please don't get the boy upset, sir," the supervisor said in a curt little voice as if she was exhausted with Asher. Asher wanted to tell her to kiss his ass. He had never told anyone that in his life and had rarely even had the thought.

KATHI OFFERED ASHER a job at her store, Hoskins' Grocery, where they had shopped his whole life, and he took it. The store was small and always held the scent of lemon Pine-Sol and overripe bananas. There were only three employees including himself and Kathi. The other one was Cherry Sizemore, who staffed the register and conducted his training.

Cherry had recently dropped out of high school to have a baby but had worked at Hoskins' since she was fifteen years old. She had the palest skin he'd ever seen—intricate networks of blue veins plainly visible in her temples and wrists—and was tiny but her belly had started to become very rounded. One evening when she lifted the green smock over her head to hang it in her locker back in the break room he had accidentally caught sight of her bulbous navel peeking out from under the hem of her shirt.

"I'm only eighteen weeks but already my belly button is poking out and so sore!" Cherry said in her cheerful way, tugging at the edge of her blouse.

"I'm sorry," he said, ashamed he had seen this private part of her, but she thought he meant he was sorry for her pain.

"It's just part of it, I reckon," Cherry said.

He had known her since she was a white-haired little girl playing in the mudholes of the church parking lot after services. Cherry's mother had kicked her out for getting knocked up and now she was living in a trailer park across the busy highway with her older sister. She walked to work and back every day, one hand on her belly as she eyed the traffic, waiting to cross. Justin had always had a crush on her.

She taught Asher how to stock the shelves, how to change out the merchandise so that the newest stuff was always at the back. She taught him how to run the little handheld machine that printed out UPC labels for the shelves. She even taught him how to run the register, although he was to do that only in emergencies. "That's usually my and Miss Kathi's territory," Cherry said, in that sweet-as-hard-candy voice of hers that made Asher think how he couldn't understand anyone—especially her mother—kicking her out on her own.

Most days he and Cherry worked in happy silence. They were both quiet people and he figured that she was as content as he was to pass the day with little conversation. Only occasionally she said something profound to him that made him think she needed someone to talk to. In the past he would've invited this—people always said he never met a stranger, could talk to anybody, which made for a good preacher—but these days he was floating through the world the best way he could. Surviving. Sometimes they both found themselves singing along to the country songs that played through the ceiling speakers.

One day as they were fixing to go home he wrung out his mop, dumped the gray mop water, and clicked off all the exterior lights. Cherry was already at the door, ready to lock up, and she kept her eyes on him as he came up the aisle to the door.

"Pastor Sharp," she said, despite the fact he had asked her many times to call him Asher and to remember that he wasn't a pastor anymore, "I've been wanting to tell you how good it was, what you said on that video."

"Thank you, Cherry. Most people 'round here don't feel that way."

"I think more than you realize do, though," she said, and her brows fretted together, her hand rushing to lay itself flat on her stomach.

"You alright?" Asher said, putting his hands out toward her arm in case she needed to steady herself.

But then a smile overtook her entire face. "Yeah, it's just little

Emmaline kicking," she said. "Lord, about took my breath there for a minute! This gal's liable to be a football player."

They laughed at that and stepped out into the cool, black night.

"You want me to walk with you?" Asher asked as she told him goodbye and waddled toward the highway. "Make sure you don't fall?"

"Naw sir, I'm just fine, I believe," she said. "Night."

There was not much traffic tonight so she was able to cross without waiting but he watched until she had disappeared into the trailer park. He stood there with his hand on the door handle of his car and looked up at the night sky. Impossible to see many stars under the cluster of streetlamps guarding the lot.

So many days had passed since he had lived with his own child. Mornings and gloamings. Sunup, sundown. The phases of the moon: waning, waxing, gibbous. The last days of summer had passed now. That glowing green had passed with them. The wildflowers, the Confederate roses, the bluestars: gone. Now the ridges were orange and yellow, the river was narrowing in its autumnal way. The first frosts would happen soon and Cherry's child would be born and before long he'd know how much he would be allowed to see his own. After a long while he got into his Jeep and drove home.

15

The Everything

The more Justin watched the clock hanging over his teacher's desk the longer the day seemed to be, the thin, black wand of the minute hand sweeping over the numbers in slow motion. The classroom smelled of dirty hair and the markers the teacher was squeaking across the whiteboard. Justin was trying to follow along and write down what she was posting up there—questions for a quiz about the Civil War—but his eyes kept going up to the clock.

Then the spitball hit him directly in the ear, miraculously lodging in the curves just above his lobe. He swung his face around and of course that boy with Rabbit was having a laughing fit behind his grubby little hands. His fingernails hadn't been clipped in ages and black lines of dirt stood under each one. Rabbit brought up the straw he had snuck in from the lunchroom and huffed into it, launching another spitball that stung the middle of Justin's forehead. Justin didn't even turn away or react. He kept his eyes on Rabbit's pink rabbit eyes to show him how bored he was with these daily acts of meanness.

Mrs. Sherman didn't catch any of the muffled laughter that was happening behind her now. She continued to write on the whiteboard, the squeak of the marker becoming increasingly annoying.

When Justin wouldn't stop staring Rabbit finally thrust his middle finger into the air and mouthed "Your daddy's a queer-lover," which was his favorite thing to say these days. Justin turned back to his notes and sighed. Some days Rabbit was such an idiot that no matter what he did Justin wasn't much bothered by it. Other days it was too much to bear. Most nights he laid awake and thought about ways to fight back.

Rabbit's family had been living on the football field here at the school, in the campers the government set up for the homeless, ever since the flood, months ago, so Rabbit thought he ran things now. He claimed to sneak into the school after dark and go through the teachers' desk drawers. Rabbit had lived in the Cumberland River Court and every one of the trailers there had floated away in a jagged line on the flood. Most folks had been able to move in with family or friends but Rabbit's parents hadn't had anyone. Rabbit had been picking on Justin for years now, long before the flood. Ever since first grade. Justin should have been used to it by now, really. But there was no getting used to something like that.

At recess was the worst. Rabbit took someone's phone and showed everyone the video of Asher. The kids all gathered close and they had a big laugh together when the video zoomed in on Asher crying out "We've got tō quit this judgment!"

Rabbit clicked the phone off right after that and they all turned their heads at once, like a family of owls, to see Justin watching them from his perch on the swing. The December air bit into his face and his nose had numbed from the cold—the teacher had said they could stay out only a few minutes, since it was so cold—but he didn't mind. The cold reminded him he was still alive and not a ghost-boy spying on the playground.

Then they were laughing and pointing and some kind of power came over him and he yelled: "Shut up, you stupid-asses!"

Rabbit ran hard toward him and before Justin realized what was happening, Rabbit had knocked him out of the swing and was on top of Justin, like a wall falling onto someone. He pinned down Justin's arms and situated his chin on the back of Justin's head, grinding his face against the soured mulch.

Most of the other kids were yelling and laughing—Justin could hear one small voice screaming "Quit! Leave him alone!" but he didn't know who that was. Then Rabbit brought his knee up into the small of Justin's back and he felt a start of electricity run all the way up his spine and into his neck. He actually saw light at the corners of his eyes. He felt like he was going to pass out but in that brief time he felt shimmering all around him and he could hear everything slowed down and magnified. He could hear the sky moving. He thought how he had lied to his father, because he didn't believe in God. Not really. This was what he believed in. The Everything.

But then: "Your daddy's a queer-lover," Rabbit whispered into his ear, his breath wet and hot, and Justin could see again, he could hear all the other kids hollering and laughing. Some of them were chanting "Fight fight fight" but their voices trailed away and then Justin was aware of the boy's weight being sucked away as the teacher plucked Rabbit off him.

Justin felt like he couldn't breathe. He willed himself to roll over onto his back and the white light of the winter sky caused him to squint. Someone was bending down over him.

"Are you okay, Justin?" his teacher was saying. "Honey, can you catch your breath?"

He managed to roll over onto his side just in time to let a pinkish-orange ribbon of vomit burst out of his mouth and slide down his jaw and neck, running down into the collar of his shirt.

Nobody was laughing now. Everyone was very quiet.

After a time Justin stood, without help. He could see Rabbit being hustled away to the principal's office by one of the other teachers. And Mrs. Sherman was at his arm, asking if he was okay, but he didn't answer her. He was thinking that he hated Rabbit. He knew you weren't supposed to hate anybody. His daddy had been telling him that his whole damn life. But he hated them all. He hated all the other kids, too. Not laughing anymore, but trying not to, their hands over their mouths, all those eyes on him. He looked away from them and more than anything he was thinking this: *I'm stronger than you.*

16

Asher was stacking cans of PET milk on a shelf when he caught sight of his son making his way up the aisle toward him. He squatted down and Justin hugged him. He drew in his son's foresty scent. Over Justin's shoulder he could see Zelda hovering at the end of the aisle like a lookout. She had to know she was breaking the law by allowing Asher to see him without the supervisor present.

"Can't you just come back home now?" Justin said.

"No, buddy. I wish I could. But I can't. From now on you'll have two homes. My house and your Mom's. Alright?"

"Things would be so much easier if you'd just come home,"

Justin said, and Asher wished that it could be that simple. He put his hand out to smooth his thumb down the side of his boy's face and then Justin said he had to go and trotted back down the aisle. Zelda raised her hand in a wave, and they were gone.

"You ought not allow her to do that again, Asher," Kathi said, standing behind him. "It'll only cause you trouble if they find out before the custody hearing."

Asher bristled but just nodded to her.

"And you're not gonna believe this, but there's a CNN van out front. I need you to get rid of 'em, Asher. I can't have them interviewing my customers. Enough people are mad at me for having you working here, anyway." Kathi saw the concern on his face and put her hand up before he could say anything. "If people don't like it that you're working here then I don't want their business nohow. But I can't have the news people harassing my customers."

Asher went outside and asked the news crew to leave. Later, online, he saw that they had set up a film crew at the Cumberland Valley Church of Life. People he had known his whole life were on there saying how they had no choice but to get rid of him, that they didn't believe "that way," that Asher had turned into a troublemaker instead of a pastor. They interviewed a man from a protest group who said that Asher now represented the "silenced progressives of rural America."

Fox News and two newspaper reporters came to his trailer but he dodged all of them.

One of the journalists seemed taken aback that he wouldn't want to capitalize on the fame. "Your video has now been viewed by almost four million people, Mr. Sharp." The man had a five-o'clock shadow and was so disheveled in his suede blazer and Kings of Leon tee shirt that Asher didn't understand how anyone would take him seriously. The reporter pushed his glasses up the bridge of his nose roughly and blinked hard. "Don't you want to take advantage of that?"

"It's not my video," Asher said. And that was all.

That weekend, during one of their supervised visits, Justin told Asher he had set up a Twitter account for him because of all the attention the video was getting.

"You shouldn't even be online!" Asher's stomach rolled at the thoughts of what all Justin had seen written about him. "I mean it."

"Please don't raise your voice to the child, sir," the supervisor said, barely looking up from the video game on her phone's screen.

"It's a tribute page," Justin said. "Your handle is 'at folk hero preacher.'"

"What's a handle mean?"

"People talk about how the video helped them, mostly." Justin produced a smartphone from his pocket that Asher had never seen before. "Mom got it for me. I had to promise to only be on it if there was an emergency, unless I'm with her."

"You know I think you're too young for that."

Both of Justin's thumbs were typing in a blur on the phone, then he held out the screen so Asher could see the top message on the account: *@folkheropreacher if only ppl would listen to your message and change their hearts. tired of the hatred. #equality #lovewins.*

"You've got 36,413 followers," Justin said, like a little businessman, as he clicked off the phone and slid it back into the pocket of his jeans.

"I know the kinds of things people say on the internet, Justin. You ought not—"

"I'm nine years old, Dad," Justin said, and his face was so serious and mature that Asher couldn't find it in himself to negate that.

THE COLD RAINS set in. Then the sleet, the first dustings of snow, the thin ones that only last past noon on the most secret ridges. Fisher told him to be patient, the hearing was only three months away. But in those three months Asher thought he might lose his mind. He didn't get to see Justin enough. Every night he thought of how he wasn't being allowed to tell his son good night in person. Mornings he awoke and realized there was nothing but the plywood walls of the trailer to greet him. He stood at the window with a cup of coffee and watched snow sift down on the gray trees crowding close to the lake bank. *Let there be light Genesis 1:3*, he thought in the mornings when the sun arose, and in the evenings he thought: *then, darkness came over the whole land Mark 15:33*. He had to work consciously to keep a madness from growing in his mind.

At work one day Cherry came in excited and told him she had seen him in *People* magazine. "They did this thing where they asked a big bunch of celebrities what they thought about your video! Nicole Kidman talked about it, Pastor Sharp! And Dolly Parton! I about died! Dolly knows who you are!" She was laughing but he felt sick to his stomach. "They're arguing about it on the news. And I was at the hair salon the other day and everybody in there was talking about it! I can't get over it."

"Well, neither can I, Cherry," Asher said, and ran his box cutter along the top of another case of Premium saltines.

"You've got the whole country talking about this." She grabbed hold of his hand, drawing his eyes back to hers. "And you know what, they *need* to be talking about it. They needed to hear a *country* preacher talking about it." She let go his hand and put fists on her hips, the way she balanced herself these days as her belly grew bigger. "All these damn bigots." She capped a hand over her mouth, her eyes large above her fingers. "I'm sorry to cuss, Pastor Sharp. But it makes me so mad. Why won't they all just hush?"

SOMETIMES WHEN ZELDA and Asher talked on the phone, she said a prayer for him, her voice passionate and intent while he waited silently for her to stop.

"I've been studying on all this and I agree with you that we shouldn't turn people away. But people don't talk about sin enough anymore, Asher," she said this time. "We can't just go around saying that people can do whatever they want. Christian folks have to be lights."

"You sound like you're just repeating all that stuff your husband used to preach," Asher said.

"I know my own mind. You've always accused me of just agreeing with whatever he said or Lydia said. But I study the Bible, too, you know. I have my own way of thinking. And I don't want to be mean to anybody. I wouldn't be. But I also don't know if I believe in accepting this way of life these men have as easy as you can."

"It's not a *way* of life, Zelda. It's just *life*. It's their *lives*."

He knew what it was like to be the minority. He remembered the arguments with his mother, trying to get her to be more accepting of Luke. But then it had become easier to just agree with her, to seek her approval. And so he had become a preacher who preached against his own brother.

"I know you feel alone right now at that church, to be one of the few who agrees with me—"

"No, honey, I've told you: I have my own thoughts on this. And Justin does need to know about sin. He does need to be shown right and wrong."

Asher took a deep breath. Something in him had known it would come to this. That he would lose her, too. "I have to go," he said.

"I do love you, Asher," Zelda said, after a pause. "I always will. You know that. Like my own."

He clicked off the phone.

Now he hadn't heard from her in two weeks. He had called her but she hadn't answered. On his breaks at work he checked the screen of his phone to see if it showed any missed calls from her.

Two days before the hearing, he went out back of the grocery on his break and stood where he could see the first hints of purpling of the redbud trees along the Cumberland River. He dialed Zelda's number again and this time she answered. A great fumbling of the old rotary phone she had seen no point in replacing.

"Hello?" she said, always that question when she answered the phone since she still had a landline and no caller identification.

"You're going to testify against me at the hearing," he said.

"Not *against* you."

"But for her. To say that I'm not fit to have joint custody. After all we've been through together, and as good as you know me, you're going to lie for her."

"Not *lie*, Asher. And she's not gonna take him away from you. You can't expect him to go back and forth all the time, half with you and half with her—"

"Why *not*?"

"A child needs his mother."

"Not when his mother is a judgmental fanatic who cares more about church than she does her own damn son!" His voice rose with each word. He tried to calm himself. He knew it was the wrong thing to say but he wasn't going to apologize. "You realize that she's asking for me to only get him once every two weeks? You know what that'll do to him."

"I'm sorry," she said. "I've prayed and prayed about this. I've struggled so hard with it, Asher. But this is what the Lord has told me to do."

He hung up on her, drew his arm back, fought the urge to throw the phone into the river.

17

As they made their way up the tiled stairwell to the courtroom, Fisher tried to prepare Asher. "So many people are opposed to what you're standing for—and that video has become so popular—that the odds have been against us from the beginning. It's not right. But—"

"Well you're not one to give your client a lot of hope before they go into the trial," Asher said.

"Hearing. Not a trial. Big difference," Fisher said, and stopped on the landing to drain her Mountain Dew. "And I'd rather you go in with low expectations than high."

At the end of the hallway Zelda stood by the large wooden doors that led into the courtroom. She was clutching the top of her purse, her face screwed up in confused grief. As Asher and Fisher walked toward her, Lydia's lawyer shuffled out of the ladies' room and took the crook of Zelda's arm, directing her into the judge's office.

Asher felt as if he didn't have any emotion in his body.

"Can you honestly say that Asher Sharp is not a good father?" Fisher asked Zelda.

"He's a real good father, but—"

"A simple yes or no, Mrs. Crosby."

Zelda struggled to keep her eyes from drifting to either Asher or Lydia. She looked down at her lap, causing her voice to be muffled, so Fisher had to ask her to repeat herself. "Mrs. Crosby. Can you honestly say that Asher Sharp is not a good father?"

"No," she said, and just before Fisher could spin on her heel and say that was all, she added: "But he's misled right now. He's all mixed up."

Asher watched as they turned off one row of lights so the video could be seen better. He watched the entire video with everyone else. The first time he had seen the whole thing. He watched as the judge made a barely visible shake of his head when it was over. He was a shiny-headed old man whose pinkish face had softened and melted in his old age, causing him to favor an old granny-woman from photographs of the Great Depression.

Lydia was dressed like a television evangelist: a bloodred dress suit, large white ruffle on her blouse that skimmed her chin anytime she talked or moved her head, hair meticulously poofed and sprayed. She looked stronger now. But when her eyes fell on Asher's he saw the hurt that still lived there.

"Your Honor, my main concern is having primary custody of

our son so I can oversee his moral and religious upbringing," she said when it was her turn to address the judge. At least she would not lie on the stand and say Asher was a bad father, either, when pressed by Fisher.

But none of it mattered and Asher drifted away somewhere when the judge came back in and awarded full custody to Lydia. Fisher capped her hand over Asher's forearm as if holding on to a stair railing. He would no longer be required to have supervised visits but he'd be able to have Justin stay overnight with him only four nights a month. "The father shall have the right to unimpeded telephone calls and the ability to write his son letters whenever he chooses," the judge said, his words gelatinous with phlegm that caused him to cough wetly, without covering his mouth. "The right to receive from the child's school . . ."

Asher didn't listen. Instead, his mind was already turning with ways to make it right. He should have stayed quiet. He should have stayed with Lydia. But as soon as these thoughts wended through his mind he knew that none of that was possible, no matter how badly he wanted it to be.

Lydia sat very straight-backed. She did not look victorious. Zelda's shoulders were hunched forward with betrayal. Her gray hair was latched in a loose knot at the back of her head and he could see the trembling of her body in it. As soon as the hearing was dismissed Asher bolted to his feet and walked out. He threw the heavy wooden door open and half ran to the stairwell, trying to get away from it all. On the landing Fisher caught up with him, took him by the elbow.

"We can appeal," Fisher said. "People think differently in

Nashville and I think we can show that they were swayed by their religious biases. I'm raring for a fight if you are. I say let's do it."

Asher steadied himself, palm flat against the green tiles of the wall. "How long would that take?"

"It could take up to a year," Fisher said. "But we'd really be making a statement—"

"A year? I couldn't stand that. I couldn't—I've lost my son."

"It would be worth the wait, though. My ex only sees our children about five days a month and it works out. They know when you love them. They know that—"

"I can't stand to be away from him that much," Asher said. "I can't even stand the thoughts of it."

"We can appeal, though," Fisher repeated. "We can get him back. And really, I've always thought we'd have to go on up, to the court of appeals, because of the way people think here."

"I've lost my boy!" Asher found the rail on the stairs, stepped down.

"It'll get easier . . ."

Asher saw himself and Justin walking on the ridge above their house. Asher pointing to the trees, Justin following the sweep of his finger. And then, their feet on the soft soil of the trail, Justin's small hand finding its way into Asher's.

Asher stopped on the stair and looked back at Fisher, standing there on the landing as if awaiting something to happen. *No, it won't ever get easier,* he thought. *Not for me* or *for him.*

"You go home, get some rest, and come in on Monday," Fisher said, "and we'll get the ball rolling."

Asher flew down the stairs, faster and faster until he was

almost in a sprint, and then finally he was outside, in the cool air of an April morning, and driving his Jeep home in complete silence, and then there was the lake and his empty trailer.

That evening he walked through the dark woods and squatted down on the rocky bank so he could hear the soft wash of the lake's small waves supping at the shore. Back at his trailer he warmed up a can of soup. He studied all the postcards that he knew were from his brother, laying them out on the carpet before him as if setting up a game of solitaire. He ran his finger over their shiny fronts, turned them over and read the words once again. He tried to pray, but still he could not. He did research online. He would be quiet, but he would work. He'd plan. He'd drive to Nashville, go over to Opry Mills and buy Justin some new clothes. Go to the bookstore for more information. Educate himself. He'd get the supplies he needed. He knew what he had to do.

18

The night was black and hot with high summer and the cicadas along the river were screaming. As he turned into Zelda's driveway Asher clicked off the headlights and his eyes adjusted to the dark; the moon had slid out from behind the silver-edged clouds and he could see well enough to roll down the steep driveway with ease. He shifted into neutral and killed the ignition.

The Jeep came to a stop near Zelda's front porch, the long ropes of the willows brushing against the car's hood. The cicadas quieted. Here their songs shook like nervous tambourines. A whip-poor-will let out its lonesome call.

"Lord have mercy," Asher said aloud, and these four breaths of words calmed him. He eased the Jeep door shut and kept his eyes on the front door of the house, willing himself to not notice Zelda's waxy red geraniums and the chimes that hung from the eaves. Still, seeing these things reminded him of his ex-mother-in-law's liver-spotted hands digging into the potting soil, of Zelda looking up with a smile on her face.

He knew Justin was here. He had been watching for days now, his car hidden in a pull-off near the river, himself perched within the cover of the willows down by the river so he could see their comings and goings. Lydia had made a big show of hugging and kissing both her mother and Justin, which meant she was going out of town for a day or two, at least.

Three sharp raps with his right hand.

He counted to three and knocked again, harder.

The door chain clattered and the knob twisted. Zelda's soft face appeared in the crack. "What is it?" she said, peering over her glasses. Asher got a tenderness for her in the center of his chest that threatened to spread easily despite her betrayal. Her small, bluish-gray eyes squinted to see better: curiosity at first, then recognition, shock.

"Let me have him, Zelda."

"You shouldn't be here, Asher. I'm—"

"Let me *have* him," he repeated. She had stood by and let this happen, but she had also been the only mother he had ever had. *Don't look at her eyes. Don't think of her gathering up her dress tail to wade in the Cumberland that day.*

Zelda hesitated, keeping her eyes on his while she tried to figure out what to do.

"You know what's right," he said. "You know she shouldn't've taken him from me."

"Asher—" Zelda said, her voice trembling now "—you'll wake him up—"

So Asher willed himself to drift outside his own mind and heart and everything he had known for all these years and he kept repeating Justin's name in his mind. He pushed himself against the door with such force that the impact knocked Zelda away, but did not break the chain. She tried to slam the door shut just as his shoulder made contact again. This time the chain broke and the door flew open and he was in Zelda's good, familiar house that always smelled like bacon grease and fresh coffee.

The door had knocked her back so that she had fallen onto the coffee table. There was a great crash of breaking things; the large orange ashtray she had kept twenty years past her smoking husband's death, the iridescent candy dish that had belonged to her great-grandmother. Once Asher had held the dish up to the sunlight and watched the milky colors change within its curves like something sanctified.

Asher saw the gash beneath Zelda's eye, a thin line of blood rising. He felt a shudder escape his throat at the understanding that the edge of the door had struck her. The nausea of guilt washed down his torso.

Zelda put her hand up to the cut, moaned, then her fingers drifted down to clutch at her lower back. She drew in a great gulp of air.

Asher wanted to help her up, to *help* her. Yet he knew he could not.

You're like a son to me, she had said, once.

Now Zelda put her hand out in front of her but Asher turned and moved down the hallway lined with framed photographs. Lydia's school pictures. Their wedding portrait, Asher's arms encircling her waist as he stood behind her. Like a different life he had lived ages ago. Then: baby pictures of Justin. Asher felt so dizzy he reached out and steadied himself against the wall.

"Justin!"

Music from an old movie played on a television down the hall.

Asher heard Zelda let out another moan. His name seeped from her: "Asher. Please."

Justin lay in the blue glow of the television, that eerie light flickering around the room. Apparently he had fallen asleep next to Zelda, watching television. On screen Ava Gardner was throwing back her head to laugh at something Richard Burton had said while palm trees swayed behind them. Justin was on his back, one arm above his head, the other resting on his chest in a tightened fist. The way he always slept.

Asher had not seen him in two weeks, an eternity. He longed to stretch out here beside his son and go to sleep. He was so exhausted. But he couldn't stop now.

He hustled Justin into his arms and headed down the hallway, rushing past all those photographs again. Trying to not look at Zelda, who still lay in the broken wood and glass of the coffee table, moaning his name. She caught sight of Asher moving toward her, carrying Justin and she reached out her arm, her face full of hurt. Not anger or malice. Grief.

"Please don't do this," she begged.

Justin slept soundly, accordioned across his father's arms.

He would remember this act of leaving her for the rest of his life.

He slid Justin onto the back seat. The child's eyes fluttered open and then closed as sleep overwhelmed him again.

A turn of the key, the slide of the gearshift, and then the Jeep was peeling out, the wisps of the willow sucked away as they moved up the driveway and onto the road, then onto the smooth purr of blacktop where Asher once again could hear the cicadas screaming along the black river in the hot, still night.

PART TWO

The Open Road

1

The red of morning streaked the eastern sky before they had even crossed the county line. Asher drove out of the little town he had known his entire life— *Good-bye, Cumberland Valley*—and into the great unknown of a new day and a new life. He hoped so, at least.

Asher drove as his boy slept on the car seat beside him.

He held on to the steering wheel with both hands, leaning forward with determination, eyeing the highway, looking over occasionally to reassure himself that Justin was still there and not just some dream he had conjured up out of his misery.

He was there. He was. Stolen. And Asher's now, again. The

news and the law would say Asher had kidnapped Justin, that a father couldn't love that strongly, that a man couldn't possibly care so much, and that the whole affair had been done simply for spite.

No. Justin is my child. My boy.

Only now, driving away with Zelda lying on the floor and most likely hurt, did he realize how much worse he had made things. But it was too late now, and he wasn't giving up Justin. He shouldn't have to.

So they would go to Key West. They'd find Luke and he would know what to do. He always had.

He drove south.

Asher had never been anywhere, really, and most of his travels had been as an evangelist before he became pastor at the church in Cumberland Valley. To Gulf Shores a few times, Atlanta twice, for church conferences, lots of little bitty churches in Northern Alabama and Southern Kentucky and East Tennessee for revivals. He had grown up less than an hour from Nashville but had never relished going downtown and tried to make trips down there as seldom as possible.

There had not been much of a way to prepare, so Asher had taken care of the basics: music and food. He had made a playlist of songs that would last eight hours, at least. Driving music. He had packed plenty of clothes and a big grocery sack full of food, a cooler crammed full of water and Mountain Dew. He had bought an oversized atlas. Had packed a suitcase full of art supplies and board games. A load of books in a canvas bag.

The road rolled on, graying in the lifting pinks and oranges of a summer morning that was already hot. The hills were lush and striped with thin lines of mist rising up from the river. Asher coasted onto I-40 and the road sliced its way on toward all the little towns that lay between them and the vast, deep ocean. Surely Zelda had been able to reach the phone and call the police by now.

That reminded him: he grabbed his phone, rolled down the window, and was about to let go. But then he thought how easy it would be to find, lying on the side of the road, and there might be something in there that would lead them to him.

There was hardly any traffic out here at this time of day so he stopped on the bridge over the Cumberland River. He got out and leaned against the concrete bridge railing and looked down to the water where a few small, white, summer leaves decorated the surface of the river. A long drop down but he could smell the water.

He let go of the phone and the river swallowed it whole.

And then, as soon as Asher got back into the car, even though he had eased shut the door, the thing he had definitely not prepared for, because he had not even thought about how he would have to explain all of this to him:

Justin awoke.

2

"Where's Granny? Where's Mom?"

"They're back home, Justin," Asher could hear how sad and tired his own voice sounded.

"Where we going?"

"To the ocean. We're getting out of here for a while."

"We're not supposed to, though," Justin said, not looking at his father.

"There's no reason we shouldn't. Sometimes the law gets it wrong. And this time, they did."

"We're gonna get in trouble," Justin said. "The law'll be after us."

"Maybe so. But you're my son."

The blacktop sang beneath them.

"You know it's not right, how this has all gone. Don't you?" Asher asked, but Justin turned to the passenger window. Asher couldn't say when he had crossed that line from being the kind of parent who avoided talking badly about Justin's mother to outright saying this. But everything was changed now.

Asher cupped the back of Justin's head tenderly. "Justin," he said, and wondered how many times he had said his son's name aloud since his birth. Thousands, probably. A hundred thousand, at least. "Answer me, buddy."

Justin seemed to have lost sight of what the question even was. "What?"

"You know that it's not right, them taking you away from me. Don't you?"

The highway beneath them. The *cuh-lump* as they passed onto a bridge and the *cad-oomph* as they glided off and back onto the road.

Justin kept his face turned to the passing land and Asher questioned himself, his own motives. Had he taken him just to get back at her? Or because he couldn't stand to be away from him? Because he really thought being with her was unhealthy? All of that. Every damn bit of it.

"I don't want to say anything bad about your mother," Asher said, although he wanted more than anything to do just that. He wanted to say: *I bought into all of it. But I can't do it anymore. I can't go through the world judging everybody else. And I couldn't leave you in that mess, being brainwashed that way.*

"I'm hungry," Justin said.

"I brought you all kinds of snacks," Asher said. "You can take your seat belt off long enough to look through them."

There were chips and some granola bars, oranges and bananas, packs of Nabs, peanuts and cashews. Apparently there was nothing Justin wanted because he slid down into his seat, clicked his seat belt back into place, and fixed his eyes on the road.

"I need a honey bun," he said. And because the boy had always had this way of saying he "needed" things instead of that he "wanted" them, like so many other children did, because Asher would do anything in the world to please him, he said they would stop at the first store they could find.

3

As soon as Asher saw the Git 'n Go he wheeled in and parked beneath the bright white lights of the gas canopy, which were still burning despite the fact that morning had completely stretched out over the world by now. Asher put his hand on the door to get out, but Justin sat motionless.

"What are you waiting for?" Asher didn't want to be here long. Any second a cop could slide into the parking lot.

"I don't have no clothes on," Justin said, and then Asher realized he was still wearing sleeping clothes: cotton shorts and a ratty Bible camp tee shirt, barefooted. But he wasn't about to leave him in the car while he went into the store. He bit his tongue against the desire to tell him to just come on, that they didn't have much time. Asher didn't want to make his child feel like he was living life on the run, although that's exactly what they were doing.

"There's nobody else here," Asher said, pawing through the bag of clothes he had packed, all brand-new. He found a pair of flip-flops. "Slip these on and let's run in right quick. You look fine."

"You always say people look lazy, going in stores in their sleeping clothes."

"It's real early, though, Justin," Asher said, but Justin had set his jaw in defiance. Asher dug down into the bag and plucked out a pair of khaki shorts and a tee shirt. Holding the clothes reminded Asher of how little Justin was for his age. Like a little old man.

"Put these on, then," Asher prodded, and glanced around the empty parking lot. "Hurry, now. Nobody'll see you."

Asher stood outside the car with his back to the driver's door to give Justin the illusion he was on the lookout for anyone who might see him changing. Justin had always been very modest.

The day had bloomed completely. The cicadas were silent, resting up for the punishing heat the day promised, when they would sing their screaming songs, letting everyone know they were alive.

The red of morning had paled into a worn blue. The color of Luke's eyes. His brother had been famous around home for his eyes. Girls had always been crazy over him to no success, saying he looked like Paul Newman.

Justin hopped out of the Jeep.

"Now you're looking sharp," Asher said, and tousled his hair. "You like that new shirt?"

Justin nodded, mumbled "Mmm-hmmm" in a not half-hearted way.

A young woman was working in the rear of the store, but their arrival brought her back to the cash register. She smiled at Asher as she went behind the counter, her dangling earrings pulling her lobes long and slender when she nodded. The morning news blared from a small television.

Justin scampered off down the aisle on the hunt for junk food.

Even though they were already far east of Nashville there was a large display of souvenirs of the city: the skyline in a snow globe, a guitar-shaped flyswatter. Pots of coffee on a big silver machine beside green hot dogs that rolled around on metal cylinders, a silver pan of sausage and biscuits wrapped in wax paper tinged pink by the glowing heat lamps above. A whole aisle was stocked with rice, salsa, tortillas, and hominy for the migrant workers who bent over in the fields all day, plucking tomatoes.

Over a shelf of Bunny Bread Asher watched the little television. The newscasters segued easily from the terrorist attack in Munich to news of a heat wave moving into the Eastern Seaboard. At any minute pictures of them could pop up on that television.

Asher turned down an aisle to find Justin crouched at the end, leaning into a small cell phone. The phone was tucked inside a blinged-out case with fake diamonds and rubies studding the back and a small rainbow sticker resting beneath Justin's finger.

"I'm with Dad and we're okay. He'll take good care of me." Justin clicked off the phone and slid it behind several packs of Pampers, then turned and saw his father.

"Justin," Asher said. "What have you done?"

"I had to call her." Justin was clutching snack cakes and

cookies to his chest as if caught with stolen goods. "Please don't be mad at me. Maybe since I called her she won't send the police."

"She will, Justin. She will, and now they'll know where we are." Asher tried to keep his voice calm. But now they had to hurry and get out of here. He didn't know whether he should feel betrayed or assisted. There was no time to study on this. "Where'd you get that phone?" His whisper was harsh.

"That lady must have left it laying back here."

"Come on," Asher said.

Justin struggled to unload his bounty on the high counter: two honey buns (one frosted), two packs of pecan twirls, a bag of Bugles, and a plastic cup of Nutter Butters.

"Got everything, now?" Asher tried to think what was normal conversation for the cashier's ears. He felt sick from the knowledge that Justin had called his mother. "We won't be stopping for a while."

The cashier peeked over the large cash register at Justin. "Oh Lordy, he got all the good stuff," she said, giggling, her accent like a little song. A red rectangle of plastic pinned to her orange smock was printed with her name: ADALIA.

Asher studied a square of foam outfitted with several cheap rings with adjustable bands, each with a different picture captured under a raised slice of resin: the Virgin Mary holding Christ, the Virgin of Guadalupe, Day of the Dead scenes, and several of Frida Kahlo. Luke had always loved Frida and liked to check out a thick book of her paintings from the library.

"Sometimes people say I look like Frida, but it's only because we're both from Mexico." Adalia rolled her dark eyes and smiled. She took one item at a time and ran it over the scanner, moving so slowly. Behind her the news anchors were in deep conversation about the presidential election. "Some folks think all brown people look just alike."

He wanted to tell her that he had to get out of there, *now*. But he had to remain calm. Only now did he notice the security camera in the corner of the store. So eventually they would know he and Justin had been here. No matter, really. They were still close to home. This wouldn't give much away besides the fact that they were east of Nashville. They could go anywhere from here.

She was now openly studying his face. "I *know* you from somewhere."

"I've got one of those faces," he said, willing himself to smile.

"Where you all headed this early on this pretty morning?" Adalia asked.

"The ocean," Asher blurted out, regretting it instantly. He was giving away everything.

"Gulf Shores, I bet."

"Yep." How easily the lie came. He had always been honest. Now he wouldn't have that anymore, either. He would have to lie every single day.

Adalia tapped the "total" button like a pianist hitting the last note on an amazing performance. "Nine dollars and eighteen cents, darlin." She shook her head. "All this stuff is overpriced in these gas stations. Terrible."

Through the plate-glass window behind Adalia: a state trooper pulling into the parking lot.

Asher's breath came out ragged. Adalia noticed; she brought her eyes up to meet his as she counted out the change.

She glanced out the window. "Rodney stops here every morning to get his coffee and a Krispy Kreme." She shook out a brown paper bag for the groceries.

Some part of Asher thought that maybe she had pushed a button under the counter to alert the cops. He fancied she had most likely seen news of the kidnapping on the morning show—the news happened instantly nowadays, after all—just before they had come in and she'd played it cool long enough to stall them.

He could feel the pulse throbbing in his neck.

Asher's mind raced with what he could do once the trooper came in: Fight back? Run? Surrender? None of these seemed an option.

"I tell him don't he know he's a walking what-do-you-call-it," Adalia said, pausing before putting the cup of cookies in the bag.

Hurry up hurry up hurry up.

"You know, the word for when somebody is expected to be a certain way."

The cop was out of his car and fishing back into the cab now, digging for something between the seats.

"A stereotype?" Justin offered.

Asher looked down at his son as if in slow motion. He wished for the noise of the blaring television, anything to distract him from the feeling of nausea and the cold sweat that ran down the backs of his arms.

"Yeah, that's it!" Adalia said. She was taking ages to put everything in the bag.

Hurry hurry hurry.

"A walking stereotype, a cop that eats the doughnuts. You're a smart one!"

Asher grabbed hold of Justin's wrist with one hand and the bag with the other as Adalia shoved it across the counter at long last. He would will his feet to move and then he would glide right on out of there. If the trooper had come for him then this was the end, already. But if he hadn't, they had to walk out of there right now.

Adalia brought her eyes up to light on Asher's. He felt as if he had known her a long while, as if their lives might forever be entangled from this moment on.

"I'll say a prayer for you, darlin," she said. "For your travels to the beach."

"I appreciate it," Asher said, like someone else was speaking.

The state trooper stepped back to hold the door wide open for Asher and Justin, his face hidden beneath the shadows of his hat.

"Hey there, little man," the cop said, and Justin stopped.

"Hello," Justin said in a small voice, and skipped to the Jeep.

Asher turned the ignition, shoved the Jeep into gear, and darted back onto the highway, fighting the urge to peel out and leave scorching black rubber behind them as they hit the open road.

4

As they sped down I-24 the heat was so thick they could see it from a long way off, a hazy mist striping the hillsides.

Only seven o'clock in the morning but they were already close to the state line. Blue mountains rose in the distance, smudged behind the wooly June heat. The Smokies.

Justin leaned on the door and let his hand float up and down on the rushing air. He had asked Asher to take the top off the Jeep but they'd be too visible. Asher wondered what all was going through Justin's mind. He was staring out the passenger window, earbuds in his ears and his music turned up so loud Asher could hear it. Then he pulled one earbud out. "Are we going to do stuff that kidnapped people do in movies?"

"You're not kidnapped, Justin. You're my son."

"But we're on the run. Ain't we?"

"Just until I can figure out how to get the judge to listen to me."

"They probably sure won't listen to you now."

"You're probably right," Asher replied.

"Are we going to dye our hair? And wear caps and sunglasses all the time?"

"What?" Asher laughed but he felt a troubling across his chest. He rolled his window up so they could talk without yelling. "No. No, we're just driving down south for a few days. To figure things out."

"This is my fault," Justin said.

"No, Justin. How can you think that?"

"If I hadn't found them men, during the flood."

"No, buddy. It's way more complicated than that."

"It's why Mom got mad at you." Justin locked his eyes on Asher's face. "Ain't that right?"

"No, it's not right. Listen to me, now. None of this is your fault."

Justin turned away again and the highway hummed on below them. Asher rolled his window back down, not so much to get the air as to reintroduce the noise. There was nothing else to say.

Near Monteagle they coasted down the exit ramp and onto a state highway that climbed mountains and sliced valleys in half, wound up and down, over and around, twisty as a gray ribbon that had been dropped from the sky.

"You're switching back and forth from the interstate to little country roads to throw the cops off?" Justin asked.

"You've been watching too many cop shows at your granny's," Asher said, and they laughed at the same time.

5

Along the road: tiger lilies growing in the ditch-lines. *Flags*, Asher's mother had called them. He remembered her cupping one in her thin hand, a moment of real tenderness. *Look how pretty, Asher. They're perfect.*

If only someone had gotten Asher away from his mother. Because a strange sort of brainwashing had happened after Luke went away. She had convinced him that Luke didn't care about them, that she had been trying to save his soul from hellfire by pulling that gun on him. Tough love, she called it. The kind of love God had shown to the world when He flooded it, when only Noah had heeded His call. The kind of love God had shown Abraham when He had convinced him to kill his own son, Isaac, before stopping him at the last minute. The kind of love Job had suffered. She had convinced Asher that an Old Testament kind of love was the best kind of all. *Pray with me now, Asher, pray with me for Luke's soul that he'll see the error of his ways.* It did no good to talk to her about how Christ had brought them the New Testament. Instead, he prayed with her.

And in that way she had made him feel loved for a while.

By the time he had figured out that she had God and judgment all mixed up he had been preaching along those same lines for years. And then he had begun to realize that he had married a woman who did not disagree with her, who was not unlike her except for the abuse. If Lydia had ever laid a hand on Justin he would've kidnapped him long before now. At least she didn't possess that kind of meanness.

They passed a scattering of small, tidy houses with red geraniums and hanging pots of wandering Jew, a collection of rockers and chairs on the porches.

Old couples hoeing corn in the gathering heat, their gardens rectangle-shaped wounds of rich brown soil among the green yards.

So far out across the fields they could not hear its engine, even if they had been standing still: an orange tractor bumping along the edge of a tobacco field.

Barns. Gray, red, white.

Abandoned houses with tiger lilies growing in the windows. *Look how perfect, Asher.* He had loved her even after she had pulled a gun on his own brother. He had become a preacher for her, to please her because Luke had not.

A small cemetery with plastic flowers on the graves, the

tombstones wiped clean recently, most likely back on Memorial Day. Country folks still took that seriously.

Spaced out every few miles, cinder-block stores with good names: Daddy and Them Grocery. Lord God Almighty Hair Salon.

Occasionally: a Confederate flag hanging on a rusty pole, or draped over a porch banister.

Church after church after church. Asher had preached in so many just like them, back when he was doing revivals. He could conjure the smells of those little churches (musty, perfumy, the scent of plug-in deodorizers or soured mop water or acrid hair spray that lodged in the back of his throat). The people coming forward, asking for prayer, his hand capped over their foreheads, their lips trembling with the Holy Ghost, dotting oil on their temples, praying like a fever let loose. The drummers—almost always women—playing so hard and fast, pianos pounding. A church's kind of rock 'n' roll. The church people dancing, cloaked in the Spirit. The electric guitars and the singers and the tambourines shaking with their ancient sounds. He had believed in all of it with everything in him. He had believed and believed and believed.

All of the churches were small, some of them with names so long they didn't fit properly on their signs.

LITTLE DOVE FULL GOSPEL CHURCH IN JESUS NAME

THE ONE TRUE GOD GOSPEL CELEBRATION CHURCH

HOLY GHOST REVIVAL CHURCH OF THE NEW SAVIOR

Most of them with shelter houses nearby, filled with picnic tables. Most of them white, but a couple redbricked, all with crosses. Only a few possessed steeples, squat and fat.

The boy looked out the open window with such concentration

that Asher wondered if he, too, was mourning the loss of Tennessee, grieving the loss of a past whose passing ought to have been celebrated.

Good-bye forever goodbye, he thought, his mother's face before him.

6

Georgia. Justin had dozed off again and Asher kept the music off so as not to disturb him. The Jeep humming a steady song on the long, gray line of I-75, the guilt straddling Asher's chest. The image of Zelda lying on the floor playing over and over in his mind.

"Forgive me," he whispered now, not to God, but to Zelda, way across the mountains and pastures.

Justin stirred beside him, his big eyes sleepy but open. "Dad?" he said.

"It's all right, buddy," Asher said. "Go back to sleep."

"You said 'forgive me,'" Justin said. "What did you do, Dad?"

Asher kept his eyes on the road. He tightened his jaw, turned on the music but Justin snapped it off, quick.

"What did you *do*?"

"Justin—"

"No, you have to tell me. Is Granny alright?"

"Yes," Asher said in his *and-that's-final* voice, turning to look Justin in the eye so the boy would know he was telling the truth. "We'll call her, once we get past Atlanta."

AS SOON AS they got on the other side of the city they began to see large red-and-yellow billboards for

TIGHTWAD'S
"THE CHEAPEST GAS IN THE SOUTH,
NOT GUARANTEED"

and after a while the Jeep carried them off the exit to find a similar, gigantic sign perched on the roof of a massive truck stop painted highway-stripe yellow.

"I'm going to call your granny right quick," Asher said, shoving the gearshift up into park. "You want to talk to her?"

"She'll just cry," Justin said. "And tell me to pray."

"Sure?" Asher was fishing quarters out of the ashtray. "It'd do her good to hear from you, little man."

"Yeah," Justin said with some amount of exhaustion, so Asher closed the door and went to the phone.

A young Cherokee woman in cutoff jeans and a red halter top strutted across the parking lot while she smoked a cigarette. Her

breasts bounced with each step she took. Her black hair struck
her at the waist and she flipped one side of it over her shoulder.
A trucker swung down out of the cab of his eighteen-wheeler and
whistled at her. "Oh, squaw woman!" he hollered, but she kept her
eyes on the truck-stop door. "You're killing me baby!" He patted his
hand against his open mouth as he yelled to make a *wo-wo-wo-wo*
sound. At this she thrusted her middle finger into the air, still
refusing to look toward him.

The coins dropped into the phone. Asher was lucky to even
remember Zelda's number, but he had learned it in the days before
cell phones. Only two rings and she answered.

"Hello? Asher?" she said, as if she had been awaiting his
call. Her voice was held back, like she couldn't catch her breath.
"Where are you?"

"Zelda? You alright?"

"My hip's hurt, but I'll make it." How easy it was to be folded
back up by someone who has been good to you.

"Your face?"

"Asher, what were you thinking?"

"Nobody's ever been as good to me as you, Zelda. And I
shouldn't have, but I didn't know any other way—"

"I know it, Asher." He could picture her, sitting at her supper
table, drinking coffee in the hot part of the day. The *nit-nit-nit* of
the yellow plastic clock on the wall.

But maybe not. Maybe cops were sitting right there with her.
Lydia with her ear pressed up to the phone receiver, listening to
every word. This was the end of their relationship, and he knew
it, grieved its passing.

"You know I was a good father."

"I should've done something. I should've talked sense more to Lydia."

The phone receiver was shaking against his ear. He steadied his nerves, glanced at Justin to make sure he was alright. The boy was studying the atlas now. In movies phones got traced or not, but always in them it depended on how long a person stayed connected. He wasn't going to take the chance of talking long.

"Asher, bring him back. Before she finds out. You can fix all of this if you just bring him back. Right now."

"You haven't called the law?"

"She doesn't know yet," Zelda whispered.

"What?" Asher couldn't believe it. They had left Cumberland Valley over six hours ago, thinking the whole time he was running from the police. "You haven't called her?"

"She's gone to Knoxville for a revival and won't call until lunchtime."

Thank you thank you thank you.

He felt the fear roll off him. If she didn't listen to her voice mail, which she never did, then she wouldn't know.

"Nobody has to know, Asher. If you'll just bring him back." Asher could picture Zelda's lower lip trembling, her violet eyes full of tears. "I was wrong, before. I set in that courtroom and let it happen. But this ain't the right way. You have to bring him back." In her own way Zelda had had the saddest life he had ever seen, always minding someone else, never thinking for herself. Seeing the way Lydia treated her had made him see that he wasn't going to live his life that way. "You know I have to call her."

"I know it," he said. "But I can't bring him back. I won't—"

"And she'll call the law."

"I know."

"Asher, please don't do this," she said. "I don't blame you for being so mad at me. At her. But please. I'm begging you."

The world tilted, spun, straightened. Asher could hear every breath he took, loud in his own ears, his blood pumping, the heat humming all around him. He could hear the gas being pumped into a farmer's truck, the electric bells chiming as the gas station door opened, the breath of hot air in the stand of pines nearby.

"Asher?" Zelda said loud and forceful, as if she had said it many times without him hearing.

"I'm here."

"Please don't take him."

Asher put his finger on the silver button to hang up but stood there holding the phone to his ear. He needed a minute before he got back in the Jeep. He was shaking all over. He had talked to Zelda and she was all right. They had a head start of six hours on the law. And this was really happening.

He put the phone on the hook but as he started toward the Jeep, he saw that a young man was heading straight for him. Bleached hair, a mangy beard, a tee shirt with the sleeves torn off, emblazoned with the face of one of those male country singers who all sounded alike.

"Thank you—for what you did," the boy said.

"I'm sorry?" Asher said.

"For what you said, on that video. It meant a lot to me." The boy—not much more than a teenager—kept his brown eyes right on Asher's face.

"I'm glad, son," he said, and realized he had not used the word *son* with a stranger since his preacher days. He put his hand out to be shaken. "I'm so glad it helped you, buddy." He let go the boy's hand. "Please don't ever tell anyone you saw me here, alright?"

"Okay," the boy said, a confused smile playing across his mouth. "I won't."

"Take care of yourself," Asher said, sliding into the Jeep.

Justin had turned the key so he could listen to music. He sang along until they got to the interstate ramp, where a skinny man with long hair and a full, red beard stood on the shoulder. He looked exhausted as he stood in the heat holding a cardboard sign. HUNGRY STRANDED had been printed on it in neat block letters. A worn backpack sat at the man's feet.

"Dad, let's help him," Justin said as they passed the man, and turned in his seat to keep his eye on him. "Let's go back to that McDonald's and buy him a fish sandwich."

"Justin, we can't, honey." Asher watched the man growing smaller and smaller in the rearview mirror. The man had turned to watch after them as if he knew they were discussing his fate. "We need to keep going."

"But he's hungry. We should help him," Justin said as the Jeep curved up the interstate ramp. Too late to turn back now.

"I'm already on the interstate, buddy."

Justin fixed his eyes on the highway. "We should have helped him."

He didn't speak to Asher down the entire length of Georgia.

Instead, he turned his face to the passenger window and watched the pinewoods and pastures pass by. Churches and homes and cows. But mostly the signs alongside the Georgia highway:

JUST AHEAD: BOILED P-NUTS

RIPE GA GROWN WATER MELUNS

THIS FLAG IS HERITAGE, NOT HATE

G

E

T

RIGHT   WITH

G

O

D

ICE-COLD WATERMELONS 5$

JAM JELLY MOLASSES

GOD HATES FAGS

BEST PEACHES 4 MILES

7

Asher sat by the window, watching the trees. There were thirsty-looking pines and short little palm trees, and the parking lot blacktop was covered with a thin layer of sand that had blown in during some time when there was actually a breeze moving around. The trees were completely still in a way that they never were back home in Tennessee and not a single bird he could see. Maybe they were way back in the deepest parts of the woods where the pine shade was cool and fragrant, a better place for winged things than out by the treeless interstate where it was nothing but rotting motels and truck stops.

They were in a motel near the Florida–Georgia border. Asher

had driven more than eight hours before he started falling asleep. He had coasted into the Shady Oaks Motel, gotten a room and had dived into a hard sleep after making Justin swear to not leave. He had fallen asleep to the sound of his son watching the television but now was awake after only a couple of hours. Justin's small snores were singing across the room to him.

At least the room offered those two hours of sleep. There was a rust stain on the floor around the toilet and the bar of soap was thin as a Hershey bar and smelled like funeral flowers. The towels were like sandpaper. He was pretty sure there was dried vomit on the carpet in the corner. Justin had said the remote felt sticky.

"It's perfect that the word 'shady' is in the motel name," Justin had said.

"Why's that?"

"This is the shadiest hellhole I've ever seen," Justin said.

Asher started to tell him to watch his mouth, that little boys weren't to handle language like that, but that was just an old habit that didn't even make sense to Asher anymore. Besides, Justin was right.

He had clicked off the television and now he sat on the air conditioner at the window.

An old dog moseyed across the parking lot. If he were a dog, Asher thought, he'd be crawling up under a cool porch somewhere or getting off that hot blacktop. There was something pitiful about the dog. Maybe because he was all alone out there. Asher reckoned he probably hadn't had a bath his entire life. He was black and white but everything about him had been grayed by dirt. The dog stopped and sniffed at the air—maybe he was out hunting food and too hungry to be lounging around under a porch—and then he turned and set his eyes right on Asher's. The dog turned and headed toward the little pinewoods and then Asher could see that his right back leg never touched the ground.

Justin's snoring piped up like a bad muffler and then he snorted and rolled over, his deep breaths hushed by the pillow. In so many ways he was like a little old man.

Asher looked back to the window but the dog was gone. Now he knew he'd be worrying about him the rest of the night.

He wondered if Lydia had listened to her voice mail by now. And Zelda had reported it by now, surely. That meant the law was most certainly after them. He could have picked up the phone and ended this whole thing before it got any worse. But then he'd have to give up Justin. He couldn't do that.

The dog was back, his limp more pronounced. His tongue lolled out and it seemed to Asher that the dog was lost. Not lost in the sense that he didn't know where he was, but that he had no idea what his next move might be, as if he had exhausted all of his options for survival.

Asher padded into the bathroom and filled a thin plastic cup with water. He slipped out of the moldy room and onto the sidewalk where a dozen air conditioners leaked thin streams that ran in jagged lines down the concrete. The heat was thick as curtains. Night was fixing to slide over the world and the cicadas were calming down for that hushed time between daylight and darkness, when crickets rosined their bows. That was what happened in the deepest parts of the pinewoods. Out here by the motel there was only the sound of eighteen-wheelers groaning down the interstate, one after another, an endless noise of commerce.

The dog lay on the narrow rectangle of grass between the sidewalk and the parking lot, his back legs splayed out and his front paws tucked under his chest. Asher leaned over, trying to not spill the full cup of water, and put his hand out so the old boy could draw in his scent. Luke had taught him how to do this as a child. The dog sniffed his fingers and latched his eyes on to Asher with a mixture of trust and suspicion.

"Hey there, buddy," Asher said in a voice like he was talking to a baby.

He set the cup on the sidewalk and the dog glanced up at him to make sure it was a gift and then his tongue lashed at the water as if his full thirst had only now overtaken him. Asher tipped the cup to the side for him to get more water and the dog continued to stare at him as he lapped up more. The whole time his eyes were saying *Thank you so much that's the best damn water I've ever had in my whole entire suffering life.*

Then the dog was going crazy, licking Asher's hand and jumping up so he would squat down and give his full attention. He smelled like he'd rolled around in something rotten and dead. Asher petted him anyway.

The dog looked like beagle, pit bull, perhaps some mountain feist. He had a strong chest and a noble head, a slender but muscular body, despite his obvious hunger. Asher patted down the dog's back and he could feel pebbles under his skin that he knew were shotgun pellets because Roscoe had had them, too. He had been out gallivanting and one of the neighbors had shot him right in the hind end for digging up her flower bed.

Asher sat down on the grass and let the dog cover him up with loving, regardless of how badly he stank. The dog climbed into his lap and licked at his face, perching one of his paws up on Asher's chest, and this was the first time Asher had been truly happy in a long while.

"Yes sir, buddy, that's a good boy, yes him is," Asher sing-songed to him, and the dog seemed to talk back by the way he wiggled around and licked Asher's hands and face when he could sneak in a kiss. There was no way he was leaving this good old boy here.

8

They drove south, through the hot, black night. Asher had taken the top off the Jeep since it was dark now, and the sticky wind twisted inside the cab. Justin couldn't sleep after his long rest at the motel. He turned the music up loud over the pummeling wind. Florida raced by them with only the gray highway visible in their headlights.

Justin had named the dog—Shady—as soon as he awoke. They had given him a bath in the motel tub and then old Shady leapt into the Jeep and curled up on the back seat like Asher and Justin had been his family as long as he could remember.

There was a sort of contentment that had settled between the three of them. Perhaps for Justin it was only resignation; Asher could tell that his son was going through all kinds of feelings about being on the run like this. He wished that he could take all of that from him, but no amount of talking about it would make it any easier.

So for hours and hours there was nothing but the road. They tried listening to the radio for a while but there was only static or gospel stations. Holy Roller programs and screaming preachers. Somehow those programs always had the best reception. Asher found it hard to believe he had once been one of those hacking preachers himself. This other life didn't seem possible to him. This other world.

He drove down the long finger of Florida with nothing to keep him from thinking about what he was going to do.

By the time they reached Key Largo, his back ached, his neck ached, his arms ached. Even his fingers were sore from gripping the steering wheel. But he had to keep driving. The sudden thought of finally arriving in Key West and not driving anymore filled him with a stark fear. What would it be like to be on an island where the road simply ended? The more Asher thought about it, the more it sounded like a trap waiting to swallow them.

The sky lightened in the east, a graying of the blackness way out over the ocean. They waited at stoplights although the roads were empty. There was nothing more lonesome than an empty, dark intersection. Even the billboards seemed lonely.

CROCODILE CROSSING JUST AHEAD

SEE THE CHRIST OF THE DEEP

GLASS BOTTOM BOAT RIDE ON THE KEY LARGO PRINCESS!

Behind this last sign a state trooper had hidden to watch for speeders. Asher felt a cold sweat on his upper lip and his heart drummed in his chest.

The air—warm even before daylight—smelled like salt water and fish and overripe watermelons.

Somewhere outside Tavernier Justin announced that he had to pee and Asher wheeled into a Tom Thumb gas station.

The cashier was a mountain of a woman with a big, brown mole and sweet, green eyes. "Good morning, darlins," she said when they entered and as they left she asked: "Are you going to the very end, then?" Asher didn't understand. "Key West," she said.

He nodded.

"Good luck, darlin," she cooed.

Back on Route 1, driving, driving. They rode along in silence for a time, listening to the road slip beneath them. Shady struggled up from the back seat and licked at Asher's face, then pressed his wet nose against Justin's cheek before pushing himself into Justin's seat. Justin kept his eyes on the road and one arm around Shady's neck. Asher could hardly bear to watch this love blooming between his son and this new dog without thinking of their sweet, old boy Roscoe.

As the light increased, Florida Bay yawned out at their right, dotted with sailboats and small yachts, lined by houses of every bright color. On the left, the Atlantic, too big to comprehend.

ISLAMORADA, the sign said. Justin pronounced the town's name aloud several times, more to himself than to Asher.

(*Eye-la-more-ah-dah*)

They passed over dozens of small Keys. They passed a hundred gas stations and motels and waters that sped by on either side. Justin begged to stop at the Theater of the Sea, and then at the Indian Key State Park, but they had to keep moving, and besides, it wasn't even seven in the morning.

Justin watched the Gulf, pointing to what he thought might be dolphins.

There was the old railroad bridge, stretching out like a concrete mystery.

Conch Key.

"Look at that!" Justin pointed to a terrible plastic mermaid on a sign, welcoming visitors to the Tiki Bar.

Justin was feeling good this morning. He turned up a Tom Petty song and danced along in his seat. Asher watched him twisting around, thrusting one arm out the passenger window, the other against the Jeep's roof, his eyes closed in satisfaction as he sang along. Asher had done the right thing and they could be happy like this every single day of their lives if everyone would just leave them alone.

"You've got good taste in music, little man," Asher told him when the song was finished.

"I know it," Justin said, and smiled.

9

The Everything

They walked out on the old bridge in the place where the Gulf waters churn against the Atlantic.

Justin dragged his hand along the rusted metal railing. The sun shone in his hair and Asher imagined how warm it would be to the touch.

The water beneath them—the Gulf of Mexico—was dark and blue, but up ahead, just past the bridge, were the emerald waves of the Atlantic. These were colors that were more than colors; they went beyond that into something magnificent. In all of Asher's thirty-five years he had never seen anything that compared.

This was a walk that called for silence, and they both knew

this somehow. The dog did, too. They listened to the waves strik-
ing the pilings, and the hustle of the morning wind past their
ears, and the occasional passing vehicle on the new bridge that ran
parallel. They were walking out into a confluence, and they could
feel that power beneath their feet.

In the middle of the bridge they stopped and looked out at
the immensity of the Atlantic. Asher stood behind his son and put
his hands on the boy's shoulders. Asher and Justin: father and son,
connected forever.

Normally in a moment like this Asher would say to Justin
that he was everything in the world to him. He wanted to tell his
son that his own existence meant nothing until he was born. He
wished Justin could know the way he felt about him, the way no
child could ever really fathom until they cherished someone else
completely. Being a parent was a constant heartache, an endless
act of making sure the child was as safe and as happy as a person
could possibly be in this life. Asher wanted to tell his son that he
would die for him, or kill for him, and everything in between.
He wished he could tell Justin that he had given his whole self to
him without question, with total sacrifice. But he didn't need to
say any of this. It was contained in the way he touched his son's
shoulders, the way they stood there together, two people alone
in this world made of nothing but endless waters and a strip of
concrete crossing them.

10

I always wanted to come here, to the Keys," Asher said as they strapped back on their seat belts.

"Why didn't you?"

Asher wheeled back onto Route 1 and then they were on the Seven Mile Bridge, crossing.

"Your mother never wanted to. Couldn't hardly get her out of Tennessee unless it was for a revival."

Shady stood on Justin's lap, his front paws on the door. He squared his face out into the rushing air, ears clicking at the wind.

"I miss her," Justin said.

"I'm sorry, Justin."

"I know." Justin kept his eyes on the Gulf. "But I get it."

"Do you?"

He nodded. "She lied, in court. Granny did, too."

"How do you know that?"

"Granny told me," Justin said, still not meeting Asher's eyes. He was watching as a white speedboat bounced away across the waves. A woman in a bikini was leaning against the silver boat railings, her face against the wind. "She didn't say they lied, but that they didn't tell the whole truth. Which is the same thing. Granny said she wanted me to know it was wrong."

Asher didn't know what to say, so he kept his eyes latched on the road.

"But this still doesn't feel right," Justin said, "to run off like this."

Asher took his right hand from the steering wheel and laid it atop Justin's forearm.

Who knew what would happen next. Asher would most likely never see Tennessee again. The police could pull them over at any second and throw Asher onto the blacktop and arrest him. If that happened where would Justin stay until someone came for him? In the jail, too? And would he ever see Justin again once he was carried off to prison?

Once they came off the Seven Mile Bridge there were cops all alongside the highway. He had never seen so many police officers on one stretch of road and his hands gripped the steering wheel tighter each time one of the cruisers *schwoom*ed past them.

A bunch of kids were laughing and running toward a man at the end of a pier that jutted out of the side of the highway. He was holding up a silver fish whose gills were gasping for water.

"Oh no," Justin said, his hands rushing to the door as if he might pull on the handle and open it. "Dad, go back."

"What is it?" But Asher knew what he was going to say.

"Go back, and get that man to throw that fish back in the ocean."

"I can't do that, buddy," Asher laughed a little. "Come on, now, turn around."

But Justin couldn't stop looking back. He turned in his seat and watched for as long as he could. Asher watched by way of the rearview mirror for long enough to see that the kids were jumping around the stupid man, like letting this fish die right there in front of them was the most fun they'd had in ages.

"God, I hate people," Justin said. "People suck."

Asher thought perhaps he should tell his son to not say that, but he didn't. He let him be. If there was a parent who always had the correct comeback he'd like to meet them. But Justin was so wracked with guilt at not having helped the fish. He had twisted his head around, still looking back although the man and the kids and the fish were long out of their sight now.

"Justin," Asher said, and tapped his knee. "Come on, now, buddy. We can't control everything in the world. Wish we could."

"I hope I hope I hope," Justin was saying out loud without realizing it and so Asher put his hand gently on the nape of his son's neck.

"It's alright, little man." Asher patted the back of Justin's head.

Three cop cars in a row, all with their lights on and their sirens screaming (*whyo! whyo! whyo! whyo!*), *schwoom schwoom schwoom* they went by.

Asher paled and held the steering wheel tight and looked up at the rearview mirror, afraid of what he might see, but the siren sounds got farther and farther away until they couldn't hear them at all. They were not turning around to catch them.

Telephone poles along the highway, topped with huge piles of sticks and twigs. Osprey nests. Asher had read about these.

KEY WEST: 20 MILES AHEAD.

The Haitian Baptist Church with yellow doors.

A white heron fishing in the shallow waters of the ocean.

Stock Island.

Trailer parks and Kentucky Fried Chicken.

One more bridge—no more than a second—and then, they were in Key West.

PART THREE

Little Fire

1

Key West is coming awake when they arrive.

Once they cross over onto the island and there is the opportunity to turn right or left, Asher chooses left for no real reason and then they are beside the ocean again, where people are jogging and riding bicycles and pushing baby carriages. The Atlantic burns a greenish-blue back to the horizon. He realizes he has no idea what to do next.

On past two or three beaches (empty this early in the day), hotels and motels and guesthouses and resorts.

All at once there are many different streets and Asher keeps making turns that will keep them near the ocean. Just seeing it has become a sort of security he is already not willing to abandon.

And he knows it offers some sense of direction. Justin watches everything in silence, sizing up the place.

After some time the traffic slows near a giant red, black, and yellow concrete buoy that sits on the shore where people are having their pictures taken. Asher knows it from researching the island online. Scooters zoom every which way. The Jeep idles behind a mess of tourists who are trying to navigate a rented electric car into a small parking space and Asher and Justin watch the people gathered around the marker. Families. Man, woman, and child. Couples. Two men, holding hands, which Asher has never seen before. Never. Despite himself he feels nervous about Justin seeing this. There is also a man and woman kissing.

And here I am, he thinks, *on the run, a criminal now, with my confused child.*

Across the fake buoy is written:

THE CONCH REPUBLIC

90 MILES TO

CUBA

SOUTHERNMOST

POINT

CONTINENTAL

U.S.A.

KEY WEST, FL

HOME OF THE SUNSET

Asher's legs have turned to planks of lumber and all at once he feels as if his body is shutting down. The exhaustion has caught up with him at last, now that they have arrived. He feels like he is speaking through a wad of cotton that has been shoved into his mouth. "I need to get somewhere and rest for a little bit," he says, wheeling the car back onto the street, not knowing where he intends to go. His arms are jerking with exhaustion.

But Justin is so excited to finally be here that there is no way he is going to nap. The heat, even this early, is too dominant to simply pull over and take a nap in the Jeep. But if Asher can stretch out for a few minutes, he will be alright. He believes he can will himself to not go to sleep.

Asher turns down one street and then another and somehow they end up back on the waterfront. The water is a throbbing bluish green, so shallow he can see waves of seaweed swaying just beneath the surface. A lone sailboat sits tied up in the shoals, bobbing on the small, steady waves. When Asher sees the beach he pulls into an empty spot alongside the sidewalk.

"We get to go swimming?" Justin says, excited.

"No," Asher slurs, "let's just rest for a little bit. Okay?"

But it's too hot in the car and Justin is begging to let him go to the water.

Asher somehow manages to grab the throw from the back seat and open the door. Justin is scurrying down the sidewalk, Shady running alongside him, darting away so fast that enough energy flares in Asher to holler out: "Justin! Stop!"

Justin slows but does not come back to him, so Asher tries to push on, feeling as if he is wading through muck, the way the ground was for days after the floodwaters went down. Up the steps and past a bathhouse built of sea rocks and coral, and then there is the nearly empty beach. The sky is too cloudy for most people to come out, and the smell of an oncoming rain marks the air. Far down the sand a young family is settling themselves beneath a large white umbrella—man and woman, two children, a baby lying in a car seat on a towel—and even farther down a group of boys have just begun a game of volleyball. But that is all.

Justin runs to the water's edge, laughing, hollering out. Shady barks at the waves, then sticks his nose into the water and sneezes. Asher finds a shadowed place beneath the palms lining the beach; the morning is new enough that the air isn't too thick in the shade.

Only when Asher bends to spread out the throw does he notice the wind pummeling the beach. The throw bucks like a possessed thing. He falls to his knees atop one end and manages to pin the throw down long enough to take a seat. He has never been drunk before but he imagines this is how it must feel, the world shifting and leveling, then sliding back off-kilter again. He puts the flat edge of his hand up to his brow so he can gaze out toward the ocean, and watches Justin and Shady as they run down to the water's edge.

There are few things that fill him up more than seeing his boy running free, but as soon as this thought blossoms in his mind, he also realizes how neither of them will ever really be free again.

He has taken that from Justin, because what freedom is there in being on the run from the police? He hasn't thought this through enough. What will they do when school starts back? There's no way to enroll him without it becoming known. What will they do if Justin gets sick and has to go to the hospital? What if Asher himself gets sick?

"Justin, come back!" Asher hollers, as Justin heads down

toward the breaking water and the volleyball game. He minds, and starts back. Asher sees all of this through a thick haze, as if a fine mist lies over everything. "Come here, right now!"

As Justin runs up the beach there is nothing but goodness on his face.

Asher can't stand it anymore. He lies back on the throw and locks his fingers together over his belly. If he can only rest for a few minutes . . .

Justin is standing over him, his face shadowed as the sun blazes white behind his head.

"Won't you lay down with me for a little bit, hmm? Let's rest awhile, buddy."

"No, I want to get in the water."

"Not yet," Asher mutters. He can't keep his eyes open. "You don't have your swimming trunks—"

"I can go get them. They have a shower house, I saw it, it's made out of rocks—"

"No, now. Let's just rest awhile."

"I want to get in," Justin says, fed up. "I've been in that car for two days! I'm tired of it!"

Asher isn't even able to make his mouth work correctly now. He is beyond tired; he is weary down into every muscle and bone. He hasn't rested for months. "I'm sorry," Asher hears himself say, as if from very far away, and even as he says the words he knows this is a mistake, that he can't go to sleep, that he can't allow Justin to be alone here on this beach. He tries to say: "Stay real close."

Asher is asleep before Justin has even turned to run back to the surf.

2

The Everything

Justin used to think the trees were God. But today, right here, he thinks the ocean might be God. All that power and weakness, spread out for us to see. The ocean can do so much when it wants to, and sometimes it can do nothing but go in and out, waves and smoothness. The ocean is a mystery and so is God. They are both so big we cannot see all of them at the same time but we can catch pieces of them here and there. Justin believes God is big like the ocean. Even bigger. But lots of people don't. They think He's small enough to fit in a church house or an offering plate or an ancient book. He's not, and His mind is even bigger than Him. People look at the ocean and they usually see only blueness. But there are so many other colors. Right now Justin can see ten different shades of blue, and lots of greens. There are lines of brown and the white lips of the waves. When the light hits the water in a certain way there will be even more colors: red, orange, peach, purple. At night there will be gray and the farther he could swim out into the ocean he could find the water darker and darker until it was black on a cloudy night. Justin thinks God's eyes are that color: everycolor. This is the kind of talk that would horrify his mother, but he believes God is in everything and everybody. Pieces of him. He doesn't just mean the spirit, he means the actual chunks of God. He thinks He's not only in the ocean, but also in Shady, and the sand, and the trees, and every person on this beach, every person in the world. Today, right this minute, Justin can see nothing but ocean, and that is Everything. And Justin can feel the Everything beneath his hand where he is resting his palm on Shady's chest and Shady's heart thrums in a steady rhythm like the waves on the beach. He can feel the Everything under himself in the gritty sand. He can smell it in the seaweedy smell smoothing over his face. He can hear it in the laughter of the teenagers down the beach and in the crying of that baby and the metal sound of the airplane sliding over them all and the water coming in and out in and out. The ocean is God but so are we all.

But this isn't the kind of thing he can say out loud to anyone. He knows it's the kind of talk he can say to himself in his own mind when he is sitting on a beach a thousand miles from home, not knowing what will come next.

3

His face is covered by thousands of tiny red ants.

He parts his lips to holler out but no sound comes; his tongue feels like a rusty jar lid.

His arms are leaden, too much weight to move so he can sweep away the swarm overtaking his head and neck.

His eyes are so heavy he has to conjure up all of his strength to pry them open and as soon as he does the world is all whiteness until finally he can make out the white ball of sun and the sky around it and the lifting fronds of palm trees above.

Then he feels the sand biting into him, being driven at him with such force by the ocean's wind that each grain feels as if it is boring into his skin. The sand clicks at his teeth, gathers in little whirlpools at the base of his nostrils, burrows into the corners of his eyes.

There is a split second of relief when he realizes the ants are only sand, but then Asher thinks of Justin and draws in such a quick breath that he is choked by the grit he has sucked down his throat.

He rises up and sprints down the beach for Justin.

Asher doesn't see him anywhere. He is looking this way and that, his head darting about like a scared bird. He has no idea how long he had been asleep but everything looks just the same: the volleyball game, the shape of the sky, the startlingly pale family with the baby, the ocean kicking little tufts of waves in the wind. He can't have dozed off for more than five minutes from the looks of things, but maybe it has been longer.

He feels as if he's been punched in the stomach.

I've lost him.

Asher turns around and his eyes fall on the very spot where he has been sleeping. He sees that Justin and Shady have been lying on the throw next to him the entire time. Shady raises his head and cocks his ears. Justin is sound asleep, but Asher is so scared and glad that he shakes him awake, barking out his name.

"What is it?" Justin says, cowering away from Asher, his eyes suddenly wide.

"How long was I asleep?"

"I don' know." Justin rolls over onto his side. Shady crowds in as close as he can get to him and tucks his nose into the nape of Justin's neck. "Twenty minutes, maybe."

A wave of relief sweeps over him. He bends to kiss Justin's forehead—he hasn't done this in months—and then lies beside him on the throw again, despite the pounding sand. They have not taken a nap together in so long.

Asher fixes the top of the throw up around their heads so the sand won't get into their ears, and he rests.

4

S ky huge and tight with blueness.
Wind.
Ocean.

Asher guesses they slept about an hour, and he feels more rested than he has in ages. Neither of them has moved a muscle in their sleeping and as soon as Asher opens his eyes he sees that Justin is completely still. A little old man lying there asleep.

Asher knows he has to get up and see this place, to feel it and smell it and hear it and taste it. He has to find Luke. And Asher has to get up and press on for himself, too. For Justin.

That's when he hears the sirens.

He stands, ready for them, accepting that this is over, his mind racing but not telling him anything. The family nearby is watching him with some amount of unease, he thinks. Maybe his face is all over the news now; he has no way of knowing. He needs to get to a television. The mother holds the baby close to her chest, eyeing Asher over her shoulder. But maybe he's just being paranoid.

Shady howls at the passing sirens, his head thrown back. Justin does not flinch, lost to exhaustion.

And then the three police cruisers zoom on by, speeding to something on the other end of the island.

Asher sinks back down on the throw. Vomit rises up in his throat. He coughs the acid off the back of his tongue and wipes his mouth on his forearm. Cold sweat lines his forehead and he puts his head between his knees to keep from throwing up again. Shady pads over to Asher and licks at his ear. After a time Asher gives Justin a little shake.

"Come on, buddy," Asher says, acting as brave as he can. "Let's get this all figured out."

On their way to the car they pass a concession stand trailer. Hand-lettered signs cover the side:

2 HOT DOGS FRIES COKE $5
COLD COLD KEY LIMEADE $2
FAMOUS SMATHERS BURGER $3
FRIED PLANTAINS $3

A window is cut into the side of the trailer and a man leans on a small Formica counter, reading a battered paperback. This is as good a place to start as any. Asher asks Justin if he wants anything.

"No," Justin says. "I'm good."

"I'm gonna have a limeade. You sure you don't want one?"

"No," Justin shakes his head, "gross." He is watching the swaying fronds of palms above them as if hypnotized.

"Hello, boss," the concessions man says when Asher approaches, laying aside his book. The cover shows the title: *Piedra de Sol.* "What can I do you for?"

Asher orders the drink and watches as the man pours the limeade from a clear plastic pitcher with lime slices floating within. Asher's mouth waters at the prospect. By the time the man hands over the wax-paper cup its sides are already sweating from the heat.

Asher gives him two dollar bills. And then, too abruptly: "You don't know of any work around here, do you?"

"There's always plenty work in Key West." The man's eyes are very black. He leans his elbows on the counter, his shoulders rising under his ears. "But most of the work down here you wouldn't want to do."

"Why not?" Asher is surprised, but masks it by taking a long pull on his straw. The limeade is tart and delicious.

"Most of the jobs I know about are done by us brown folks." The man laughs.

"I'm willing to do anything," Asher says. "I've got to make a living."

Justin is pulling at his shirt. "I'm burning *up*," he stage-whispers.

"My cousin used to work at the Casa Marina and they were good to him. They got employee housing, too. I'd start there."

Asher thanks the man, then thinks, *Why not?*

"You wouldn't happen to know a man named Luke Sharp, would you?"

"No," he says, shaking his head. "I don't believe so."

"He's my brother. I'm looking for him."

"I'm sorry," the man says, and takes hold of his paperback again.

"I 'ppreciate ye," Asher says, the country way of saying thanks suddenly on his lips.

"It's nothing, señor."

THE HUGE, LUMBERING woman at the Casa Marina says they have no work, but she directs Asher to the Blue Marlin.

The Blue Marlin maids—flirty, pretty, laughing, Indian, Cuban, Mexican—sit on a stone wall like birds on an electric line during their break. They tell him to look around down at the Harbor.

The men at the Harbor, scattered about the deck of a boat called *The Lonesome Dove*, pluck their cigarettes from their mouths and all talk at the same time. "The paper." "The classifieds." "The *Citizen*."

And in the newspaper Asher finds ads for several jobs, most of them restaurant and housekeeping work, but also calls for everything from data-entry clerks to medical technicians. Almost all of the ads demand that the applicant speak English. The one that draws his attention, however, is for a place called Song to a Seagull.

> *Help Wanted. No Keys Disease Tolerated.*
> *Apply only if you are ready to work hard*
> *and are a good person. I'll know if you're not.*
> *Song to a Seagull Cottages.*
> *184 Olivia Street.*

Asher has no idea what Keys Disease is but he's pretty sure he doesn't have it. And he likes the mystery of the ad. Help wanted for what? *I'll know if you're not.* Something about the vagueness is intriguing.

So they head to Olivia Street.

5

As they turn onto Olivia Street, Justin sounds it out slow, aloud, as if learning to pronounce a foreign word: "O-liv-eeee-uh," like exhaling four little breaths.

There's a white fence with tall palm trees and the eaves of three roofs behind it. Pink and purple flowers drip over the fence. Asher finds the gate and there's a cardboard sign taped there—HELP WANTED—so they know for sure this is the right place.

Asher pushes the gate open, easing his way into a courtyard. They are swallowed up in trees and flowers and birdcall. "Bougainvillea," he says, putting his finger to a small purple flower. He had read about these when researching the island. There's a bubbling fountain and a still pool. A glass patio table is loaded with all kinds of breakfast food: muffins, a glass pitcher of orange juice, a coffee machine and bowls heaped with fruit—bananas, oranges, apples, grapefruits, grapes. Asher's mouth waters at the sight of the pink grapefruit.

In front of them there's a big old house, painted a pale orange, with the windows outlined in dark green and bright white banisters around the porch. There's a green swing and a few rocking chairs painted a finger-paint-bright yellow.

A little metal sign decorated with bright painted crabs— OFFICE THIS WAY—hangs from the limbs of a gigantic plant, so they make their way down a gravel path where they push tree limbs and pink or purple blossoms aside as if they are walking through a jungle. They come upon what looks like a little tool shed with a hand-painted board hanging over the open doorway: OFFICE.

Inside the shed an enormous woman about the age of Zelda is spread out at a desk stacked with towers of papers and books and receipts. The whole inside of the shed looks like it belongs to one of those hoarders Asher has seen on television. She's wearing a muumuu that is the color of red Kool-Aid and he thinks of Zelda because they are her favorite things. The woman's black hair is heaped on top of her head and it is threatening to topple over if she moves her head too quick. She has placed little purple flowers into the clump.

She scribbles out a list on a scrap of paper before she notices them.

"Whatta you say, boys?" she says, glancing up. Back home only men say hello this way. She snatches off her glasses, pulls the muumuu out to wipe the lenses. Asher likes the way she moves, like a queen. "Needing a room?"

"No, ma'am," Asher says.

"What can I help you with, then?"

"I could use work."

"You ever done any cleaning work before?"

"I've been cleaning my own house my entire life."

Asher doesn't know any other men back home who clean the house, but he always has. He likes for things to be very, very neat. In fact, the tumult of this office is making him nervous. Back home if Asher had said he cleaned his own house, women would have laughed at him and patted his back as if he didn't really understand what cleaning meant. Especially the women at church.

"You keep a good clean house, then?" She looks at Asher over her replaced glasses like she's making sure he's not lying.

"I believe I do," Asher says.

"Now who's this little feller here?"

"This here is Justin—" Asher says, and cuts the end of Justin's name off quick, realizing he probably should have used a fake name. "He's nine."

"Oh, he's real little for his age," she says, eyeing Justin. She doesn't seem as big when she stands. She takes a dainty step forward and puts her hand out to be shaken by Justin, who takes it without hesitation. "I'm Bell," she says, "B-E-L-L, like what you ring." Then she shakes Asher's hand. "I'm real pleased to meet you both."

"And this'n here?" She nods her chin at Shady.

"We couldn't leave him on the side of the road," Justin says.

"Where you from, baby?" Bell asks Asher.

"Tennessee," Asher blurts out.

"I could tell it, from your accent. I'm from Notasulga, Lower Alabama."

Asher nods. "Don't know it, but I've been all over northern Alabama." He doesn't tell her that he had been to Holy Roller church meetings there, plenty of times, especially up on Sand Mountain. Lydia hates it when he says *Holy Roller* but that's what they are (or at least used to be), so why not just own it? What she *still* is.

"You don't mind cleaning up after strangers, then?" Bell asks.

"I'd rather clean up after strangers than people I know."

"Why's that, now?" Bell's head is cocked to the side as if she sizing him up.

"I guess because it's more interesting."

"That's one way of looking at it, I reckon."

"And because when I know somebody I would tell them to clean up after their own self."

Bell laughs at that. "Amen," she says and she laughs some more and her large breasts shake. "I agree with you on both counts." She sinks down to sit on the step up into the shed. Shady strolls over to her, settling himself against her hip and closing his eyes as soon as she starts rubbing his belly. "Human beings can be wonderful and terrible but most of them are disgusting creatures, I'll just tell you. I reckon you know that already."

"I've been knowing that my whole life," Asher says.

"So you like this old boy?" Bell looks to Justin, still petting on Shady.

He nods.

"You can sit right here with me," she says, scooting over.

Justin sits next to her and Shady stirs, nuzzles his head so that his face rests against Justin's leg and his belly's pressed tight to Bell. He grunts in the back of his throat, too lazy and relaxed to bother with opening his mouth.

"Oh yes sir, you've got you a friend for life in this'n," Bell says. Her voice is softer now. Dogs did that to people. Asher reckons that's what he likes most about them. "He's like everybody else. Just wants to be loved on."

Then she's picking right up where she left off: "I can't get over some of the messes folks leave."

Asher swallows hard and smiles around it, trying to get his bearings. He is still swimmy-headed and suddenly cottonmouthed.

"I have a guest cottage and then five guest rooms that I let out. Sometimes people think they have to party big-time because they're in Key West," Bell is saying. "But a little guest cottage and rooms like this attract the better quality of traveler, you know. I don't allow guests to bring kids but I can make an exception for your little boy. All the real terrible ones—the college kids trying to get as drunk as they possibly can and the in-debts trying to impress their girlfriends—they stay at the big chains."

"Yeah, that's real good," Asher says.

"So you'd have to clean the rooms and the cottage, and go to the store for me. Any kind of errand I needed. I like things done when I want them done."

Asher nodded. "Yes, ma'am," he says.

"You don't need to call me 'ma'am.'"

"Alright."

"Evona takes care of the pool and the grounds. You'll end up working at least forty hours a week, sometimes more. Would that be alright with you?"

"I'll do whatever you need me to do," Asher says. He sounds desperate, even to himself. "I'm not afraid of hard work."

"Well, sounds like we're in agreement so far. So it's yours if you want it."

"A man at the beach said that sometimes inns offer their workers a place to stay."

She eyed them all for a moment. Asher, Justin, the dog, then back to Asher. "Well, I do have one side of the worker's cottage. You'd be sharing the house with Evona. Totally separate, two different entrances. She likes to keep to herself."

"Me, too," Asher says.

Apparently Justin has made a little game of watching the two of them talk, Asher notices. The boy's eyes move back and forth between whoever is speaking.

"Y'all would have to share the porch, that's all. Evona is honest, I can tell you that."

"That sounds alright to me," Asher says, although he is suddenly thinking how dangerous it could be to share a house with a strange woman who might eavesdrop or try to get to know them. But what he wants more than anything in the world is somewhere for them to lay their heads down at night.

"That's a deal, then," Bell says.

They talk money. How much an hour. How much she'll charge for rent on the cottage—it will take most of his pay—and she welcomes them to eat with her every evening. "I like to cook, but I don't like to eat by myself," she says. "Easier to cook for a big bunch. We put breakfast out by the pool every morning for the guests, so y'all are welcome to eat from that, too."

"Would you care to pay me in cash?" Asher asks quickly.

"You in trouble?" Bell asks, and looks at him as if memorizing him.

"No," Asher says. "But I'm not wanting to be found."

"I know all about that," Bell says, nodding. She pushes herself up with a grunt, like a big old machine unlatching itself from being still too long.

"I'm in dire need of groceries, so how about you go on down to Fausto's. There's bicycles over by the side entrance, or you can take the Vespa. Up to you."

"What is Fausto's?" Asher asks.

Bell stops, swings herself around. "How long you been here, sugar?"

"We drove into town this morning."

Bell considers this and takes off for the office again. "Fausto's is the only grocery store where I'll trade. Just go up this street here." She thrusts a tourist's map at Asher. She settles herself back at the desk and puts on her glasses. "Dog can stay right here with me." Shady slumps down at her feet and curls up like he can speak her language. "He'll be fine. And take the Vespa. It's faster."

So Asher has a job. And they have a home. On Olivia Street with the bougainvillea. "Olivia Bougainvillea," Justin says, as if he has read his father's mind. Asher lets out a wearied breath. They have either reached a dead end or a whole new beginning.

6

Asher has never been on a scooter before, but he figures out how to run the Vespa. Once or twice Bell leans out the doorway to see if he is going to be able to start it, but she doesn't offer any instructions, and he doesn't ask. When the engine finally fires, he tells Justin to hold on, and they are off.

Two days ago Asher had been going crazy in that little trailer out on Cheatham Lake, and now he feels as if they are in a different country.

They pass houses the color of beads on a bracelet—pink and turquoise and yellow and orange—behind white fences. An old, black couple sits on their porch stringing beans, children play in a yard, a skinny rooster struts down the sidewalk, flowers open like red or purple promises. A woman does a little dance as she sweeps her porch, in a bikini and white earbuds. A small grayish-yellow Methodist church sitting close to the street.

Asher scans the faces of every person they pass in case he sees Luke, wondering what he would say if he actually saw his brother again. He has a strange dread that he might actually find him while also wanting desperately to find him. How would he feel about seeing Luke holding a man's hand? The thought makes his stomach roil.

At Whitehead Street they come into more businesses. There is the courthouse and the post office. The salty air settles on their skin. At one of the stoplights Asher glances down to his waist where Justin's small hands are latched, his fingers laced together and his little thumbs clenched.

The grocery has narrow aisles, small metal buggies, fruit and vegetables priced sky-high. The mangos are a kind of pinkish-red that causes his mouth to water even though he has never tasted one before. He realizes for the first time that he is famished. He made Justin eat some fruit before they left but he's had nothing.

There is a whole section of key-lime products, all kinds of brands and foods Asher has never seen before.

People crowd in at the glass case in front of the deli and order up chicken salad and olives and something called hummus. An old man glances down at Justin. "Hello there, little man," he says in a faraway accent. Wisconsin or the Dakotas, maybe. Asher doesn't know. Justin puts out his hand and the man laughs with surprise, takes it. As a church child Justin has been taught to greet older men this way. "That's a real gent," the man says, looking up at Asher with pale, watery eyes. Harmless.

Still, Asher puts his hand on Justin's shoulder, nods to the old man with a tight grin. For all he knows there are posters of them all up and down the interstates between here and Tennessee. Every person they see might report them if they look into their faces long enough. Asher had momentarily felt safe in not being recognized from the breakdown video because Key West felt so exotic—he had briefly fancied that they might as well be in a foreign country. But they are still in America, and the crowd at the deli is at least half tourists, who could be from anywhere, even back home.

A woman turns from the deli with a plastic bowl in hand and beams down at Justin. "Hey," she says, a clipped little voice like a bird, her small lipsticked mouth pinching together in a small smile.

"Hidy," Justin says. As she clicks away on kitten heels Justin looks up at Asher. "I like this place," he says.

The cashier has purple nails—so long that Asher watches in amazement as she taps at the register keys—and eye shadow to match her polish, bleached curls, and enough wrinkles to show a lifetime of drinking, smoking, and sun. Her voice sounds out each word as a hoarse scratch.

"Where y'all visiting from?" she rasps.

"Tennessee. We—" Justin stops, interpreting Asher's finger pressing into his back. They will have to talk about this, about how much to say to people. But he doesn't know what to tell his son. Asher doesn't like the idea of Justin lying, but he ought to

have thought about that before kidnapping the boy. Too late now.
Turns out that kidnapping a child is a lot like having one, period:
you have to figure it out as you go along.

"I've been there," the cashier says. "It's pretty country."

"Yeah, I like it," Justin says, causing the cashier to look up at
Asher and smile, her whole craggy face becoming twice as wrinkled in the doing.

Then:

The low buzz of the scooter.

The island changing with the deepening of light, preparing
for evening. Tourists, leaving the Hemingway House, waddling
toward Duval Street wearing white visors and white socks with
white tennis shoes.

Justin leaning against his father's back as the Vespa slices down
the street.

The smell of the ocean.

ASHER LETS JUSTIN play with Shady on the porch while
he carries the groceries into Bell's cottage. Bell leaves only the
screen door closed behind them, and Asher can hear Justin chattering to the dog.

Bell's house has white walls and orange-brown tiled floors
like glazed terra-cotta pots. Large, healthy plants stand near all
the windows. There are lots of colorful paintings that don't make
any sense but are still nice to look at, framed photographs here
and there. Asher tries to study them without appearing to be
nosey. A black-and-white picture of a tough-looking woman, a
younger Bell, with one foot propped up on the bumper of a truck,

a cigarette planted in her mouth; a baby in a just-born hospital picture, the color of the early 1970s; several children sitting on the ground around a worn-out-looking woman in a kitchen chair that had been brought out onto a dusty front yard. A beautiful black woman in a red dress, blowing a kiss toward the camera; a magnolia blossom is shoved into her hair above her right ear.

In the front room there is an upright piano, rich maple wood, not unlike the one at the Cumberland Valley Church of Life.

"Do you play?"

"Yes," Bell says, barreling on toward the kitchen.

Asher hasn't played in years, but he has not missed his fingers on the keys until this very moment. Once upon a time he could not go a day without playing for an hour or so. Once he had sat at a piano like this and felt God in his fingers, had felt the music washing out of him, and in those times everything else floated away and he became the music and he believed, he believed, he believed.

"You play, too?" Bell asks as she unloads the groceries.

"Not anymore," Asher answers.

"I can finish here. You go on and get settled," she says, suddenly radiant in the brightness of the yellow kitchen.

"I think we'll turn in early tonight," Asher says.

"Not gonna eat with us? You'll miss a good meal."

"I appreciate the offer," he says, already backing toward the door. It's going to be hard to not be social at this place. But he has too much to worry about. "I'll see you first thing in the morning."

As he slips out the door and onto the porch he looks back just in time to see her watching him on his way out.

MOST EVERYTHING IN the cottage is wicker: couch, love
seat, coffee table, bed headboards.

A small bathroom with a frosted window, a bedroom for Asher
and a smaller one for Justin. No dining room, but an old Formica
eating table in the big kitchen so much like the one he grew up
with.

Asher is pleased by how little they possess. There is a freedom
in not having anything. They have every single thing they need
and not one bit more, and that's how Asher has always wanted to
live, really.

The porch runs the entire length of the house's front side. A
wall of lattice divides it in two so they have their own side and the
woman has hers. Evona. Nobody could forget a name like that.
There is plenty of cushioned wicker furniture and a couple of
wooden rockers and a swing, a set of chimes that ring against one
another in the slight breeze coming in off the Atlantic.

Asher watches the light and shadows move down the porch
floor as darkness fully overtakes the island. All is quiet here, no
sound other than the chimes and the brush of palm fronds, the
occasional murmur of Justin inside as he talks to Shady. This has
been the longest day of Asher's life, but maybe the best. There had
been a time when he would have thought this serendipity happened because God was on his side. Now he sees the arrogance of
that thought.

There is a clomping on the porch. He catches sight of the
woman breezing past the latticed divider and into her side of the
cottage. As soon as she gets inside she turns on music, as if she has
rushed home for this sole purpose.

Violins, drums, the Mamas and the Papas.

You gotta go where you wanna go

She is singing along, her voice harmonizing with the recorded ones. A rectangle of yellow light falls onto the porch floor from her living room and occasionally Asher can see her silhouette passing in front of it.

Once he goes back inside he finds that Justin is asleep, sprawled out across his bed still wearing his Chuck Taylors, lamplight illuminating his face. Shady lifts his head and acknowledges Asher with his good brown eyes (*I am too bone-tired to get up*) then settles his muzzle back on Justin's chest. Asher sits on the edge of the bed and watches his son sleep.

7

He leaves a note by Justin's bed—*I'm working; stay in the house.*

Bell meets Asher in the courtyard, wearing a seagull-patterned muumuu. Asher studies the knot of tiny pink flowers pushed into her hair at the back of her head and she says, "Frangipani. My favorite. Smell."

Asher feels awkward leaning into the back of her head, but he draws in the scent—like the magnolias back home, but more fruity.

"They smell the best at night," she says, and takes off across the courtyard. "First thing is we need to set up breakfast."

And so Asher's workday begins. Bell shows him how to do

everything: lay out breakfast, clean the rooms, do the laundry, sweep all the porches, put out evening wine-and-cheese service, be on call if folks need pillows or anything else.

Bell sits heavily in one of the metal chairs and dots her sweating forehead with a handkerchief, cross-stitched at its edges. There is a wall of purple bougainvillea and aloe plants big as tree stumps, and all manner of nature closing in on them at all sides.

"Evona will tend to the flowers and trees, wash down the walkways, fix anything that needs fixing."

"How long she been with you?"

"Long while," Bell says. "Best not to ask too many questions of her, and she'll do the same for you."

Asher nods, relieved.

"The main thing you need to know about Evona is that one day she'll be as happy as a lark and the next day she'll be real low." Bell fixes her eyes on him. "You need to know that. Alright?"

He nods again. "Can I ask you a question?"

"Yes, but I may or may not answer it."

"That's fair enough."

Bell waits, closes her eyes as a breeze moves through the yard.

"Have you ever heard of anybody here named Luke Sharp?"

"No. I'd remember a name like that," she says. "Who is he?"

"He's somebody I'd like to find."

"Because you hate him or love him?"

Asher wants to tell her Luke is his brother but then he will have to reveal his own last name. Besides, the less she knows, the better. For Asher and for her. "I'd give anything to see him," Asher says, "and I think he's in Key West."

"I wish I could help you," she says. "I don't believe I know a

person in this world named Luke. But I keep to myself most of
the time. Except for church."

"Where do you go?"

"Saint Paul's. The big Episcopal church down on Duval. But
I don't like to go out at all now. I've not gone in years and years.
They bring me communion on Sundays."

Asher wants to ask why she stays at home but that seems too
personal. When folks don't want to get out of the house they most
likely don't want to explain why, he reasons. So he asks if he can
pull the Jeep into the garage. He tells her he'd like to get it out of
the weather because of its soft top but she is no fool.

"Long as you can clear out a place for it," she says. "There's
all kinds of junk piled up in there but if you stack it up neat there
might be room." Bell slaps at his knee and rises. "You think you're
ready to get started, then?"

"I reckon so," Asher says.

"Just holler if there's something you can't figure out."

Asher goes about his work. The guests show up as soon as
breakfast is set out. A woman dressed in silk pajamas and a silk
robe piles a plate with one of everything and rushes back to her
room. An old liver-spotted man comes for coffee and nothing
else. Asher speaks to them but keeps his head down as much as
possible. They don't care. To them he is just the help, someone
there whose purpose in life is to put out their breakfast and clean
their rooms.

The silk-robe woman isn't happy when Asher shows up to
clean her room but after he has been turned away twice she finally
agrees to sit on the porch and read while he does his work. "Please

leave on the radio so I may listen to it while I wait," she says, each of her words tight and close like they are each alone. Then she puts her hand out, and he doesn't know if she wants it to be kissed or shaken. He shakes it, briefly. Her smile is a tightening of her mouth. "I am Mrs. Lewis."

"Hello, ma'am. I'm Asher," he says.

She has tuned into a news station and they are rattling off all the things that are wrong in the world. Israel and Palestine at odds like they have been ever since Asher can remember. The president fighting with Congress. Hostages. Kim Davis campaigning against gay marriage. A car bombing outside an American embassy. Another movie theater shooting. The local news is mostly about the weather—rain in the forecast—and talk of oil still showing up in the Gulf and how cruise ships are impacting the reef. No mention of a man who has kidnapped his son and was last spotted shopping at Fausto's.

At least this lady is clean, Asher thinks, even if she isn't very friendly. She has draped thin, colored scarves over the lamps. Dozens of bottles, tubes, and tubs of makeup are lined up in neat rows on the bathroom sink. She has cleared everything off the desk by the front window. There is a box filled with a dozen or so pens and five white legal pads crowded with slanted cursive writing. She has even made her own bed, but when Asher asks her if she wants fresh sheets she says "Of course" as if it is crazy to think she can use the same set two days in a row.

Asher loves finding the symmetry of bedsheets, the finality of clean dishes in a drainer. When he was growing up he had been the one who kept their house. His mother had worked like a mule

and been treated like a dog at the high school, where she had
been the janitor. The students made fun of her, made messes just
so she had to clean them up. She had spent her days scrubbing
toilets and scraping dried snot and gravels of gum off the bottoms of desks. More than once his face had burned with shame
when he dashed by her in the school hallway as she spread sawdust
over vomit or cleaned vulgar graffiti off lockers. Luke had fought
people in school when they insulted her. He was suspended for
fistfights three times, all in her defense. But Asher, he thinks now,
had been a coward.

As he leaves Mrs. Lewis's room she puts her hand on the crook
of his arm.

"Wait. I *know* your face. You look so familiar. Were you ever
on TV?"

"I've just got one of those faces, ma'am," he says, and slips
away, his heart pounding.

By the time Asher gets to the other rooms the guests have
gone to the beach or out to eat. He cleans the bathrooms, gathers the towels (the most disgusting part, to his mind), makes the
beds, dusts, sanitizes the remotes, Windexes the windows, mirrors,
and television screens, puts fresh plastic bags in the ice buckets,
new bags in the trash cans, restocks the soaps and bottles, runs
the vacuum.

The thought drifts through his mind that he has become his
mother in this aspect: cleaning up after others, being the help. He
will not let it make him bitter and angry, though, the way it had
her. There is an importance to making things right.

Most of Asher's afternoons are taken up by the laundry but he makes a habit of going back to the cottage for a quick lunch. Most of the mornings Justin trails behind him at his insistence, helping Asher here and there, but as the days pass he begs to stay at the house alone. Asher spends a long time each morning emphasizing how Justin can't go past the porch, he isn't to talk to any guests, and that he can't use the pool while unattended because this might draw too much attention to him, a child swimming alone.

Already Mrs. Lewis is being nosey.

"Is that your child?" she asks as Asher is leaving her room one day.

He says yes but offers no more information. She doesn't ask any more questions, but nods firmly, as if this had been a very important question and now she has an important answer.

Lunch becomes a time for Asher to check in on Justin while the sheets and towels are in the washing machines.

After they have been in Key West a week, Evona has still not really made herself known, simply nodding when they pass each other in the yard. She takes her meals with Bell in the evenings and then plays records far into the night. But Bell is becoming more and more familiar. Asher goes home for lunch one day to find Justin visiting with her. When the cottage comes into sight Asher sees them on the porch together, sitting across from each other on the wicker furniture. They are talking quietly while each of them leans over to pet on Shady.

Asher quickens his step. *Oh God Oh God Oh God,* he thinks, *please don't let him have given us away.*

"Justin!" Asher hollers while he is still out by the pool, and even he can hear how sharp his own tone is, how his loudness causes both to whip around like something is wrong.

Shady jumps up and barks deeply three times.

"It's alright, little buddy," Justin says, rubbing Shady's head, and the dog settles again, thumps his tail against the porch floorboards. "It's just Asher."

Asher smarts at hearing the boy call him by his first name. "Justin, go on into the house."

"Why?"

"Go on, Justin," Asher says, firm. "Mind me, now."

Justin shakes his head, looking up at his father with those big green eyes. He throws a glance to Bell as if they have a secret between them, then leaves.

Bell stands, put her hands together in front of her.

"Is something wrong?" she asks.

"I need to get Justin's lunch."

"I was just visiting with him."

Asher is trembling. "Bell, if I'm going to work here for you, I just need us to keep to ourselves."

"I wasn't pumping him for information," she says, a little laugh in her voice. "I couldn't care less what you're up to as long as—"

"I'm not up to anything."

Bell fixes a knowing look on him. "Well, that's not how you're acting," she says. She steps off the porch without another word.

Justin is lying on his belly on his bed, Shady snuggled close in beside him.

"What was she asking you?"

"Nothing!" Justin shouts into the mattress.

Asher sits on the bed beside him. "Justin, it's important you tell me."

"We were just talking about Shady."

"What about him?"

"What's *wrong* with you?" Justin yells.

"Be quiet!" Asher takes hold of his arms (so small), thinks better of it and lets go. "Calm down. Why are you so upset?"

His eyes are red; he looks like he might cry. "You're the one freaking out."

"We have to be careful, Justin. We can't talk to people. We can't—"

"And I'm supposed to stay locked up in this house all day while you work. It's *summer*time. I need to be outside. I can't stay in the house—"

"I don't have any other choice."

"We can't even eat supper with Bell and Evona. We can't even be friends with *them*—"

"We can't—"

"Because the law is after us. Right?"

For a moment there is nothing but the sound of their breathing.

"We have to be careful. We have to make sure—"

"We wouldn't be in this mess if you and Mom could get along! If you all wouldn't act so stupid!"

"Your mother and I can't stay married—"

"You two can't even have a conversation! You can't even be in the same room with each other!"

"Because she took you away from me!"

Justin jumps to his feet, standing by the bed, his hands balled into tight little fists so that his whole body turns red. "Because you went crazy!" These words boom out of him. "And it was all over the internet!"

"You don't understand," Asher starts to say, but he has no idea how he might explain to a nine-year-old boy what it's like to be convinced your whole life that your purpose is to judge others instead of being kind to them. How can he tell his son that one day he awoke, but that this awakening took years? That living like that for so long nearly made him into a hollow thing? That the hollowing out caused him to collapse?

"Now I'm your prisoner," Justin says, dropping to the bed again, scooting up against the wall like he can't get far enough away from his father. He is acting like a wild thing. "I can't even get online!"

"It won't always be this way," Asher says, but he isn't so sure of that.

A decision straightens Justin's shoulders. "Soon as I can I'll call the law and tell them." He is wild-eyed now. "I'll run away from you."

Asher grabs hold of Justin's arm and jerks him off the bed. Justin is kicking at the air but he hits Asher's shins instead. Two words escape his mouth—*Please Daddy*—and that causes Asher to freeze with Justin hanging out in front, draped at the waist over Asher's forearm. He sees his mother holding Luke like this as she struck the backs of his legs, sees himself as a child, crying and begging her to stop.

Asher puts Justin down. But the damage is already done.

He realizes now that Shady is standing on the bed, growling and baring his teeth. The dog is ready to attack for Justin, but once he sees that Asher has calmed down, he does too. Shady licks the tears on Justin's face but even this doesn't still his son.

"I *hate* you," Justin says, his lips trembling while tears streak down his red face. "I hate you so much."

8

After a while Asher eases back into Justin's room holding a paper towel with a peanut butter and jelly sandwich on it. He sits a peach Nehi (Justin's favorite) on the nightstand and tosses a bag of potato chips onto the bed beside Justin.

"You need to eat," Asher says, and holds out the sandwich and chips for Justin.

Justin turns his head away. Shady makes a move for the food so Asher sets it on the nightstand out of Shady's reach.

"I know I messed up, Justin. You're right. But it's too late to fix it now. If I take you back now, I'll never see you again. They'll put me in prison for a long time, and, I just can't stand the thought of losing those years with you."

Asher's standing there in the middle of the room, feeling like a fool while Justin keeps his back to him.

"I've tried to be a good man all of my life, buddy," Asher says. "I tried following all of the rules and doing everything by the book. But the whole time, it was making me a harder person instead of a better one. That ain't no way to live, son."

Asher stops and puts his hands into his pockets, trying to figure out what to say next, his frustration rising; he can actually feel it moving through his body. "Justin, do you hear me?" He tugs at Justin's shoulder, conscious of how small his bones are. "Justin! First you say the worst thing anyone can say to another person and now you just ignore me? Why are you doing this?"

Justin gets up and kneels on the bed and Shady goes to full alert beside him, ears up. "I'm stuck in this shitty cottage all day!" Justin blurts out. He is empowered by letting this forbidden word fly free, and he goes on, unstoppable. "You brought me down here so we can have a good life together and this is what you planned? You working all day and me sitting here alone? If you don't have a better plan than this then just take me to the bus station and I'll go back home."

"Justin," he says, and lets a time pass quietly between them. He doesn't know what else to say. Asher knows that already his son is feeling bad about what he has said.

"But I don't want to leave you," Justin says in a small voice. "I want you both."

Justin grabs the sandwich and bites into it. Shady edges in

close to Justin's mouth while he eats, taking deep breaths like that peanut butter is the best thing he's ever smelled in his entire life. Justin holds the sandwich high up in the air between bites.

"If I hadn't run off that night, you and Mom'd still be together," Justin says, and then swallows down the mouthful of food.

Asher takes hold of Justin's arms and looks him in the eye. "No, buddy, no," aching at the sight of the sadness on his son's face. "None of this is your fault. Do you hear me, Justin?"

Justin shakes his head, a barely seeable affirmation.

"Not a bit of it. Sometimes people just can't make it work. Your mom and me, we tried. But we failed. We're the only ones at fault here. Not you. Never you."

"But if I hadn't run off to look for Roscoe—"

"Listen to me." Asher puts his face very close to Justin's, locks their eyes together. "I want you to put that out of your mind right now, alright? You're the best thing that ever happened to me or your mother."

"She can't even stand me," Justin says, and he looks past Asher as if he is seeing the ghost of his mother standing in the doorway, a ghost with a firmly set mouth and crossed arms. "She wishes I was never born."

"Stop that, now, Justin. That's not true. Your mom and I don't agree on a whole lot of stuff but she loves you, little man. We both love you more than anything in this world. Don't you know that? You *have* to know that."

Asher is thinking *This is too hard I can't do it I don't know how to do this*, but he keeps talking as if someone else has taken over.

"There's never been a doubt in the world about that," Asher

says, then runs his thumb over one of Justin's eyebrows. Somehow that's always been a comfort to Justin and somehow Asher knows that.

"How about if we go to the beach today, when I finish working?" Asher asks. "You like that?"

"I guess," Justin says, but it's clear by the brightening of his face that the main thing he needs right now is to get out of this cottage, to move.

9

The Everything

They are leaving the beach and the warm air has already dried them completely. Justin's beach towel is hung around his neck and one end of it flaps in the wind behind them like a flag.

Justin knows they can't go on like this very long. He is imagining how it will happen when the cops finally catch up with them. He can see it all in his mind, so he closes his eyes, washing the image away, and then opens them again: At the far eastern edges of the yellow sky there is a green feathering of clouds moving in low, hovering just above the water. A storm approaching. Very far away, still, but moving fast.

They ride the scooter by houses with sandy yards. Then to streets lined with shotgun houses painted pink, yellow, green, purple. Past people on their porches, coming out to see the gloaming settle over the island. Music pumps out of one of the houses—a thrumming bass and drums—and two men are dancing on the front porch, caught up in the song, unaware of each other. As the scooter zips by, Justin turns his head and watches the dancers until the turquoise-colored house is out of his sight.

A rooster struts down the sidewalk as if on its way to the grocery. The green streaks of cloud are taking over the sky and the smell of rain spreads itself out over the island and people pause and sniff at the air. The first drops glisten on the orange-brown feathers that run down the back of the rooster's neck, but he pays this no mind.

Around a corner and then they are at the giant buoy they had first seen when they arrived. Justin begs to stop and since it's easy enough to park the scooter on the sidewalk, Asher obliges.

"Will you take my picture?" Justin says, rushing around to stand by the buoy, and for a split second Asher goes to pat his pockets for his phone, but it is lying on the bottom of the Cumberland River, back home.

Justin looks so small standing there that Asher pauses. Small, and scared, and confident, all at the same time.

"You gonna take it?" the boy asks, expectant, hopeful.

"I don't have a camera. I threw my phone away."

A huge wave crashes against the barrier behind them and sends a wall of spray up into the air. The tourists scatter with peals of delight.

Then the sky opens up, allowing the rain to pound down like coins, and the tourists squeal and run for shelter. But Justin and Asher do not move. They stand very close near the low concrete wall and look out toward Cuba while the rain pounds against them. The water is rocking and white-capping but the rain is warm and the wind coming off the ocean is somehow comforting. An occasional wave laps itself up over the little wall and splashes them, overwhelming the air with saltiness.

Then the rain moves on past the island, out over the Gulf of Mexico.

"Luke is here," Asher says.

"Uncle Luke?" Justin watches the darkening water. "How do you know?"

"He sent me some postcards from here. It's why I chose this place to come," Asher says. "When we came, I wasn't absolutely sure. But now, I know. He's here. We're going to find him."

"If y'all are so close why'd he leave?"

"We fell out."

"Why?" Justin's eyes are on him now.

"It's complicated—"

"Why didn't he come back when I was born? Didn't he want to meet me?"

"He didn't know you existed."

"He should've been checking in on you, then," Justin says.

"Well, it's more complicated than that, buddy."

"Why?"

Asher doesn't reply. He watches the darkness gathering out over the ocean. "We better head on back and check on Shady. It's late."

When they are settled back on the scooter, Justin holds on to his father as they speed away. He is watching the sky again, his head leaned back. That's the way people should pray, he thinks. Instead of bowing their heads, tucking their chins into their chests. They should lean back and expose their faces to the sky. Justin can see the clouds as they meander away, roiling and turning from green to a deep gray, the yellow behind deepening into the dark rose of the beginnings of night.

10

The breeze from the Atlantic laces through the palm fronds. The plants breathe in the darkness, moving closer to the cottages in the nighttime, easing their vines and tendrils and green points toward the walls of the houses. The pool water is still in its concrete rectangle.

Asher and Justin sit on the porch, playing rummy. Shady has spread himself on the wicker love seat next to Justin, who keeps his hand on Shady's head when he isn't making a play. He has inherited his card-shark abilities from his grandmother, as Zelda is an expert rummy player and taught Asher how to play. Cards had not been allowed in Asher's house as a child.

Earlier, Asher heard the ice in Evona's glass tinkling on the other side of the lattice, but Asher has made no attempt to invite her to join them. The fewer connections they make the better and he's been lucky to be here this long without talking to the woman. He knows he has already revealed too much to Bell. Now Asher realizes that she is standing next to the lattice, studying them.

"My mother and I used to play rummy in the evenings," Evona says when Asher turns to meet her eyes. She is a slender woman but somehow makes for a big presence. There is a sadness in her movements. Even in the shadows her eyes stand out, green as the Cumberland River.

"Is that right?" Asher says, not knowing what else to say.

"That's right," Evona says, and nods with emphasis.

Asher watches Justin's face as he glances up over his fan of cards to look Evona in the eye. Asher can't tell what Justin thinks of her just yet, but he sees his son considering her carefully, to make sure he has her figured before he decides whether to like her or not.

"I was lucky to have a real good mother," Evona says, at last, as if knowing that every day Asher strives to understand his own. She is a very pretty woman, tall and long-limbed. Heart-shaped face with eyes that cause Asher to look directly at her longer than is proper. The thing that makes her the most attractive, though, is that she is so at ease in her own body. She leans against the porch post with one bare foot atop the other. And then, to Justin: "Looks like you've got you a good daddy, too, buddy."

Justin gives a half smile, puts his green eyes back on the cards.

"Y'all should join us for supper tomorrow night. You can't keep turning Bell down or you'll hurt her feelings."

Asher nods.

"She sure can cook."

The polite thing would be to ask now if she wants to join them but Asher doesn't want to. "Have a good night, then," he says, finally, hearing how rude this sounds as soon as the words escape his mouth. He might as well have said, *Get lost, lady.*

"Alright then," she says with a little, good-natured laugh, taking the hint instantly, and raises her short glass in a little, half-hearted toast—tipping it toward Asher just a bit so that the golden whiskey unlevels, ice cubes clinking—as she slips into the shadows and settles back on her side of the porch. Asher hears the creak of the rocker as she sits, another whine of wood as she shifts to pick up something off the table near her.

"Why'd you do that?" Justin whispers, his forehead wrinkled in aggravation. He is a terrible whisperer and Asher is sure Evona can hear him. He puts his finger to his lips to shush his son, but Justin rolls his eyes.

Later, Asher gets up to use the toilet. He hurries, always rushing whenever Justin is not in his sight. Living like that is exhausting, but also necessary for his peace of mind.

When Asher comes back out, he finds Justin standing by the lattice divider, his eye to one of the holes, spying on Evona. Shady stands at his side, nose pointed up, tail wagging fast.

Asher snaps his fingers to get Justin's attention, but he doesn't turn, so Asher sneaks up behind him and eases his hand onto Justin's shoulder so that he turns to look back.

Come on, Asher mouths, lips half lost to the shadows.

Justin caps his hand over his mouth and points to the lattice, tickled by having this conversation so close to Evona's back. She is sitting in a rocker not six inches away from them, reading a book. Asher can see through the lattice clearly, the yellow light from her window falling over her shoulders. She is holding a paperback and he wishes he could see the cover.

Asher thinks how Evona must have been able to easily see them, too, with their porch light burning over the card-playing table, when she stood at the divider. Asher pictures her, eyeing them before stepping over to comment on how she and her mother used to play cards, too, a line so telling and inviting that she might as well have announced that she was lonesome and wanted company. And he had simply dismissed her.

NOW! Asher mouths, arching his eyebrows for emphasis. *STOP!* A widening of his eyes, to let Justin know he is getting angry, although he can't help being tickled, too.

Justin is laughing at Asher now. He does a little dance to emphasize the fact that they are so close to Evona that it's ridiculous they aren't being noticed.

Come on now, Asher mouths, trying to not laugh, but then he straightens himself and gives the look Justin knows by heart: *I mean it, Justin.*

Justin relents, and trudges back to the card table. Shady follows closely behind, his nose always right at Justin's heel.

"Your turn to deal," Asher says, shuffles the cards, then scoots the stack toward Justin.

Yet while they play Asher continues to think about Evona over there, reading, alone, and the way Justin had been amazed to see someone doing this. The only reader Asher had ever really known was Luke, who read everything, all the time. For most of his life Asher had devoted all of his reading to the Bible, of course. That had been expected of him, to read the Bible and nothing else. His congregation had hired him because he had *not* been to seminary. Only recently had he realized the way books could give a person wings.

He thinks about the man he had been, just a couple years ago. Judging and preaching and telling others how to live, filled up with the weight of thinking he knew what God wanted.

11

The dark, rocking water. Overturned cars zooming by on the swollen river, entire trees with their green leaves still intact. The bright yellow lumber from houses that had exploded in the flood. The Cumberland River filling the entire valley. Then: Luke thrashing in the water, screaming. But the roar of the churning water overtaking his voice. A wave overtakes his face, filling his mouth with water, and he is spluttering, fighting, struggling to keep his head above the deluge. And then, he's gone. Asher: standing on the ridge, unable to move. A coward paralyzed by fear.

Asher startles awake, sits up in bed and is surprised to find his

face wet. He has not cried since before he got Justin back. There
had been nights in that barren trailer out on Cheatham Lake that
he had lain awake on his back with tears falling into his ears.
But that seems like ages ago now. And he has not wept in a very
long time.

Now the grief—of losing Luke, of losing Justin, of what it has
taken to get Justin back—climbs up from his chest. Asher doesn't
want Justin to hear, so he slips outside. He eases the door closed
and the mourning breaks out of him. He tries to cough the tears
into his cupped hands, but the large grief cannot be contained.

"You alright?"

Asher bolts up and slides into the rocker, as if she hasn't heard
every bit of his outburst. He looks across the shadowy porch but
there is only the lattice, no sign of her at all. Evona must have already been sitting out there, watching the bluing darkness. Night
never becomes as thickly dark on Key West as it did back home;
the light is different here, even at night, as if the water surround-
ing them illuminates the sky.

"You alright?" she repeats.

"I'm okay."

"You want company?"

"I'm okay," he repeats.

Evona comes around the lattice anyway, bends, and sits on the
porch floor by his leg. She cranes her neck back to look up at him.
"You don't seem alright."

"I've been holding it in for a while."

"A person can't do that," Evona says, and lights a cigarette.
"You want one?"

He shakes his head.

"I know. They're terrible. I only allow myself one a month. But this, now—" she holds up a small glass and he can hear the tinkling of watery ice "—I do believe Jameson's is good for the soul."

"That I might need," he says.

"Oh, let me get you a glass," she shoots up and slides around the lattice divide, in and out of the house, and produces a glass identical to hers, full of ice cubes, all in less than thirty seconds. She shoves the glass into his hand, then splashes in whiskey; he catches sight of the green bottle in the moonlight. Then she is clicking her glass against his and downing a drink while her last word— *"Sláinte"*—still lingers on the air between them.

He takes a small sip so he can savor the whiskey on the roof of his mouth and let it soak into his tongue. Smoky and oaky and sharp and soft, all at the same time. He takes a bigger drink and then breathes out a hot breath of satisfaction. "I haven't had a drink in years."

"Why?"

"I don't know. I never took to it." He doesn't want to tell her he has been a preacher all these years. No use in opening that door. People get nervous around preachers, even ex-ones (*especially* ex-ones, he imagines). They feel judged. No wonder.

"Does this help?" she says, and he looks down at her, not knowing exactly what she means. She is looking out at the courtyard, not at him.

"What's that?" he asks.

"Does my coming over here and distracting you and giving you a drink help? Does it help with what you were crying over?"

"I wasn't really cr—"

"You were," Evona says, and leans briefly against his leg. "It's alright. Sometimes we laugh and sometimes we cry and as long as we're alive, we can deal with everything else. You know?"

So she is drunk, he realizes. He's surprised he hadn't noticed the slur of her speech until just now. And why shouldn't she be drunk if she wanted to be, at four o'clock in the morning? She isn't hurting anyone. And she's right, they *are* alive, and sometimes a person has to get numb and deny it all. And sometimes a person has to forget, and sometimes forgive.

"I'm sorry," she says, when he doesn't reply. "I'm a little drunk."

"It's alright."

"I don't do this often," she says. "Turns out we both had a bad night on the same night. That's all. I've had a real bad week. That's why I've been so unfriendly. Sometimes I have bad nights and sometimes I have bad weeks."

"It's alright, really—"

"Yeah, you keep saying that," she says, sounding annoyed enough to make him stop talking.

A silence falls between them for a time and there is nothing in the night except the wind chimes over on Bell's porch. Then, far down the street toward the Hemingway House, there is the whine of a scooter motor.

"Your little boy is a handsome one," Evona says, sounding more sober. She splashes another drink into her glass, then drains the entire thing in one long slide. "He's different, though. I can tell."

"What do you mean?"

"He's like a little old man. In a good way." A silence. The

scooter is gone, now, out of earshot. Only the wind chimes. "Like he knows things he's not old enough for yet."

Asher doesn't know what to say because she has captured Justin in a way he has never been able to say out loud.

"I didn't mean any offense."

"It's alright."

"God, if you say that again, I'll scream." She lets out one big laugh, then caps both hands over her mouth. "Shit! Did I say that out loud? Sorry. *Sor-eeeee*." She collapses into laughter. Serious now: "I'm not a drunk. Alright? I only do this once in a blue moon. You got me?"

"Yes, I believe you."

"Do you?"

"Yeah."

"You *feel* me?" she says, laughing. She is cracking herself up. "You feel what I'm saying, Mister?"

"Yeah, but we need to quiet down a little." She is having such a good time that he can't help smiling.

"Alright then," she says and nods, putting a finger against her lips in a shushing manner. She is barely able to keep her eyes open. "Let's hush. Let's listen." She cocks her head like she is waiting for some perfect sound, but the night is silent. So she bursts out laughing again.

He reckons that last drink has finished her off. In fact, she is much more drunk than he had thought. She wears herself out laughing and then collapses against his leg, her body limp.

Asher hasn't felt anybody against him in a long, long time. And he sure hasn't felt anyone against him that he wanted there.

He stands and leans down to shake her shoulder. "Hey there," he whispers. He takes note of the sadness that shapes her face. "Come on, now," he says, quiet.

Evona's eyes flutter open and focus on him. "What is it?"

"I'm gonna help you get to bed."

She puts out one limp arm and he helps her stand so she can lean against him. She smells musky and sweet, the way hickory nuts smell when broken open in the woods of autumn. She smells like the woods back home.

"Hey, what're you doing, mystery man?" she mumbles. Her eyes are still closed even though she is taking little shuffling steps. He has to put his arm around her waist to steady her. She's putting all of her weight on him, her head against his shoulder.

"I'm going to put you in your bed, alright?"

"Yep." She nods.

Asher has some trouble opening the screen door while holding her up, but he manages. A lamp lights the living room dimly. Books are stacked everywhere. A record is spinning on the record player and only now he hears the Cuban music playing, as she has turned the volume down very low, probably to keep from waking up Justin and him. Trumpets quaver and a woman sings *"Tamborilero!"* in a voice she pulls up from the bottom of her belly.

Evona starts moving her hips in a feeble attempt to dance, the music prodding her awake. "Let's dance," she says, pulling his hands to settle on her hips, then locks her hands behind his neck. She is dancing now, but still has trouble keeping her eyes open. She struggles to focus on Asher, squinting hard, laughing.

"You're not dancing," she says.

"I don't know how."

"Aw, shit, yes you do." She grabs his hips, pushes them back and forth. She might as well try to get some moves out of a tree stump. She laughs at his awkwardness.

Now men are singing along with the woman, *"Tamborilero!"* over and over.

"Come *on*! You can do better'n that!" Evona shakes at his hips again and he responds with a brief motion just to pacify her.

"Dance, dammit!" But then she has lost her burst of energy and has to lean against him again, sliding her arms around his sides to lock at the small of his back. She lays her head on his shoulder. "I'm not a drunk. I should be. But I'm not."

"I don't think you are." Asher finds himself moving his feet so that they're turning in the room in a little box step. She feels so good against him, breathing, sad, and most of all, alive.

The arm of the record player lifts itself at the end of the song and before it can click back and settle its needle on the first track Evona stumbles away. "Yeah, I better go on to bed," she stammers. "I can't remember your name."

"Asher."

"Yeah," she says, and falls into the door frame, slurring out his first name. He goes to help her but she has passed out standing up this time. He gathers her up in his arms—she is light as a child—and carries her into her room.

The bedroom is dark but washed in hints of whitish-gray light that falls in the open windows where curtains breathe in a passing breeze from the Atlantic. There are three framed pictures on the nightstand, all of the same little boy.

Her words drift away as he eases her down onto the unmade bed and pulls a quilt up over her bare legs where her skirt has worked itself up high on her thighs. He does not want to think that she is beautiful, but he does. He pauses, trying to figure out if he should turn her on her side in case she gets sick and needs to throw up. He reckons it is best to leave her but as soon as he takes a step back, she stirs.

"Where you going?" She raises her hand and starts to grab his wrist but drops it weakly. "Please."

He steps out of the bedroom and puts the record player out of its repetitive misery. He places the needle on its perch, clicks off the machine and closes the door behind him.

She has left the bottle on the porch, so he pours himself a little more of the Irish whiskey. He watches as the sky turns from a dark blue to a dark purple to a bluish-lavender glow. Another Key West morning. He thinks again of Zelda and he feels sick to his stomach at what he has done to her, leaving her there in the middle of the floor like she was nothing or nobody. He deserves to go to jail. He deserves whatever is coming.

He finishes the whiskey and goes into his side of the house. He slips into Justin's bed with him and the boy doesn't flinch, his breathing an even purr. He lies there, worrying for all of them as light moves around the walls and ceiling, claiming the world again.

12

Asher spies on Bell while she receives communion from the priest who brings it to her from the big church down on Duval. They carry it to shut-ins and sick folks. Asher doesn't know if Bell is sick or if she just doesn't want to fool with the world but every Sunday around three o'clock here comes the little man in the white robe that flutters out behind him, glowing in the afternoon sunshine like a moth. Asher reads his lips when he holds the bread up for her (*the body of Christ*) and then when he put the wine to her lips (*the cup of salvation*).

It has been too long since Asher took communion. He wonders

if he would be able to feel the bread and wine spreading all through his body like light.

He has paused behind an enormous aloe vera plant and a wall of bougainvillea dripping over a low wall to watch and feels it would be wrong to move until the Eucharist is completely finished, so he stays very still while the priest says the concluding prayers, then rushes off to the house so he'll have some time to rest before supper. Justin is in the pool when he gets to the cottage, swimming back and forth with his face down in the water.

They have been in Key West three weeks now. Rain almost every evening or morning but there is hardly ever lightning like back home and sometimes Justin swims even during the rain showers. There are fewer guests now so Asher doesn't worry so much about leaving him alone there. Sometimes Justin trails along behind Asher during the workday and helps. He loves seeing what disgusting things he can find in the rooms when people leave. But mostly he stays at the cottage, or in the pool. He does a lot of drawing. He has three sketchbooks full of drawings he won't allow Asher to see.

"Hey," Asher says, when Justin finally comes up for air. "It's almost suppertime. You better go change clothes."

He's finally agreed to have supper at Bell's, which Justin is excited about since he's taken a liking to both Bell and Evona. He climbs out of the pool immediately and the water pours from the legs of his swimming trunks as he runs a beach towel over his hair.

"You can't say too much about who we are at supper tonight," Asher says, settling into a rocker, "and you especially can't say our last name, even if you're asked point-blank."

"You want me to lie?"

"No," Asher says, although that's exactly what he's telling Justin to do. "Just don't volunteer it. That's something they might ask me, but I can't imagine anyone asking you."

"And will you lie?"

"No," Asher says, not knowing what he will do. "I'll probably just tell them that's my own business."

"That'll sound rude," Justin tells him.

"Justin, listen to me."

But then Asher can't think of what to say. He is leaned down close with his eyes right on Justin's but he needs a moment to gather his words.

"What is it?"

"I'm sorry I've done this. I know that it was wrong. You know that I don't like lying. It's wrong—"

"I *know*," Justin says, as if to say: *God, I've heard this shit about a thousand times.* "Let's go."

WHEN THEY SIT down to eat at Bell's she asks Asher if he will pray. He freezes. He has been trying to pray in his mind for so long now, finding only silence.

"I'll say the blessing," Justin says.

Evona lets out a delighted little laugh.

"Well, good!" Bell says. "Go on then, buddy."

Justin puts his hands out to the others the way they always had at home, back when Asher said the prayer before every meal and they all joined hands. What seems like ages ago now, when Asher was a pastor and they prayed all the time. Even when they went out to eat, right in the middle of the restaurant. Had he been showing off, making sure others knew that he was a preacher? Now he wasn't sure.

Justin is sitting between Bell and Evona so he takes hold of their hands.

"Thank you for this food and these people," Justin says, squeezing his eyes closed. "Thank you to the Everything. Amen."

"Amen," they all say together.

"That's a pretty perfect prayer," Evona tells Justin.

From the time Justin was very small Asher has taught him how to say a simple but succinct prayer of always being thankful for the food and the people who were gathered to eat it. For so many years Asher worried about making sure Justin understood the Bible and attended church, although over the last year he hasn't attended to his ways of believing at all, resigned himself to the fact that Lydia was going overboard with it all. Somehow Justin has already come up with his own way of thinking.

There is red beans and rice, corn bread, chunks of tomatoes and cucumbers swimming in vinegar, avocados picked from the tree by Bell's front porch, sliced and drizzled with balsamic vinegar. Neither Asher nor Justin has ever eaten an avocado before.

After they fill up their plates and start eating, Evona tells a long, funny story about a time when Bell's back had gone out on her and Bell laid in the courtyard for hours until Evona returned from the beach to find her.

"I was trying to help her up but I was too weak—"

"That's her nice way of saying I was too fat!" Bell says.

"And once I got her up she just couldn't even move her legs, bless her heart. Her back was gone—"

"And so then we both just sort of folded down onto the gravel path out there and by this time it was dark—"

"We just sort of slid down on the ground with me on top of Bell—"

Then they are both so tickled that Asher finds himself laughing in a contagious way and he catches Justin laughing, too.

"I was trying to get out from under her," Bell says, "and there we laid all tangled up about the time a couple of the guests came home from the beach—"

"And they were about the worst guests we ever had," Evona says. She is laughing so hard now that tears are in her eyes. She can hardly contain herself.

"They had complained about everything their whole stay," Bell says.

"I don't know how long we laid there laughing, but long enough that Bell's back was okay by the time we finished."

Asher keeps his eyes on Evona a beat too long, and she catches him looking.

"We've got dessert," Bell says, pushing down on the table to stand up. "Blackberry pie."

Evona starts gathering up plates. Asher stands and fixes his eyes on Justin so he'll know to offer his help, too.

"Oh, thank you," Evona says, as Justin picks up the silverware. "What a gentleman you've raised, Asher," she says.

Back home most of the women wouldn't have let a man carry dishes into the kitchen. They would have insisted that the men sit down while they took care of everything. Asher could recall only one memory of his father; he had left when Asher was so small. They had just finished supper and his father sat at the table. He pulled out his false teeth and sucked at them while Asher's mother cleaned up everything. Then he went into the living room and watched the news and hollered at Luke to not be in there with her. "That's women's work," he had said, and winked at Asher.

"Bell, won't you let us do all of this? Go on," Evona says. "We'll do these dishes, then have our pie and coffee."

"I won't argue with you," Bell says, and struggles away. Lately she has a hard time walking and seems to be in pain. Now often when she rises from a chair she winces.

Evona looks at Asher with worry, a quick glance that tells him everything.

In the kitchen, Justin, Asher and Evona clean up, the dishes and silverware clinking between them. Asher watches the sink fill with hot, soapy water, the suds growing so big they look like they'll spill out onto the floor. He draws in the clean lemon scent, a smell that always makes him think of Zelda. Every single day he regrets that one moment. He had been out of his mind.

"Go clear the rest of the table, buddy," Asher tells Justin.

"He's a special boy," Evona says, and eases her hands into the dishwater, testing it for heat. "That prayer," she says. "Like a little man."

Out in the living room Bell plays the piano. Justin stands behind her as her shoulders undulate, her head swaying back and forth. Her eyes are closed, her hands moving like waves on the ocean, her whole face feeling every note.

AFTER THAT, ALMOST every evening is like that. A good meal and Evona laughing and Bell plays a Joni Mitchell song for them and then they eat peach ice cream or lemon cookies and at some point in the night Asher finds himself looking at Evona the way he never looked at Lydia. Sometimes Evona sings while Bell plays. Asher likes it best when Evona sings Mama Cass songs. Other times they all talk on the porch while Justin lies on the ground with Shady, watching the stars.

Some nights Evona can't come out of her room for supper and later he can hear her softly crying.

Some nights he feels paralyzed by fear: fear they'll be found; fear he will never find Luke; fear that he will find him.

Some nights it's easy to forget that Tennessee even exists.

Some nights Asher thinks Key West is the whole world and that the people who are sitting there with him eating pie or watching the night are the only ones left.

Some nights he thinks they are just a dream God is having.

Sometimes he thinks there may not be a God at all. This is perhaps the most frightening thing of all for him.

Other times Asher looks at the blue-black sky and imagines Zelda watching the stars, thinking about him and Justin, and he can hardly stand it. He thinks about the way Lydia would never go out and look at the night sky but how she is probably awfully lonesome now.

He hates thinking of Lydia being lonesome, even if he has to battle hating her. It seems to him she's afraid of everything in the world and doesn't know what to do about it.

Some nights he thinks Tennessee is just a dream he had one time, with green hills and cows chewing their cuds and cicadas screaming in the hot night.

13

_____

The three of them ride their bicycles down the narrow streets, zigzagging beneath the tunnel of tree limbs lush with leaves and purple flowers. They ride past the graveyard where the tombstones glow in the gray shadows, then ride faster once they near the ocean and catch its salted scent.

Evona leads the way, turning down one street and then another, sometimes standing on her pedals while she sings.

(*My Dixie darling, listen to the song I sing*)

Sometimes daring Asher to race her, sometimes coasting along quiet. Asher likes to watch her when she is feeling everything in a big way. She is either happy in a big way or sad in a big way.

Asher is like that, too, but no one knows that except him. That's the difference between himself and Evona: she hides nothing and he reveals hardly anything. That's the way he has always survived. Sometimes even hiding the truth from himself.

They ride all the way out to the end of the White Street Pier where people are fishing and the wind stammers in steadily from the choppy Atlantic, its whitecaps particularly bright against the dark water. A big pelican is picking at itself on the concrete railing but as soon as Justin zooms by the bird rises, tucking up its legs and flapping away, perturbed at the disturbance. The three of them stand straddling their bikes, and look out at the endless black ocean. Very far away are a few boat lights but mostly there is nothing but the darkness and the warm wind and the sound of the waves supping at the cement pier.

Asher feels exposed here, though, because there are too many bright streetlamps. Nearby stands an older couple, fishing, wearing matching airbrushed tee shirts. The man tries to control the long fishing pole in the pummeling wind. The woman, maybe bored with watching him fight the rod-and-reel, keeps looking over her shoulder at the threesome as if fearing she and her husband are about to be mugged. But Asher thinks that perhaps she is wondering why he looks so familiar.

Justin takes off and Evona follows, pedaling away without a word. Asher rushes to catch up and rides behind them both, watching Justin's strong little legs pump the pedals, feeling safer once they are back in the cover of darkness. Then Evona is singing the chorus of "My Sweet Lord" and Justin joins in with her.

Some nights Asher feels like they have lived in Key West much longer than a month. Nights like these he wishes they could stay here forever. But he knows that is impossible. Every day that becomes clearer.

They ride along in streets striped by deep shadows, past small, pastel-colored houses with people on their porches smoking or laughing or singing. Often the doors are open or the windows are uncurtained so that Asher can see into each golden-lighted room (people watching television, eating late suppers, a woman pointing her finger at a man seated in a recliner, her mouth contorted by anger) and see all the little dramas happening to each person in the world.

He still looks for Luke. He cruises the streets and hopes to happen upon him. He searches the internet and he occasionally asks a stranger on the street if they know a Luke Sharp. But he has no more leads tonight than he had before he got here.

They leave the neighborhood of closely aligned houses and then are flanked on either side by a thick woods of palm and pine trees. He is aware of the ocean breathing close by again although he cannot be quite sure how; by now his senses have adapted to island life so that he is simply aware, as if the pulse between his feet and the ground changes when he is near the edges of the land. He has not been in such darkness since arriving on this island, where there always seems to be a light behind the sky.

"Park your bikes and be quiet," Evona whispers.

"Why?"

"If you want to see the stars the best then we have to sneak out onto this beach where there are no lights. But it's a private beach."

"We can't be breaking the law."

"It'll be fine, Asher," she says. She sounds halfway put out by him and halfway amused. "I've done it a hundred times."

"Come on, Dad," Justin says, already walking toward the sound of the water. Asher's eyes have adjusted to the darkness enough that he can at least make out his son's shape in the front.

"I promise. We're way down on the far corner of a big resort," Evona says, and puts out her hand. Her face is touched by the shadows of palm leaves so that a thin, gray light shows only on her eyes and her outstretched fingers. "They'll never know."

Asher doesn't take her hand and she withdraws it.

"It's against the law," he whispers.

Her eyes flare in the shadows. "Well, it ought to be illegal for them to fence in a wild thing. Sometimes the law isn't right." She turns and he follows her, mostly because Justin is already out of his sight. "Justin," Asher hisses, trying to be quiet, but Justin doesn't answer and after a few steps they have arrived at a chain-link fence where someone has taken wire snips to make an opening. Asher wonders if Evona has done this herself. He wouldn't doubt it. She slides through like a child, then holds back the little flap of fence so Justin can ease through, too.

"Watch the ends, buddy," she says in a quiet, tender way, and he knows for sure then that she was once a mother. Or perhaps still is. There is something in her words, in her body. "So you don't get cut."

The smell of the pines takes Asher back home, to Tennessee, when he used to carry Justin on his shoulders in the woods along the Cumberland River, to his childhood when he and Luke played in the same woods, when things—the good and the bad—made sense to him. Or when he and Lydia first started courting and went for a walk in the woods after church one night. Asher closes his eyes and draws in the scent, filling himself with Tennessee, with the home that he misses and does not miss.

He steps out of the dark woods and finds the beach is just as shadowy. There is a necklace of white and yellow lights in the distance where the resort spreads itself on a curve of the island. Justin and Evona are running down to the surf. By the time Asher reaches them they are lying on the sand with their feet in the water. Justin has his arms behind his head and his face seems lit by a distant light.

Justin sticks his finger into the air. "Look, Dad." Asher turns toward the sky and his eyes find the most stars he has seen since the flood, when all of the electricity had been knocked out by the high water and he stayed out far into the night, helping neighbors and looking for Roscoe.

Asher lies down beside his boy.

There are so many stars this night that the sky seems as much silver as blue black, a sky not so much pocked by stars as made from them. There is no moon, which makes the stars even brighter, and when Asher is very still he can pick out satellites zooming across to point out to Justin. They watch in silence, except when Justin sees a shooting star or Evona whispers the names of constellations. They feel the earth turn beneath them.

All Asher can think is what he is always thinking: that he has to memorize everything about this moment, because soon Justin will be taken from him. He has gotten to the point where he can hardly enjoy anything without mourning its loss while it is happening.

And then Justin is up and running and jumping in the night surf. Evona sits up, watching him, the ocean wind sweeping back her hair in a black tangle.

"My God this place is beautiful," she says, looking out at the dark ocean.

Asher thinks: *So are you.* But just as quickly he thinks: *You can't be thinking that way.*

Evona rests her hand atop his and he jerks away as if he's put his fingers too close to a fire.

"We're attracted to each other, so why not?" Evona says. There is no anger in her voice. "Life is so short, Asher. It's just way too damn short to not enjoy it every little bit you can."

"All I can think about right now is Justin."

Asher knows she is in the dark, that she has no idea why they have come to Key West, but he can't tell her. He can't trust anyone with that information.

"That boy will be much happier once you are," she says.

"It's more complicated than that."

"Asher, I know." She looks at him like she is taking in his entire face.

"What do you mean?"

"I *know.*"

He waits, not breathing.

"I recognized you as soon as you came here. I remembered your face from the news back when that video went viral. But I wasn't absolutely sure. So I googled any 'Asher' and 'Justin' that might be in the news. You should've at least changed your first names."

Asher bolts to his feet, blood thumping in his ears, his first instinct to grab up Justin and simply run. But Evona is on her feet, too, her hands out in front of her as if about to calm a wild animal. Justin is skipping along the edge of the water, away from them.

She puts both her hands on Asher's forearms. "It's all right. You're safe with me. It's not hard to figure out why you'd take him, after what happened at your church." She pauses, shakes her head. "The more I looked, the clearer that became. The news said she used that video against you but what you said on there—it was all just right. It all *needed* to be said. She used it to show that you were incompetent but to me it shows exactly how sane you *are*. Lots of folks think you're a hero for what you said on there."

Asher can't help feeling betrayed, even if her words are soothing. He pictures her sitting up all night, learning all about them.

"How could you do that? Read up on us like that?"

"It's not like that. I'm living right next door to you. Just one wall between us," she says. "Bell may go on her gut instinct, but I've been through too much to take chances like that. I'd have been crazy not to have looked you up."

He can't argue with her there.

"To an old judge in a little Tennessee town what I was saying *was* crazy," Asher says.

"Well, they're wrong. I don't see how anyone who spent five minutes around you and that boy couldn't see the connection between you. It's awful bright."

"Did Bell recognize me? Is that why she took us in?"

"No," Evona says, and nothing else.

Justin is running back their way so Asher lowers his voice, sits back down on the sand. "Do you think we should leave?"

"I think you're lucky to be in a tourist town where people mostly aren't watching the news. Although locals are, and locals go to the beach, too. They work at Fausto's. So eventually somebody's going to recognize you. Most of the articles online make you out to be a crazy man, and people want to help little children get back to their mothers."

Asher listens to the waves washing ashore for a time. "Evona!" Justin yells.

"I know what it's like. To lose your child," she says, but then she turns away. "You're safe with me and Bell."

Justin runs back to them, stands with his hands on his hips, panting. "The water's warm," he says. "Warmer than it is in the daytime. Let's go swimming."

"Let's go!" Evona stands ready to bolt off with him.

"Wait, now," Asher calls, always uncertain of the ocean. "I don't know about that. Swimming at night."

"It'll be fine," Evona says.

Justin and Evona run out into the water. He wades out behind them and the small waves wash against him like bathwater. Above him the stars are endless. Justin and Evona are laughing and splashing in the darkness but Asher feels his own quiet building around him as he walks farther out, even past them, until the water is at his chin and he tastes salt on his lips.

14

Justin finds a pair of red panties bunched up at the bottom of the sheets one morning when he's helping Asher clean rooms.

"How'd they get down there?" he asks.

Asher shrugs.

"Hey, wait a minute!" Justin shouts when he sees there is a pair of men's underwear down there, too. Blue boxer briefs with *EXPRESS* written around the waistband. He stands there studying on this discovery a long moment, as if figuring out a math problem. "They must have pulled them off while they were in bed and forgot about them," he says. "Why'd they do that?" Then as soon as the last word is out of his mouth, he realizes, and his face goes red.

Justin pinches one corner of the panties and holds them up for Asher, asking him what they should do with them. Asher rushes over, holding the garbage can out like an offering plate. "Drop them in here, Justin. Now!"

In that same room Justin finds two used rubbers, one in the garbage can and one on the floor beside it (people are always just barely missing the garbage can in these rooms, but when they miss they don't bother to pick it up like they would at home). Each of them had been tied into a knot and looked like water balloons that had slowly deflated.

Asher catches Justin staring at them and tells him to go play, but he doesn't, as this is all far too interesting.

A sink in another room is filled with beard stubble where somebody has shaved without washing out the bowl. People think they can do anything in a rented room.

Guests are always leaving stuff. Especially little things, which Justin finds especially interesting. If Asher says he can keep a find, Justin puts it in his Keds shoe box that also houses his nature collection. He has shells, sea glass, bird feathers, pressed flowers, a pale-blue bird's egg (empty, with one tiny hole in the shell as if something sucked out all the juice).

The cottage-finds item Justin seems to cherish most is a small silver medallion. He thought it was a dime when he first found it lying on one of the room's tiled bathroom floors. There is a man in a robe stamped onto it. He's holding his arms up in the air and there are animals all around him: a dog, a fox, a squirrel. There are birds on both of his shoulders and on one of his hands.

Sometimes in the evenings when he is going through his collection, Justin takes the medallion out of his shoe box and holds it between his index finger and thumb.

Asher loves it when Justin lays his collection all out on the wicker table on the porch in the pink light of late evening. In some strange way he even covets the treasures his son has found. There is a metal pencil sharpener that looks like a globe, with lots of bright colors for countries. A book of matches (on the cover: drag queens standing in for the *I*'s and *E*'s of the words *AQUA NIGHTCLUB KEY WEST*). A wallet-sized picture, deliberately left behind, of a woman from the 1950s, holding a metal stringer with about a dozen little fish hanging from it. She is wearing white capris and a white sleeveless blouse, a white headband in her black hair. She's smiling but she looks sad. On the back someone has written *Thelma* in a crooked mix of cursive and printed handwriting. Asher knew it would fit right in with Justin's collection. Asher figured Thelma had been wild and sad every day, sometimes at the same exact time, and she went dancing in a red dress and she liked dogs, and sometimes she would sit on the riverbank while she was fishing and tears would fall out of her eyes while she thought of someone she loved but had lost. There is also a tiny little blue bottle of cologne: *Davidoff Paris, Cool Water, .5 fl. oz.* Justin likes to hold the bottle up to the sunlight. He says it is the blue of a thundercloud made into glass. He sprayed the cologne on his neck once and it did smell like cool water, somehow, but it was so strong Asher made him go wash it off.

Some days Asher is alone throughout the day and spends his time memorizing everything, fearful of the day he may not have this freedom anymore. Sometimes when guests are getting their breakfast or having their free wine in the evenings he watches them. He thinks how lucky they are to be living their lives without being on the run. Yesterday Asher watched a woman stick her hand down the front of a man's pants during wine time. He led her off to their room with her hand still in his britches. He saw a man slip his hand inside his girlfriend's bathing-suit top and cup her breast and she laughed and then leaned in and kissed him on the mouth. Today in the pool a woman slapped her boyfriend's face, and then took off on her scooter in her wet bathing suit. Asher studies on how things like this have never happened to him in his own quiet life. Until he kidnapped his own child, of course. He feels he has had two lives: Before and After.

Bell is often at her desk, holding her papers up very close to her eyes because her glasses don't work right and she doesn't want to go to the eye doctor to get new ones. But Evona and Asher are always moving, Evona singing while she works (*My love is like a red red rose*). Asher works nonstop. He thinks if he works hard enough he'll burn all the worry and sadness out of himself.

Asher limits seeing Evona to suppertime at Bell's. When he doesn't see her it's easier to not think about the way she makes him feel something he's never felt before.

Asher can sense that this kind of happiness and peace isn't possible for much longer. His comeuppance is coming. Sometimes he thinks he can almost hear it, a hum that increases in volume throughout the day, becoming loudest at night when he is desperate to fall asleep.

Luke would be able to tell him what to do. If Asher could just find his brother, that'd make everything alright. But he's done everything he knows to do. Asked everyone he can, driven every street on the scooter, looking into every face.

15

The Everything

The morning before the day when everything starts to unravel, the dog finds a very long and very old iguana that has died under the porch.

Shady crawls halfway to it and is frozen in his barking, unable to tear himself away from his discovery. Justin maneuvers under the porch and finds the lizard lying a few feet from Shady, who is crouched down on his belly with his paws parked in front of him, a low growl in the back of his throat between deep barks. Justin hooks one of the iguana's claws with a stick and drags it out.

Bell comes out to see what's the matter with Shady and when she sees the iguana—its skin green like limes except for the black blocks running down its tail, eyes open and milky white—she says "Oh no," sadder than Justin has ever heard her be before. "I've been knowing that old man for a long time."

Justin asks if she had named him.

"Oh, no. I don't believe in naming wild things," she says, leaning down with her hands atop her knees. "Me and this old man came to an understanding. Every once in a while I left him a treat—leftover collards or mangoes—and so he returned the favor by not eating my garden vegetables."

"For real?" Justin asks.

Bell nods. "When you respect a wild thing, they return the favor," she says. "Mostly."

The iguana is almost the length of Justin's arm, tail and all, but she says he was actually kind of small for a full-grown one. "I've been here twenty years and he's been here at least fifteen of them," Bell says. "Poor old thing."

Justin can't stop looking at its little claws, which are all curled up, very pitiful.

Bell steps down from the porch and puts her hand on Justin's shoulder while they look down at the iguana. Justin misses his granny then because allowing this silence to bloom between them is like something she would have done.

Shady edges nervously forward, then takes a step back with his nose near to the ground, wanting to get close enough to get a good whiff of the death-smell but too afraid to venture all the way for fear the iguana might spring back to life and swipe at him.

"Get back!" Bell hollers, very sharp. Afraid that Shady might try to snatch up the iguana, Justin reckons. Shady clicks his ears flat and sits, yawns to feign nonchalance and perches his head atop his paws.

"Should we bury him?"

Bell nods and tells Justin to go ask Evona for the shovel. Evona is in the middle of dividing an enormous aloe vera plant that is too big for its pot, and she points toward the toolshed.

On his way back Justin passes his father, hanging sheets out on the clothesline. Asher watches Justin over the clothespins he's latching to the line.

"Where you headed with that shovel, buddy?"

"Bell needs it."

"Love you, little man," he calls after Justin. Sometimes he says that too much. Justin knows it good and well so there's no use in him saying it twenty thousand times a day.

Justin looks up at the sky where clouds like bruises are moving slow and low over the island.

Bell has fetched a shoe box and now she has already lain the iguana inside and attached the lid.

They choose a spot at the side of Bell's house. Justin digs awhile but isn't much good at it, so Bell shows him how to stand on the shovel to get the blade to go deeper, how to tug up on it to throw the dirt aside. "Hard to use a shovel properly when you're wearing flip-flops," she complains, but seems to be doing just fine despite her sandals. She is good at digging, her shoulders and arms moving like that big metal piece on the side of old-timey railroad engines that joins all the wheels together. Justin doesn't know what that's called but he can picture it in his mind. He tells her what he is thinking.

"I've worked these old arms plenty enough. I don't believe they's a job I haven't done to make my way in this world."

Shady watches from a good distance away, now sitting at full attention, his ears up like he knows something is dead and being buried.

When they have a good-sized hole they put the shoe box in and rake the dirt back over, the clods making little *tap-tap-taps* and *clup-clups* on the lid until there is a dark mound. Bell pats the dirt down with the toe of her shoe and then they stand there again, not knowing what to do next.

"Should we say a prayer or something?" Justin asks.

"You can, I reckon," Bell says. "You're better at it than I am."

In Justin's mind he knows what he wants to say: *Everything, thank you for giving us this good old iguana. He was beautiful. Amen.* But he can't say that out loud, not even in front of Bell.

When Bell sees that Justin isn't able to speak, she puts her hand on his shoulder again—he can feel her sadness working its way from her fingers into his skin, an old sorrow that the iguana has conjured back up for her—and says: "Everything that is, is holy."

"Amen," Justin says, so quiet he isn't sure if he has said this aloud or not. He thinks: *Olivia Bougainvillea Iguana.*

Justin and Bell sit on the porch afterward. Shady jumps up on the wicker love seat and sits with him. Bell rocks in her bright yellow rocker like a queen and looks out where the gray clouds are crowding together to turn the sky a dark blue.

"You feel things in a real deep way, don't you?" Bell says after a while.

"I can't help it."

"It's nothing to be ashamed of. But sometimes it's a lot to carry around."

"Why are you so sad?" he asks.

"Everybody in this world has troubles," she says. "Not a person who don't."

"My granny always says that a person has to live until they die." Justin doesn't add that ever since he can remember he's been trying to figure out what that means. Sometimes he thinks she means that the living is harder than the dying. But other times he thinks she means we have to live as much as we can before we die. He tries to not think about dying, though. Sometimes he lies awake at night and thinks about eternity and even if he's thinking that's going to be a good thing, the thought still makes him feel like throwing up after a while.

"Well, I agree with her. Life shouldn't be feared any more than dying. I've never been afraid of either one. But when my time comes I sure will miss all of it."

"All of what?"

Bell swept one hand out in front of her, indicating the trees, the sky, everything. The clouds have moved on and the world is brightly lit once again. "All of it."

As long as Justin can remember people have been talking to him this way. There's something about him that makes people treat him like he's an old man. Maybe that's why all the kids at school hate him even if they don't know why. Once Rabbit held him down in the bathroom and dipped a wad of toilet paper in the commode and shoved it in his mouth and got very close so that his words spat on Justin's face: *Eat that you weirdo bitch.* For no reason at all. Justin hadn't done anything to him.

"I wasted a lot of years being mad. Don't you do that. Alright?"

"I won't," he says.

Then Bell leans her head on the back of the rocker and closes her eyes. Justin watches her enjoying the sunshine. He wishes that she and his granny could know each other. He thinks they'd be real good friends. He thinks they'd have a fine time together.

16

An arrogant brood of hens pecks at the lawn of the Key West Post Office. They're not like chickens back home. Here they strut around as if they own the place. Zelda has a few chickens back home—"laying hens," she calls them—and hers are jerky, always on the edge of darting off with their heads pumping and wings tucked, clucking a ruckus if anyone gets too close. One of Justin's favorite things has always been to go check for eggs in the mornings. The roosters are the worst here, swaggering along the streets; even the chickens of Key West show very little concern for the people approaching them.

They park their bikes and Justin runs ahead of Asher, hunching down, spreading out his arms as he rushes toward them. "I am the Chicken King!" he hollers. "I can do anything!"

The chickens barely look up.

"Leave them be," Asher says, but there's a little laugh in his voice.

Nine o'clock in the morning and already the heat has settled down over the island like a yellow bowl meant especially for brewing more heat. The post office stands in a still pool of air.

Inside the post office the air conditioning is far too cold. All the clerks are wearing sweaters. Justin zooms straight to a big plate-glass window that is frosted over and puts out his finger to write in the milky dew.

"Don't, Justin," Asher says. "That makes the windows look nasty."

Justin minds him, but with some hesitation. Justin has a weakness for surfaces that beg to be written upon. Once, at the Dollar General back home, on a dusty pickup he wrote *In trunk! Call cops!*

Asher hustles down to Bell's post office box to check the mail but glances behind him because Justin is dawdling behind. He watches as Justin puts his finger to the cold glass and writes: *HELP*. And just as Asher reaches him he finishes: *I'VE BEEN KIDNAPPED!*

Asher swoops across the slick polished tiles and rakes his hand across the window, wiping away the words.

"Why did you do that?" he whispers angrily.

Justin is small and cowering there before him. "Not because I *have* been kidnapped. Just because it's a funny thing to write. The way you'd do if it was the trunk of a car."

"But it's not the trunk of a car, Justin." He struggles to keep his voice low. "And we can't be drawing attention—"

"I'm sorry," Justin says, frightened, small.

"It's alright," Asher says.

Yesterday Bell was on her porch taking communion and Asher snuck into her office and got online. He googled his and Justin's names and there they were, all over the place. Their pictures. Lots of the articles got everything wrong. More than a couple reported that Asher had assaulted Zelda. Which he had.

Most all of them were like this:

An Amber Alert has been issued for a nine year-old boy in Middle Tennessee who was kidnapped by his father.

Justin Kyle Sharp was spending the night at the home of his grandmother, Zelda Crosby, near the community of Cumberland Valley when he was taken by his father, Asher Sharp, 35, a former pastor who gained notoriety one year ago after his emotional breakdown in front of his church congregation was recorded and became a viral sensation on the internet. Sharp was hailed as a folk hero by many within the gay rights movement.

According to the alert, Sharp left Cumberland Valley in the early morning hours of June 7 in a midnight-blue 2012 Jeep Wrangler with Tennessee license plate 4S47EY. Justin Sharp is described as very small for his age. He is about 4'2" and weighs about 56 pounds. He has dark brown hair, green eyes and freckles. Asher Sharp is described as dark-haired with green eyes, 5'11", weighing about 165 pounds. He is considered armed and dangerous . . .

Almost all of the articles had a snippet of the video where Asher fell apart in front of the church but they showed only the worst part, where he broke down. Asher had watched only a couple before realizing they would all show the same section, the part that made him look crazy.

And they linked to a short piece of the voice mail Justin had left his mother. All they played was him whispering "I'm with Dad." They left out all the rest, where he promised her they were okay and said that Asher would take good care of him.

One of the news stations had a video of Lydia, standing out in front of their house. So strange to see his own yard, the one he had mowed hundreds of times, the house he had built standing behind her looking just as it always had. Somehow he had thought everything might have changed in his absence.

"Asher," Lydia said, looking right into the camera, "if you're watching this, I'm begging you: please bring Justin back to us. Please don't hurt him." Then she started crying and the newswoman took the microphone away from her, looking very compassionate.

Anger had flared in Asher's chest. She knew he would never, ever hurt Justin. He could only imagine how this would play for people who didn't know her, or him. They'd think Asher was a monster.

Still, there was a new kind of sorrow in her face. He was tempted to call her, just to let her know Justin was alright. Bell's phone was right there beside the keyboard. But the thing was, she always blamed everybody else, never took responsibility for her own part in things.

In the post office, Justin is standing there looking up at him with those big eyes and his small nose and mouth, waiting, and it is all Asher's fault. There is a dripping rectangle across the wet window, a collection of words wiped from existence with one motion of his hand.

17

Years later, looking back, Asher sometimes thought he heard the little gold key slide into its place in the post-office box. In his memory the sound was much like that of old-fashioned prison keys in the movies: the exaggerated sound of metal on metal when filmmakers wanted to drive home the fact that somebody was being locked away. By this time Asher was already a prisoner, too, and he would not be able to rid himself of that feeling for a long while. He had been terrified for an entire month, of course, but that moment in the post office was the beginning of the end. Easy to see now.

A TURN OF his wrist, the grainy grind of the small hinges, his hand diving into the post-office box.

Tucked into the dip of a roll of circulars, there is a utility bill, an issue of *Time* magazine, what appears to be a letter from Guntersville, Alabama, and then: a rectangular card. One side is blank save this address:

RESIDENT
KEY WEST, FL 33040

On the other side, in huge letters along the top:

HAVE YOU SEEN THIS CHILD?

Below that, a picture of Justin that Asher himself took almost a year ago. Justin is looking right into the camera, big eyes and open face, his full beauty exposed. A revealing picture of him, one that had been chosen because that shining look is on his face. He had taken the perfect picture for a card announcing a kidnapping: completely innocent, appearing younger than his true age, small. The kind of child anyone would want to help save.

What the picture does not show, since it has been cropped down to only his face: Justin had been standing on the banks of Cheatham Lake behind Asher's rented trailer. Since the photo has been made black and white by the card makers, the peach-orange light of near-sunset has been lost, too.

That day, Asher had packed them a lunch: peanut butter and jelly sandwich for Justin, a ham sandwich for himself, a bag of chips for them both, and two cans of peach Nehi that Asher kept cold in a Bunny Bread bag full of ice.

That day they had eaten their lunch beneath the willows,

watching the small waves sup at the bank. Then he had taught Justin how to skip rocks.

It's all in the choosing of the rock. Look at this one, it's perfect.

The sky had turned a deep golden pink, and the light on Justin's face had made him look like he was glowing from inside, like some kind of modern child-saint.

Don't move. No, don't, now. Daddy's gonna take your picture.

The click of the camera, the moment caught forever.

Then they had lain back on the quilt and let the sun set and listened to the lake. A perfect day. A day Asher had immediately known he would always remember.

And now a day they are using against him.

Below the photo there is Justin's full name, birth date, height, weight, eye and hair color.

And then, a picture of Asher. The worst possible one they could find. He is looking just past the camera, sad, a moment of terrible depression caught on film.

He doesn't know where they have even found such a picture; he has never seen it before. Zelda was always snapping away at every family gathering, so most likely it had come from her collection of poorly composed and out-of-focus pictures. Asher figures that in the original photograph, he had not been the subject, but was just caught in the frame as he stood in the background behind Justin (Zelda's favorite—and really, her only—subject).

Beneath this picture is all of Asher's information, too. Birth date, height, weight, eye color, hair color, no tattoos, no piercings. All of it on this card that would go out all over the eastern United States.

Below both the pictures, in big block letters like a scream: *KIDNAPPED!*

Asher takes in everything on the card: the pictures and words causing pistons to pump in his brain, flashing from here to there, all the thoughts firing back and forth until the feeling of dread floods him like adrenaline, leaving him exhausted. He has to draw in a deep breath and steady himself by leaning against the wall of post-office boxes.

Asher can see the shape of Justin in his peripheral vision: he has found something to busy himself, as he is always able to find something of interest no matter the situation.

If there is one of these in Bell's box, there is certainly one for every person in Key West.

Then Asher sees the trash can, around which cards are scattered. People trying to get rid of their junk mail in a hurry, not noticing or caring about it. Maybe they hadn't even glanced at the *Kidnapped!* card. But most likely they had given it at least a look. Pictures of little stolen boys have a way of burning themselves into people's minds.

Asher snaps up each card.

He is aware of his labored breathing and then Justin is humming as he peers out the window, watching the chickens.

"Justin!" Asher can hear the firmness in his own voice. "Let's go. Right now."

ASHER STEERS JUSTIN down the sidewalk with his hand capped over the boy's shoulder, toward the rack where they left their bicycles.

A couple of tourists are strolling across the parking lot. "Look at the chickens!" the woman cries out like a child. She is dressed for a day of golf. Only people with money can afford to go around all dressed in white. That's what Evona told him one day when they were watching guests leaving for a day out on the island.

Asher gets ahold of Justin's shoulders and turns him around so he won't face them.

"What'd you do that for?" Justin says, loud, and Asher shushes him.

"Be quiet," he says, and starts to say more, but then, all at once, Asher is stumbling sideways and then falls, catching himself with one hand that lands palm-spread-out.

"Daddy!" Justin hollers out. "You okay?"

Asher is hunched over, shaking his head, little beads of sweat standing above his lip.

"It's alright," he says, and dusts the grit from his palm. "I just got dizzy a minute."

Asher climbs onto his bike. He knows it doesn't make much sense to climb on a bicycle right after a dizzy spell, but they need to get back to the cottage.

"Let's go," Asher says, and nods to Justin's bike so he will get on. "I'll stay close behind you."

Their legs pump them up Whitehead, back toward Olivia Street, back to what passes for home.

18

While Justin is cannonballing into the pool Asher is searching the kitchen drawers for a box of matches. When his eyes aren't on Justin, he hears him splash in the water, but he turns back to the front door after every drawer search, checking on the boy.

In the farthest reach of the last drawer, Asher finds matches in a small red box. *Galatoire's New Orleans.*

He has managed to gather up three or four dozen cards from the post-office floor and garbage can. He tears them into small strips, watching Justin's photographed face as he shreds the papers, and stacks them into a large, black ashtray on the porch. He strikes at the flinted side of the matchbox several times and then finally the flame startles to life. Asher shoots a nervous glance at Justin, who is racing back and forth in the pool (always alone—never a child to play with).

Luke, where are you? I'm alone. I need you.

The small squares of the card smolder and he has to keep lighting matches to the pile until they flame into a brilliant orangeness.

"Everything alright, darlin?"

Bell stands with one foot on the step, her eyes alternating between him and the pile of ashen-edged paper in the ashtray. He maneuvers around to stand between Bell and the cards.

"Just mind your own business," Asher says. He hasn't even realized he had that kind of rudeness in his mouth. But he says nothing else.

Bell comes closer, then pulls Asher toward her, swallowing him up with her big arms and her muumuu and her scent.

Asher can't help it, he relaxes there, settling against her. He lets loose a breath he has been holding for weeks now and this feels like a tight fist unclenching. He feels the breath leave his body and travel past the porch, brushing past plants and easing through the leaves of trees, his grief unleashing until it catches the wind and is carried out to the sea. Bell holds on to him and there is only their breathing. Asher realizes he has closed his eyes. He can hear Justin splashing in the pool.

Bell steps back. "I saw the card," she says. "We get mail here, too." He hadn't thought of that, even though he has seen the mail carrier come plenty of times. "The P.O. box is for personal mail; this one's for business."

He waits, watching her.

"And I've read some of the news reports. Have you done all the things they say?"

"No." A lie. "Yes, but the way they make it all sound. It's—"

"Why would you take him away from his mother, though, Asher? Was she mean to him?"

"No, not like that. But—"

"I know things are always more complicated than they appear," she says. "But you can't raise your boy like this."

"I don't know what else to do."

"Are you alone in this world?"

"Except for Justin," he says. "My brother, but I did him wrong."

"Now you have me, too." She isn't smiling, but a tenderness overtakes her face. "People like us have to stick together."

"What do you mean?"

"I know what it's like to be on the run."

Asher nods. How is it that a stranger can feel more like family than folks he has known his whole life?

"Try not to get so wrought up," she says. "He can feel it. And right now, you're a mess. You've got to get yourself together."

"I know it," Asher says. Then: "I'll try to figure out how to get out of here as soon as I can, if you can—"

"You landed in a safe place." She eases into the rocker, wincing as she sits back. "A blind man could see what a good daddy you are to that little boy. That's good enough for me."

"Thank you," Asher repeats, thinking *thank you thank you thank you.*

19

There are clumps of seaweed all along the water's edge, rocking endlessly back and forth as the little waves come in and go out, in and out. The waves aren't as heavy on this side as over on the beach at Fort Zachary Taylor because of the protective reef. Seagulls puff their white chests out toward the Atlantic, watching the ocean, soldiers waiting for reinforcements to arrive. Curmudgeonly pelicans flap overhead, their eyes firmly set.

Up the beach a loud group of college kids are vacationing on their parents' dime. They have been raised with too much money to simply be still and seem to think themselves the only people in the world who matter, so there is no need to lower their voices. One of the boys—his hairless chest and legs oiled and glistening in the sun like a seal's skin—drinks rum from a white bottle so that everyone can see him. A girl in a blinding-pink string bikini chides him in her Valley-Girl-by-way-of-Atlanta speech, but he shouts "This is Key West, Aimee. Everything is allowed."

Asher has been here long enough to resent that kind of thinking. A biplane slices the sky, silent, far out over the sea.

"Can I get in, Dad?" Justin asks, barely audible over the constant, warm wind. Asher nods, and unfurls his beach towel, which flaps and snaps at the air until he manages to settle it on the white sand. He has brought along a book Zelda had insisted he read—*Jonah's Gourd Vine*, by Zora Neale Hurston (*It's about a preacher who loses his way, too*, she said, shoving the novel into his hands) —but he is too paranoid to take his eyes off Justin.

So Asher watches his son and everyone else. This is the off-season, August, and most schools have started back, so the beach is not very crowded. Except for the college kids, most everyone seems to be a local. No fanny packs, no electric rental cars parked crooked at the curve.

A very fat man strolls by in a Speedo. So fat that only one thin, black line of the bathing suit can actually be seen in the front, and then, in the back: total flatness, as if his back goes straight to the tops of his thighs. Not far behind him is a woman in a shimmering gold bathing suit, complete with a matching, floppy-brimmed hat. A pair of gold-colored flip-flops dangle from the fingers of her right hand. She is talking on a cell phone as she twists along the water's edge. Two teenaged girls—confident in a way that Asher had never been, not ever—sashay by, giggling. So much like girls back home. Asher reckons teenaged girls are the same everywhere: either totally confident or not at all, but surely always giggling when they find one of their own kind.

Justin splashes into the water, pausing to study a white rock at the edge of the surf. He reaches down and runs his hand over its surface. God lives in rocks and water and sky for Justin. Asher knows this without ever having been told.

A Cuban woman and her grandson approach and make their place nearby. Asher homes in on the music of their talking. The grandmother is still curvy enough to make Asher aware that she had once been a stunning knockout. She has rolled her Levi's up to her knees and tucked her blouse under the bottom of her bra, exposing a pale hunk of belly fat. She speaks to her grandson in a pretty rat-a-tat-tat: *"¿Jesús, meterte al agua conmigo? ¿O tienes miedo?"*

A heron wanders the dunes, amazing in its clean whiteness.

The sun broils down, boils down, a punishing, comforting heat unlike anything that Asher has ever known back in Tennessee. A fierceness of heat.

He watches Justin, and the Cuban grandmother, and the ignorant, spoiled kids with their tight gym abs and long brown legs, an old woman with sagging breasts, the flat-rumped man as he strolls in the distance down the beach. As far down the strip of sand as he can see, there are people, each of them with their own stories and hurts and joys. And he loves every one of them.

At long last he believes he understands the poem he has been saying to himself ever since Luke's postcard made him look it up:

the poem about a sandpiper wandering the beach, taking note of every little thing, naming things specifically. That was the way back to believing: being conscious, seeing the God in everything and not just the Bible or the Church. That was the way back. He had to be like the sandpiper, running to the south—as far as he could drive—to find out the answers, and the way back.

He keeps his eyes on the people down the beach and he knows there is something living in each of them. Some people might call it God. Some might not have a name for it. What he knows is that they all have the good and the bad in them. He does, too. But that's where the God of his understanding lives—not just in the goodness and not in the badness, but in the shimmering knot of the two.

Asher thinks of

Lydia

Zelda

Jimmy

Stephen

Kathi

Cherry

Caleb Carey

Rosalee Carey

The girl who filmed him

The congregation, watching him

Jane Fisher

Adalia, the cashier at the Git 'n Go

The man who thanked him in Georgia

The Cherokee girl at the truck stop

The cashier who said a prayer for him

The hungry people on the side of the road along the way

Shady

Bell

Evona

And first and last is Justin. Always, there is Justin for him.

For a long while Asher hasn't known how to believe. Because how does a person keep their faith intact when they lose their child? How can we believe in a God that would allow a father and a son who love each other to be separated unfairly? Where is the goodness when a man turns his back on his brother for being who he was made to be? How can God sit by and let evil twitch itself out over the world?

That's God, he thinks, looking out at Justin standing in the water, the sun behind him so that Asher can make out only his shape, a shape he has memorized, has burned into his mind's eye. *Because God is in my son.*

Justin has walked a long way out but the water is so shallow the ocean still does not strike him higher than his chest. He turns to Asher and raises his arm, motioning for him to join.

Asher slips off his red flip-flops and runs down the beach and into the warm, silky water and joins his boy. Justin rakes his hand across the waves and splashes him when he comes near. Asher dives under and the ocean swallows him whole.

20

They pedal home slow and easy in the gathering shadows of the twilight. The sun and water have exhausted them, so they are taking their time. The island is very quiet tonight, a weeknight after one of the hottest days of the year. Asher reckons that everybody is worn out from the heat. He can hear the click of their bicycle chains over everything else and they don't speak a word the entire way.

There is some kind of sadness on Justin's shoulders but Asher knows he won't tell what is wrong. He doesn't bring it up for fear of what the boy might say: that he wants to go home, that he misses his mother too much, that he hates Asher.

The guilt is worse now that school has started back. Every

morning Asher thinks of how he used to always drive Justin to school, the little pang of pride and hurt when Justin would shuffle into the building, his backpack seeming bigger than him. He has thought about going to the library to get some books to at least continue Justin's education but the prospect of homeschooling seems ridiculous. He knows that these are the last days. Yet when Asher thinks about this fact he is filled with a terrible feeling of purgatory.

Darkness has settled over Key West by the time they return to Song to a Seagull. As soon as they enter the gate they can hear Bell playing the piano, a familiar tune but one Asher cannot place. The courtyard is dark except for the yellow-lit windows of Bell's cottage.

Asher and Justin both stand in the yard after they have put down their kickstands, listening, and the music becomes louder by their stilling. The music causes Asher to picture the willow trees down by the Cumberland River, back home, the way they looked when the late evening breeze traveled across their leaves, making its way down the course of the river, following the water. Asher knows the melody so well he can almost sing the words, but he still can't place the song.

"What is that?" Asher whispers.

"Something sad," Justin says.

They are almost to their own porch before Asher sees Evona sitting on the steps, barefoot, all the windows of their house dark behind her. Shady is lying against her and one of her hands is buried in his fur.

"It's 'Blue' by Joni Mitchell," she says, and Asher thinks *Of course*. This had been one of Luke's favorites.

"She's crazy over that singer, ain't she?" Justin says.

"Joni's songs remind her of somebody." Evona says this in such a way that Asher knows not to ask for more explanation. Bell is a mystery and a secret. She has respected his privacy and he figures he should do the same for her. These are the only people he has ever known who let him be who he is, no questions asked.

Asher tells Justin to go on and get a shower and he minds without any arguing although he usually hates to be left out of any interaction with Evona. His skin must feel as tight with sand and salt as Asher's.

Asher sits down on the step beside Evona and gives Shady a good pat on the head.

"You were on the national news tonight," she says. "Your ex-wife was on. She's out of her mind with worry." She takes her hand away from Shady, leaning forward so that he can no longer see her face. "I'd read before that your mother-in-law got hurt in the scuffle but tonight they showed pictures of her face. Tell me you didn't do that, Asher."

"I didn't mean to," Asher says.

"Oh God—" Evona puts her hands on her face as if this is too much to bear. "One whole side of her face was blue, Asher."

"She got knocked down when I broke down the door. It was an accident."

"You didn't do that *to* her, intentionally?"

"She forgave me. She knew I didn't mean to."

"Asher—" she says, and he can hear in her voice that she is ashamed of him.

"I talked to her," he says. "I begged her forgiveness."

"Why didn't you tell me?"

"The less you all know the better off we all are." His voice is shaking. Bell has stopped playing the piano and the absence of the music seems a widening thing.

"What else don't I know?"

"There's nothing." He shakes his head no. "What all did they say about me?"

"They showed a little bit of that video from you in the church—the part that makes you look the worst."

He nods, but she isn't looking at him.

He puts his hand atop hers to see if she will let it stay. "Please, believe me," he says.

She eases her hand away and there is no tenderness or malice in her voice. "What're you going to do?"

"I've got to take him back."

She shakes her head, her eyes on the ground. "Just lay low for a little bit," she says. Her voice comes from the back of her throat. "Let this pass."

"I can't raise him on the run," he says, as if she needs convincing. He has had this conversation with himself so many times before, but never anyone else. "When I took him, I just thought, 'I can't be away from my boy. I can't stand it.' I should have listened to my lawyer. She said we could appeal. But I couldn't stand the thought of a whole year without being with him properly." Now he is just talking out loud. "When I take him back, they'll put me away. I'll never get to see him."

Help me, he thinks.

Evona puts her hand on his back with some amount of hesitation, then moves her palm around in a circle. His mother had done this, long long ago, when he was little and sick. He had always been her pick. She had always been affectionate with him in a way she had never shown Luke, but he had resented her for it instead of relishing it. He recalled one time when she had touched him in this comforting way. He had been on the bathroom floor, his head against the cool porcelain of the toilet after vomiting with a stomach virus, and she had folded herself down in the little space beside him, rubbing his back. *Bless your heart, honey,* she'd said in a soft voice. He had forgotten that voice until just now because that was before she became so terrible. When someone turns mean, do we lose all that good that was in them, just as they do? He thinks that maybe we do, although we hold on to it as long as we can, hoping.

"I sure don't want y'all to go," Evona says. "I kind of like having you two around." She takes her hand away from his back, folds it atop her other one on her lap. "But her face, Asher. You've got to make this right."

Far out over the ocean there is the rumbling of thunder and seconds later lightning illuminates the night.

He keeps his eyes on her slender hands. There couldn't have been a less convenient time for him to find somebody he cared about. The thought of that is impossible, but he still can't deny what he feels. He knows how foolish it is to even entertain the thought of wanting her, in this time and place, when he has made a complete mess of everything. But he also knows he has only this one life and now that he's found someone he needs to hold on to her.

He leans in to kiss her. But just when he is close enough to feel her breath on his mouth, he pulls away. He stands and looks out into the night as rain begins to peck at the shadowy yard.

"Why did you do that?" she says from behind him.

He doesn't know if she is asking why he started to kiss her or why he pulled away. He can't figure which has upset her. "I'm sorry," he mutters. When he turns he sees that her face has changed, squared by a new kind of pain.

"Ten years ago, I lost my little boy," she says. "He was sick, for a long time. So every day he died a little bit more. But still, when he went, I wasn't ready. They told me I'd have time to prepare myself. But there's no way. So I shut myself down for years and years, after I lost him. I wanted to die. I kept thinking there might be some chance that I'd see him again if I did. But instead, I came here. And somehow I found Bell. You don't know how similar you two are."

He is sick to his stomach from the knowledge of what she has gone through. He doesn't know how anyone gets over that. But this explains so much: all the times he can hear her crying on her side of the house, the sleepless nights she spends on the porch, the days when she disappears. But also, the way she launches into the world on her good days.

After a time he asks: "What do you mean, how similar we are?"

"More like how similar she is to your brother. She was running away, too. From loving somebody. From parents who would have rather seen her dead than with a woman."

"I would've never thought—"

"They don't all act alike, Asher," she says, impatient with him.

Then: "And for the longest time, it was just me, and Bell. We worked hard every day. We ate supper together in the evenings. We learned how to talk to each other, and how to be quiet. The best part is we accepted each other for who we were, no questions asked. And even though every morning when I woke up and realized all over again that this was real, that my little perfect boy was dead and buried in the cold ground—" Her voice breaks but she does not cry. "—I did the best I could. Despite everything, I thought, I'll live, for him. See what each day had to offer since he couldn't. I don't know if I believe in God, Asher. I don't. Which scares the hell out of me. But I believe in something. I don't know what. Music. Something."

Asher doesn't know what to say. All this time he has been feeling sorry for himself, thinking about the mess he's in, and not even thinking about the grief that Evona or Bell might be carrying around.

"When you and Justin came, at first I thought there was no way I could bear having a little boy around here. I thought: I can't do it; it'll remind me too much. But Bell knew what she was doing. It was time. You all saved me." She takes his hand again, gingerly. "Does that make sense?"

"Yes." He breathes the word against her face as he draws her to him. He puts his arms around her, holding her tight, her lips so soft, the smell of her, her cool ears beneath his palms, her breasts small and firm against his chest. He kisses her mouth, her chin, her forehead. When he kisses her cheeks he finds she is crying. So he kisses her eyes, too, the salt tangy on his lips.

21

The room is lit with white morning light and Justin squints as Asher shakes him awake.

"Justin, come on—" His voice is trembling. "—we have to go, we have to leave."

Evona is hollering from the living room. "Go, Asher, go. You have to go."

Asher wants to take the time to explain, but there is no time. And if he stays here with Evona he will most likely lose Justin forever.

"Come on, buddy, hurry. We have to hide."

"I'm tired of hiding," Justin mutters, sleep in his throat. He is staring up at Asher with a furrowed brow that might as well be stamped with the words *Enough is enough.*

"We have to, Justin," he says, trying to sound calm, but his whole body is thrumming with fear and sadness. "Please, little man. Come on."

Asher can see the moment of recognition in his son's eyes (*this is serious*), and then Justin sits up on the edge of the bed, pulls on his shorts, shoves his feet into his Chucks, glancing around the room.

"Where's Shady?"

"He ran out as soon as I came in," Asher says. The dog had darted past him as if he knew what was happening. "Come on, buddy!"

When Justin gets to the living room Evona is leaning in the front door. She's been crying and her face looks like it's been scrubbed clean with a rough washrag, her eyes pink, her cheeks rosy. When she sees Justin she turns her face away.

"What is it?" Justin asks but nobody answers him.

"Just go," she says, trying to control her mouth and making her words sound like two big bubbles breaking on the air.

Asher holds on to the door frame for a moment, too.

"I can't just leave you like this," he says to Evona. "With all of this to tend—"

"*Go,*" she says, firm and hard, pushing him away, pretending to be mean about it so he will listen. She's strong Evona again, the Evona that Asher knows, the Evona who walks with determination even if she's just crossing the yard to tend to some flowers. "*Now.* They'll be here any minute."

"Who?" Justin yells this, stopping in the yard.

Asher leans over from behind and he has a hold of Justin's elbows. There is no other way to do this. "Bell's passed away—" His voice against Justin's ear.

Something in Justin's face changes, squares, hardens.

"—she passed before the ambulance could get here and now Evona thinks the police might come. So we have to go. We have to get out of here right now. We'll be able to come back."

"But I'll never ever see her again!" Justin cries out.

Asher put his hands out toward him, as if knowing what he would do, and he does: Justin runs. He runs to the cottage to see her.

"No, Justin! You can't!" Asher hollers.

Justin stops on the porch when Asher manages to grab hold of his wrist. He can't let him go in there and see her lying dead like that. But when Justin turns to face him there is something strong and magnificent about the way he looks up at Asher and Evona.

"I've always been losing somebody. Roscoe, and you"— he says directly to Asher—"but you never thought about that, did you?"

I did, I did know, Asher wants to say to him, a prayer, but he doesn't interrupt.

"I used to sit up all night, missing you," he says. "And then I lost Granny. And Mom. Tennessee and the woods and the ridge and the river. And I'm gonna lose you sometime soon, again, ain't I? You know I am."

Asher doesn't respond. He concentrates on the small bones in his son's wrist.

"Let me see her."

Asher lets go of Justin and follows him into the house. And there is Bell, looking like a queen lying there asleep. There is a stillness in the room that exists only where the dead lie. Asher recalls it from his own mother's death, from the many death beds he attended as a pastor. Justin leans over and kisses Bell on the cheek. Asher can smell the flowers Bell always wore in her hair, she wore them so long that she started to smell like them even when the flowers weren't there.

Then he hears Justin whisper: "Olivia Bougainvillea Iguana."

Justin turns to leave but Asher folds himself down and takes hold of him.

Justin buries his face against Asher's chest. Evona caps her hand over Justin's head. Asher thinks about when he was the pastor and at the end of the service people would go to the altar and he'd anoint their heads with oil. The congregation would gather around the person who needed praying for and they'd lay hands on the person's head and pray out loud in shivering sentences.

"Shady knew before anybody," Justin says, and he is off again, running outside to find the dog. Outside, Asher and Evona see Justin's legs sticking out from under the house as he squeezes under. They don't have time for this. They have to go, Asher knows. Evona will take care of Shady. "Justin!" he yells, too loudly, angry now. They have to go. "Come on, right now!"

Asher gets down on his hands and knees, peering back into the darkness and Justin is sliding on his belly to the dog, who is lying back there in the shadows of the farthest corner, curled up right under Bell's bedroom.

"Come on, little buddy," Justin says, clucking his tongue. "I'm here now. It's okay, Shady-boy."

The dog blinks at him. As if saying, *No, it's* not *alright. Not by a long shot. Bell's gone. She's* gone, *and she ain't coming back.*

Justin scooches toward Shady, ignoring Asher's pleas, and there's no way Asher can get back there. Justin manages to get his head and chest back past the two front rooms but beyond that he can't do it. Shady is watching Justin as if he is very, very concerned.

"Justin, please!" Asher pleads.

And Shady recognizes the urgency and moves forward.

"That's it, buddy," Justin soothes. "Come on, come on out."

Shady crawls toward him and Justin eases backward, urging the dog forward until they are all out on the yard. Shady spoons against Justin, their breath rising and falling at the same time in exhaustion. They lie there only a few seconds, but it seems much longer.

Asher squats down beside Justin and Evona is crying again, standing behind him. "Come on, Justin," he whispers, softly. "Let's go, just for a little while. Shady will be fine here with Evona."

Shady flops his tail twice, so Justin stands up, and they go.

22

Justin lays his head against Asher's back as they speed away on the Vespa, turning here and there because Asher doesn't know where to go. Little dots of rain tap against his face and the sun fights the dark clouds above them. There has been much rain in the night so that some of the streets on the south side of the island are completely flooded, standing like still rivers. But a flood here is only an inch deep, not like back home, so the Vespa zips right through the water.

Asher's thumb presses the accelerator all the way down but the Vespa will go only so fast. He wants to drive as hard and fast as he can, not to escape, but to outrun what has happened. Bell has been so good to them for no reason at all, without any promise of reward. And now she is gone.

He drives to the Atlantic and stops in a sandy place on the side of the road where the White Street Pier points out into the ocean. The clouds are low and gray and mean-looking over the water and waves churn below in a deep grayish blue.

"What're we doing?" Justin says. "We can't stop here."

But Asher doesn't know where to go.

He thinks about going to the cemetery but that seems too close to home. They could take a tour out to the Dry Tortugas but they aren't dressed for a whole day out and he worries about the chance of being recognized by one of the locals working the boats.

Right now what he wants more than anything is the woods. He wants someplace that reminds him of Tennessee. Asher remembers the private beach where Evona took them but he can't risk trespassing and being approached by a security guard. The closest they are going to get to the woods on this island is at Zachary Taylor Beach, where a little grove of pine trees stands close to the ocean. Turtles nest on the beach, roped off by the game wardens for protection. The guards at the ticket booth see so many faces they must all run together. He needs the woods, and he convinces himself it will be safe. He needs the trees. So he points the little Vespa that way. Justin clutches his waist as Asher guns the gas again.

THERE ARE ONLY a handful of people there so early in the gray morning. Asher sits on a picnic table overlooking the confluence of the Gulf of Mexico and the Atlantic, trying to think what they might do next. He breathes in the scent of the pines, a balm. He feels like a sleepwalker, awake but not awake, caught beneath some veil that won't let him function properly. Justin walks down the beach, gathering shells and rocks for his nature collection.

Asher thinks and thinks and thinks, not figuring out anything, his mind going in circles. There is no way out of this. He is going to jail and he knows it. Justin will be sent back to Lydia. She'll put him on those pills and wipe that extra-goodness out of him and he'll be like everybody else in the whole boring cynical world, missing the wonder of everything.

Asher can't stand the thoughts, but there is no avoiding them.

But maybe Justin is stronger now.

Maybe this trip will have taught him something about defiance. About taking chances.

Eventually Justin comes back and slumps against Asher, drained from his grief. Asher puts his arm around his son's shoulder and the boy leans into him. Small, real, alive, here, now.

Cherish this, Asher thinks, and he does, he does, he does. He memorizes this moment as if it is his last. The feel of Justin's shoulder beneath his hand, the way his hair moves light as dandelion fluff in the breeze coming in off the mixture of the Gulf and the Atlantic. Asher draws in his son's scent. He catches the pines, and the salt air, seaweed and sand. But most of all there is Justin, that smell of his that is always there, unchanging since he was a baby. Warm, sweet, musky. The smell of Tennessee riverbanks and long summer evenings lying in a field, the scent of home.

Surely there is a light in that boy that will never go out, no matter what he has to face along the way. That's all a father can hope for his child, that a little fire will burn in them to keep them going, to keep them strong.

They stay there for hours. The sun comes out and with it the tourists. Beach towels are spread, flapping on the ocean breeze. Golden bodies lather themselves in oil, children laugh, gulls gather close to the foolish people who feed them Cheetos.

Asher rents them two chairs and an umbrella where they can doze, worn out from grief and fear. They awake and Asher buys thick Cuban sandwiches and thin fried plantains from the beach café. Asher wolfs down his food, wiping up sour cream with his last plantain but Justin simply stares at his sandwich.

"Eat, Justin. You'll be starving later."

"I can't," he says. He won't look at Asher and his eyes are hidden behind the big, cheap sunglasses Asher bought at the café to hide his face from anyone who might take note of them. "I can't just sit here and eat while she's *laying* there, *dead*."

"We have to keep living, buddy," Asher says.

"She was so good to me," Justin says, his voice breaking. "And to Shady. She always made a little extra bacon just for him."

"I know it. We were lucky to know her."

"We should be there with Evona," he says, turning to his father. Asher finds only himself reflected in the lenses of the sunglasses. "It's not right."

"Just a little while longer," Asher says.

Justin dabs one of the plantains into the sour cream and chews it without any kind of enjoyment. "I can't," he whispers, and spits the food out. "I feel like I'm gonna be sick."

After a while Justin falls asleep on his side with his hands folded beneath his cheek, his mouth open in mournful exhaustion.

Asher watches him. What a failure of a father he has become. He has reduced his child to hiding all day on a beach, sleeping in a plastic chair by the ocean, on the run. He has turned him into someone who can't even mourn a person he loves without being whisked away into hiding.

He is a coward for leaving Evona. He shouldn't have, even if she did insist. He has been a coward his entire life, always afraid to do the right thing. He will never forgive himself for leaving her, the same way he will never really get over knocking Zelda down, the way he can't get over not being brave enough to marry Jimmy and Stephen, the same way he'll never be able to take back the day he turned away Luke for being himself. Some things we can't take back, no matter how hard we wish.

23

The low growl of thunder wakes him and when his eyes come open he sees that Justin is curled up in his beach towel resting peacefully. All down the beach people are snatching up their towels and coolers and chairs while the wind plucks them back, carrying some of these things tumbling down the sand and into the water. The boy who rented the chairs and umbrella to them is trying to wrangle everything off the beach before the wind takes it all.

Greenish-black clouds hover low over the ocean, grumbling toward land. Lightning kicks around in the bottoms of the clouds.

"Hurry!" a woman cries out to her little boy, who is still in the water. She's holding a white safari hat to her head so it won't blow away and Asher is thinking *Let that go.*

The umbrella planted between Asher and Justin is rocking in the wind. A rainbow-flag beach towel blows past, settling on Justin's face for only the briefest second but long enough for him to rise up like he's coming from deep water, about to drown.

"What is it?" he hollers out just as the corner of the towel slips from his face and sails on down the beach, stretching its corners out like a magic carpet.

The umbrella rental boy runs to them. "Sorry, folks, but I have to get this stuff in." He has to holler over the wind. His white polo shirt works up his back in the wind. "Y'all should get off the beach."

Lightning zigzags down and touches its tips to the waves of the ocean, causing the last remaining people to get a move on. A couple women and kids let out little yips as they run past.

Asher hustles his chair back up to the stack to help out the rental boy, who's standing back on the beach, holding Justin's chair and watching as their umbrella sails away, bouncing once on the sand before hitting the water.

"Justin!" Asher yells over the thunder. The clouds have taken the sun so it's almost dark except for the glimmers of lightning. "Come on right now!"

The sky opens up just as they reach the Vespa and the rain falls in big cold blocks. Asher has felt rain like this only the day of the flood. Before they knew how high the water would rise, he had stood on the porch while bolts of lightning like these had split the sky in two purple halves. Asher fires the engine and puts the gas to the Vespa and they speed away, like a zipper being unzipped, through the black parking lot. Asher drives them through the rain, hunched over so he can see as the raindrops sting his face. Justin curls against his back.

He is wetter and colder (that rain came from some place not of this earth, some cold, high place) than he has ever been before, even during the flood. He can't stop thinking of Bell and how soon she will be lying under the wet ground in storms like this and the rain will pound on the dirt and seep down through the soil until it eats into her casket and fills her mouth and eyes with water and sand and rocks. He thinks of how only a couple days ago she was tapping away on her piano and making such pretty music. Justin hugs his father's back and Asher thinks his son might be crying a little while they ride along. He wishes he could, too. He needs to, but the tears won't come, even though this would be the perfect time, when nobody would be able to tell his crying from the rain on his face.

Asher is trying to get back to the cottage but the rain is falling too thin and hard, like needles into his eyeballs. Lightning crashes silver all around them. All he can see is the big old church up ahead of them on Duval, so he pulls in there and makes a run for the door, pulling Justin alongside him.

24

As soon as the doors close behind them the world quiets. Several people have taken refuge in the church, but they are all sitting still and silent in the pews, some of them with their heads bowed. Yellow lights dot the sanctuary in the dim gray of the afternoon but occasionally the big stained-glass windows are lit by lightning, showing off their bright colors: reds and blues and greens as rich as pieces of hard Christmas candy.

In one window Asher sees the Sermon on the Mount. Christ stands tall and straighter and brighter than anyone else, dressed in red while the others in the scene keep their eyes on Him. His favorite passage in the Bible, the passage that stayed true to him no matter how he believed.

There is a huge white shell offering holy water at the door. Since he has never been taught to use holy water or cross himself it is best to not do either. Bell once told him that what she loved most about the Episcopal Church in Key West was that everyone was welcome and that nobody *had* to do anything.

But they are soaked to the bone and Asher hates to get the wooden pews wet, so he and Justin stand in the foyer. Besides, Asher is embarrassed to be in a church wearing swimming trunks, a drenched tee shirt, and flip-flops. He has never felt so ridiculous or out of place. Asher riffles his hand through Justin's hair and uses the end of his drenched shirt to wipe at his son's face and get some of the water out of his eyes. Already a little puddle has formed on the tiled floor around Justin's feet and he is shivering.

A priest appears with a couple of towels. At least Asher figures he is a priest because of his white robe and the green sash draped around his neck. He offers the towels up on his palms like a little treasure.

"Thanks so much," Asher whispers, seeing how long the priest's eyes linger on his face. The man recognizes Asher; he is sure of it.

He nods, smiles down at Justin, then looks Asher in the eye again.

"The Holy Eucharist will be given at five-thirty," he says. He is probably in his early seventies but there is something youthful about him. No lines on his face at all, and a kind of boyishness in his eyes. "You're very welcome to stay with us."

Asher tries to help Justin get dried off but the boy pushes his hands aside. "I can do it," he says. "I'm not a baby."

They sit in the pews with the towels under their wet shorts. More people come down the aisle. One of the women bows to the altar before she slides into her pew. The man with her crosses himself before following her. Forehead, heart, left shoulder and then the right. Asher watches and a strange sort of envy warms his chest. Envy because these people are so certain in their way of worship. He isn't sure if he had ever truly been that way.

Outside, the storm is lifting. Weak light eases through the stained-glass windows and Asher can no longer hear the rain pounding on the roof.

Another man appears up front and sits at the organ where he plays "Wondrous Love," one of Asher's favorite songs. Sometimes after Sunday dinner Zelda had put it on her old record player. Asher can feel the vibrations of the organ in the wooden seat of the pew even though they are far in the back of the church, and this sensation is so large to him that he feels the music has become God and God has spread through every part of the church, even into the floor. When the choir rises—he hasn't even noticed them until they stand—to sing the words, Asher thinks he might not make it through the entire song without breaking down. Hearing the song makes him feel as if Zelda has walked into the room and is staring him down, reminding him of what he has done to get Justin away from her.

Asher realizes that everyone in the pews is standing and singing, too. When people lift their voices at the same time, when they join together to pray, God pauses. That's what Asher believes.

"What wondrous love is this, O my soul, o my soul," they sing.

Asher thinks about how thickly Bell had believed even when so many people were telling her there was no use, that no God believed in her.

Three priests or deacons—Asher doesn't know which—prepare the communion table with a red cloth and lots of gold. They have certainly never had any gold in the Cumberland Valley Church of Life. Asher isn't sure how he feels about that, but he likes the ceremony of it all, even though he has a hard time seeing everything from the back pew. He thinks one of the men looks a lot like the deacon who used to bring communion out to Bell's on Sunday evenings, but there is a long distance up to the sanctuary and he can't be sure.

Everyone in the church is still and silent and the air feels expectant.

Asher can think only of Bell. He recalls an early morning when he had swept her porch, collecting sand and dirt from the floorboards, moving it all into a neat little pile which he brushed up onto the dustpan and then sprinkled into the ambrosia at the corner of the steps.

The sounds of morning in Key West sounded like prayers. They especially had on that morning. Strange birds in the palm trees, singing high, sharp notes. The supping of the colored water against the sides of the pool. Asher had loved everything, even the sounds of bicycles rolling along the street, and the crow of a rooster hopping among the tombstones in the cemetery, or the purr of an airplane (a silver chip on the sky, catching sunlight) coming in, bringing new people, or one leaving, taking away the ones whose time on the island had come and gone.

That morning, Bell was playing "All Creatures of Our God and King."

She had left her front door wide open to let in the morning air, so he could see her at the piano, arching her shoulders into the music, head thrown back and eyes closed. Usually she only played but this morning she had sung: a big, solid voice like the resounding notes on an organ. Asher had moved his lips to the lyrics, audible only in his own mind:

Thou rising morn, in praise rejoice
Ye lights of evening, find a voice.
O praise Him! O praise Him!
Alleluia, alleluia

Asher thought *alleluia* the most beautiful word he had ever heard. Bell swayed her head back and forth, feeling Alleluia, savoring it. He had tasted Alleluia on the air that morning.

He wants more than anything to go forward and receive communion. It has been too long.

The row in front of them has already moved into the line.

Asher knows this is foolish of him, to tempt the priest that way, to stand in display of all these people, many of whom are most likely local. But he stands and motions for Justin to follow him. They wait in the line and watch what everyone else is doing because this is not how communion is done in their church at all.

They kneel at the rail and put out their hands like the others, keep their heads bowed. Asher realizes no one is looking at them; everyone is concentrating on the holy task at hand. Then the wafer is dissolving on his tongue

(*The body of Christ*, the priest says)

and Asher's lips are on the golden cup being held out to him

(*The cup of salvation*, a whisper, but something familiar about the voice)

and he is taking communion with his own child, a thousand miles from home, on the run, in hiding. He feels as if he is taking his first full breath in a long while.

When he has swallowed the wafer and the wine Asher looks up before moving out of the way for the next row of people to take their place at the communion rail. And there before him, the cup trembling in his hand, is his brother.

Luke.

ASHER STEPS AWAY from the rail and into the small room off the side of the sanctuary. He can't believe it as he watches Luke hand off the cup to another priest so he can rush out to them. He can't seem to catch his breath. Right here, all this time. Right under his nose, just waiting for him to find the church, the place he should have gone first. But Luke, a priest? He would have never thought *that*. Not that. Only when Justin hisses up at him "What is it?" does he realize he is standing there with both his hands over his mouth.

Then there is Luke with his white robe ballooning out around him because of his haste. As soon as Luke reaches him, he wraps Asher up in his arms. They are hugging and there are no words and although Asher always imagined that he would burst into tears upon finally seeing his brother again, he doesn't. He laughs in disbelief.

"Luke," he says, grinning. "Luke, Luke."

25

Darkness has taken up residence when they return. No flashing lights, no cops, nothing. They stop at the corner of Olivia and Elizabeth Streets and then ride the Vespa on up to the fence of Song to a Seagull, quiet. The tiny chatter of crickets—night sounds are so much smaller here than back home—and nothing else.

So they go on into the courtyard.

Every light in Bell's house is on, and Evona's half of their house is lit up, too. Shady trots out to them and jumps up, his front paws on Justin's chest.

"Oh God, where have you been?" Evona comes off the porch and throws her arms around Asher's neck.

"We stayed at the beach, then the church," Asher says. "I should've come back sooner. I didn't know what to do."

"It's alright," she says. "It's good you left. They were here for a couple of hours or more. Two cops, the coroner."

She motions for Justin to sit with her on the wicker love seat. Shady jumps up there with them and perches his head on Justin's lap. Evona keeps hold of Justin's hand. Asher can't stand to look at her cried-out face. He reaches out and strokes Shady's head and Shady licks at Asher's fingers, a bathing that says *I missed you, I love you, I'm so glad you're here.*

"What happened?"

"She had heart disease. She knew for a couple years, that she might not make it very long. I never thought she would go so soon. They had told her that if she ate right and took her medicine she'd be okay for a while." In the gray shadows he watches as she wipes at her face.

"Need me to check on the guests?" Asher asks.

"One set left. I guess it freaked them out. The other couple has been gone out on a boat all day. I think they went to the Dry Tortugas."

"They should be back soon, then. The boats dock at dark."

"She was all I had," Evona says abruptly, as if she has not meant to say that aloud.

Asher gives Justin the look that means for him to move over, so he hops down off the love seat and takes Shady with him down into the shadows of the yard, where they settle by the pool.

"I'm here," Asher tells her as he sits down next to her. He holds her against him and doesn't say anything else for a time.

Asher is thinking about where Bell's body is right this moment. He hopes she is not in some morgue with bright lights ticking above her. And what about Luke? Is he sitting in some small room—he doesn't even know where his brother lives despite the catching up they were able to do briefly in the church courtyard—studying about all of the years he lost with Asher and Justin? Is he thinking about how he doesn't know his nephew at all?

He can see Justin clearly in the light coming up from the pool, sitting on the edge with his feet in the water and Shady panting beside him. Every once in a while Shady quits breathing hard so he can lick at Justin's ear.

Asher listens to the little waves washing up against the edges of the pool. He looks over at Bell's house where all the lights have been left on. He knows Evona couldn't stand to look at the house with the windows all dark.

"There was something about you she took to right away," Evona says after a while. "Bell either loved people completely or she didn't like them at all. With you, it was on sight. That's worth something. To have someone like her give you their approval."

I reckon it is, Asher thinks.

26

The sky is the pink of grapefruit meat as they sit on the beach together, looking out at the Atlantic. Evenings in Key West are calm down here at Smathers, where the homeless folks gather at the turquoise picnic tables to eat and drink and tell big stories.

Asher and Luke sit just beyond the tables, on the cooling sand of the beach. Asher has slipped his feet out of his flip-flops and digs his heels into the sand but Luke's long toes are firmly planted in his leather sandals. He used to wear the same kind back in Cumberland Valley long before any other men would have even dreamed of wearing shoes that revealed their feet. Behind them the homeless men are quiet, playing a card game or eating Vienna sausages from little blue cans. There is nothing but the breeze in the palms and the lonesome cry of a gull that paces along the water's edge, looking out to sea.

Asher can't stop staring at his brother. He betrayed him, left him alone in the world all these years, but here he is. Here, alive, beautiful, the older brother who always watched over him until the day Asher turned him away. And ten years older. Lines on his face, a furrow across his brow. His hair is thinner and lighter, but his Luke-blue eyes are just the same.

He wants to touch his brother's face, even to reach out and hold his hand. Asher has wasted years and years. He has thrown away an entire decade he could have been with Luke, who always loved him for who he was. But Asher had not been able to do the same for him.

For years Asher has been practicing how he would apologize to Luke if he ever found him again, but so far his lips have not lit on the right words. Everything sounds like a cliché, or hollow.

"I wish I could take it back," he says.

The horizon has changed to the red of a geranium. Luke is watching the crimsoned waves and for a moment Asher thinks he is not going to respond. But then, he does. "Well, you can't," he says, and Asher feels like the breath has been knocked out of him by the anger that edges Luke's words. "You can't take back what you called me. And you can't take back just letting me go."

"I didn't know how to find you. I didn't even know where to start—"

Luke latches his eyes on Asher's and his gaze is hard. "Come on, now, Asher. Quit lying to yourself. You know good and well that you didn't even try."

"Not at first."

"Not for *months*," Luke says. "When I first left, I only went to Nashville. You didn't call my friends. You didn't search. And so after almost a year of living not even an hour from you and seeing that you weren't worried about me, I left Tennessee. I'd always wanted to, and you were the only thing holding me to home anyway."

"I didn't know what to say," Asher says, and he hears pleading in his own voice. "You were so mad when you left."

"You only had to say you were sorry."

"You were too stubborn for that," Asher says. "If I had found you, you would have never listened to me. Not after what I said. And I can't hardly blame you."

"But you shouldn't have stopped trying, Asher. You should have done whatever you could to make it right."

"I know," Asher says. "It took me years, but that's what I've tried to do. I've given up everything to stand up for you. My church. My marriage. Even my—"

Luke shakes his head. "Please don't sit here and tell me how much you've sacrificed for me. The good Christian laying down his life for his faggot brother."

"That's not what I mean."

"You rushed into that marriage just to please our mother. You convinced yourself that you and Lydia were the perfect couple but she always wanted something you didn't. I never much liked Lydia but I also knew it wasn't fair of you to marry her."

"Not fair of me?"

"The only thing you two ever had in common was church, man. You shouldn't have married her."

"Well, if I hadn't, I wouldn't have Justin. So I can't have any regrets about that."

They are silent for a time, listening to the small sound of the water washing up on the shore and the low talk of the men behind them. A man in denim cutoffs stumbles so close to them that he kicks sand up onto Asher's feet. He's humming as he goes along—it's "Blackbird," Asher realizes—his eyes fixed on the water.

There is a gale of laughter from the men behind them as the humming man wanders into their group and starts a drunken, barefooted tap dance to entertain them. He and Luke have brought a box of canned goods to the homeless people who gather under the shelter houses. Luke had set the box on one of the tables and walked away, not wanting to shame them or make them think he was there to convert them.

"For all you knew, I could've ended up like those men," Luke says. "I left with next to nothing. Two hundred dollars in my pocket. A gym bag of clothes and books."

"I worried about you, every day."

"I wish I could just get over it, but I can't, Asher. All those years of remembering how you acted that day. For you, all this time you've been changing and getting used to that, but for me, when I saw you yesterday, you were the same person I left ten years ago."

"I understand that," Asher says, and he does, although he has not thought of any of this until this moment.

"The funny thing is, I thought I had forgiven you a long time ago," Luke says. His face is bathed in the lavender-orange twilight. "All this time, I was congratulating myself on being such a big person that I could forgive you for turning your back on me. And now that I see you, I'm tempted to say that I did forgive you a long time ago. But the truth is that I haven't. I wish I had, but I haven't."

Asher remembers the faces of the congregation that day Jimmy and Stephen had come to church. That's who he had been, all those years ago.

"Still, I ought not have intentionally worried you. That was wrong, and I knew every single day that it was. I should have called and let you know I was alive instead of sending those postcards just to make you play a guessing game."

"Those postcards helped me change myself."

Luke has found a piece of green sea glass in the sand and now he is smoothing it between his thumb and forefinger, his eyes on the ocean.

"What have you done all this time?" Asher has a hundred questions, but they all sound generic.

"Living. Working," Luke shrugs. "Just like everybody else. When I left home"—Asher notices that Luke still refers to Tennessee as home—"I didn't have enough money to go far, so I wound up in Louisville. Thought there might be more open-minded people up there, at least, even if it was just three hours away. And there were. I got a job down on the docks, cleaning boats, and I started to think about what to do with my life besides just have a good time. Nothing ever did seem like enough for me."

Luke dancing in the kitchen. Luke reading down by the river, talking about far-off places.

"I remember," Asher says.

"And that led me to going to seminary. Just wanting to feel like there was something bigger than me. Just to prove to myself that the church we'd been raised up in wasn't the be-all and end-all of belief. Once I started taking those classes, I figured out who I really was."

"And who was that?"

"Somebody who loved the mystery of it all. Right out of seminary I got sent to a church in Grand Haven, Michigan—in wintertime it was the most lonesome place I've ever seen—and then there was an opening for an assistant rector here in Key West—"

"The place you always wanted to go," Asher says. He had never heard anybody from Tennessee utter the name of this place except for Luke.

"And a warm place after those winters up there. So I had to take it," Luke said. "Seemed too perfect."

"That's why I came here, when we ran off. Because you loved it. And because of the postcards."

"I guess I wanted to give you clues, in case you ever went looking for me."

"It worked."

The evening sky is purpling into darkness and all along the horizon the sun stretches out orange and rosy. So much to say, so hard to put it all into words.

"I've had a good life," Luke says. "Found somebody who loved me."

"I'd like to meet him," Asher offers, hoping he's ready to see his brother with a man, see Luke with his arm around someone, perhaps even kissing him.

"Found the church where I belong. The place I belong."

Asher wants to say so much. But there is time for that. He has nothing but time. "There wasn't a day I wasn't thinking of you, wishing I had had enough sense to handle it differently."

"I didn't run off to punish you. I left because you—all of you—made me feel ashamed. Do you know what it's like to walk through the world with everybody thinking they know everything about you?"

Asher wants to explain that he does, but he knows a viral video isn't the same.

"Back home people didn't *accept* me once they figured me out. They *tolerated* me. Even you. I wasn't about to live that way, as the town freak. But I probably wouldn't have found my way if you hadn't turned against me, Asher." Those words sting—*you turned against me.* "So it all worked out, I reckon."

"A priest," Asher says.

"You didn't see that one coming, did you?" Luke laughs.

"No, can't say that I did."

"I was told I was no good all my life," Luke says. His strength is magnificent to Asher in this moment. "You all wanted me to be somebody I wasn't."

"If I could change it I would—"

"But no matter how low I got, there was always this little fire burning in me," he says. "Sometimes it would be real small, but it stayed lit. I knew I was a child of God and nobody ever could put it out."

Asher moves to take his brother's hand but just as he does, Luke stands, dusts the sand from the back of his pants.

"I've missed you, Asher," he says. "Every day. But I just don't know." Luke can't seem to look at him. "I wish I could just forget it all, but I can't. Not yet."

"I want to make it right, Luke."

"I don't know, Asher. I know I'm supposed to be full of grace and all that. I preach that stuff all the time. But I'm not sure it's possible after all these years. And I don't know if you've changed as much as you think you have."

"All I can do is try," Asher says.

"But when you think about it, really think about it, can you accept it? Can you honestly say you don't believe that people like me are doomed to hell?"

"No," Asher says, loud, instant. "I do not believe that. Absolutely not."

Now Luke puts his eyes on Asher's. "Can you look at me and Sam and not think of us as different from any other couple?"

"All I can do is try my best, Luke. That's worth something, ain't it?"

"Yeah," Luke says, after a few seconds. "It is. But I don't know, Asher. I can't just flick a switch and make this alright for you."

And just like that, Luke turns and walks away, lifts his hand to the homeless men who call out to him as "Preacher!" Asher sits on the beach, not moving, until the island has surrendered to nighttime.

27

Dear Evona,

    I am hoping you will not grieve too much when I'm gone. You've had enough of that in your life.

You are the only family I have, as far as I'm concerned. My people back in Alabama might try to claim me now that I'm dead but Martha Campbell down on Truman has it all worked out for you. I've left it to you.

Have me cremated. It's already paid for. Spread most of my ashes here at Song to a Seagull, where I was as happy and free as a person can be in this life. I'd like for my pastor to say just a few words. Play a Joni song. Whichever one you want. My favorite scripture is Galatians 6:9 and it'd be nice to have that read.

But I'd like it if you could spread some of me back in Notasulga, too. They never did want me there when I was living but I always missed the place, if not the people. There is a little grove of catalpas near the water tower at Tallapoosa and Lyon Streets, where I used to be happy as a girl, and I'd like to settle there. I don't imagine too awful much has changed in Notasulga so I believe those old trees will still be standing. If not, I'll never know the difference. The thing is that I never have forgotten those catalpa trees and how cool the shade was there on the hottest days.

Thank you for everything,

Olivia Bell Williams

28

They play "Song to a Seagull" at the service. The sleeves of their shirts flap in a Gulf breeze that is moving over the island in waves. The palm leaves lift. The sky streaks lavender and red above their heads as twilight descends.

There are a dozen of them: Asher, Justin (Shady sits at his feet, watching the house like he expects Bell to come out the front door), Evona, the pastor, his wife, a handful of folks that Bell has known ever since she came to the island. Most of them hadn't seen her for years, back when she still went to the grocery store and to church. The last few years she had kept to herself more and more, mostly because she was sick, but also because she had tired of the world itself. She had cut herself off from the news or any kind of television. *The world is too much with us,* she'd told Asher the day she explained why she never left the house, never watched the evening news anymore.

The pastor looks different outside, in the sunlight, much younger. There is an elegant kindness about the way the pastor moves, and a kind of calmness about him. He wears a black cassock with a white frock, a white stole whose ends lift in the breeze, threatening to take flight. He holds the Book of Common Prayer out on his palm as if it is floating there.

Once the song ends the pastor clears his throat and reads Bell's favorite scripture.

After a brief silence, the pastor speaks again: "Everyone the Father gives to me will come to me; I will never turn away anyone who believes in me."

The pastor nods and Evona scoops her hand into the urn, gathering ashes, which look more like heavy sand. Asher has officiated at many funerals but nobody from his church had ever been cremated.

Bell had smelled of frangipani and had cooked big meals and played the piano but now she is ashes.

"In sure and certain hope of the resurrection to eternal life through our Lord Jesus Christ, we commend to Almighty God our sister Olivia Bell Williams," the pastor reads, his voice becoming more solid, more real, "and we commit her body to the elements; earth to earth, ashes to ashes, dust to dust."

Evona releases the ashes. They fall in a cloud around the frangipani tree.

"The Lord bless her and keep her, the Lord make His face to

shine upon her and be gracious to her, the Lord lift up His coun-
tenance upon her and give her peace."

Evona shakes the remaining ashes from the urn, moving backward around the tree. She has saved the Alabama ashes in a small
wooden box.

"Join me in the Lord's Prayer," the pastor says, and everyone
obeys, all of their voices lifting together. Although Asher's head is
bowed, he opens his eyes so he can look down at Justin. His son is
watching the sky, not joining in for the prayer, although he knows
it as well as Asher does.

"Grant eternal rest to her, O Lord; and let light perpetual
shine upon her. May her soul and the souls of all the departed,
through the mercy of God, rest in peace. Amen."

"Amen," they say in unison, and this time Asher can hear
Justin's small voice in the mix.

Asher and Evona have laid out a lunch on the tables by the
pool. They had moved around in Bell's kitchen together like parts
on the same machine. Silent while Justin sat at Bell's piano, figuring out how to play a Tom Petty song. He is picking it up on his
own and pecks on the keys every time they are at her house.

Asher has taken his chances in being part of the memorial
service but now he motions for Justin and they go back to the
house. It is too dangerous to be mixing and mingling with people
right now; anyone might recognize them after the cards and how
much they've been on the news lately. Asher stands in the shadows
of the porch for a time, watching the people eating and talking in
the yard, Evona seeing to all of them. Behind him, Shady is whin-
ing. When he turns back to Justin he finds that the boy is sitting

on the wicker rocker, clenching at his throat, trying to catch his breath. He can't breathe.

Asher rushes over to him and finds that Justin is covered in cold sweat; his dress shirt is soaking wet. All he knows to do is say his son's name over and over, but that doesn't change anything. Justin is struggling to talk and eventually Asher figures out that he is saying he can't breathe. Shady barks once, then whines some more, as if telling Asher he has to do something. Asher pulls Justin to him, holds on to him as tightly as he can and feels Justin's heart pounding against his chest.

Evona is beside him, grabbing hold of Justin's hand. "I think he's having an anxiety attack," she says. "Breathe really slow, Justin. Don't think about anything but your breathing, okay?"

"Just hold on, little man," Asher says, and the tighter he holds on to him, the calmer Justin becomes. A time passes and at last Justin has become completely still. Justin moves back into the wicker rocker, leaning over with his hands clutched before him.

"I need to talk to Granny," he says in a monotone, calm and measured. "I need to see her. And Mom. I need to see them."

"I wish you could, buddy," Asher says. "But that's not possible right now."

Justin doesn't argue. He goes into his room with Shady trotting along behind him, and by the time Asher has followed he finds that Justin has closed and locked his bedroom door.

29

The Everything

When the sun breaks through the clouds this morning Justin is already awake and outside with Shady leaning against his leg. He can reach down and fit his hand right atop the dog's head. Neither one of them has been able to sleep. Shady has been just as upset as Justin. Dogs know things. They know and know and know.

Every time Justin closed his eyes to find sleep he kept seeing Bell (in her muumuu strolling across the yard, in her rocker, at the piano, cooking at the stove, in her messy office, laughing, sitting with her feet in the pool, taking communion when they brought it from the church on Sunday evenings). And realizing that Bell was gone (forever) made him miss his grandmother and his mother in an aching way he had never felt before. Especially Granny. If he could just talk to her, he'd feel better.

A couple times his father had come to the door and twisted the knob, rapped his knuckles on the wood. "Justin? Answer me, I'm worried." The last time Justin had gone to the door and opened it wide enough to say that he was alright.

"Can't you sleep?" Asher asked.

"I was until you knocked," Justin lied.

After that, Shady wouldn't stop nudging at him with his cold, wet nose, like he wanted to go out.

So they had gone outside in the middle of the quiet night. They sat still on the porch while nothing moved about the island except the Everything.

At daybreak, the light was so orange and big that Justin expected a sound to come with it. He reckoned the waves must have shifted and shimmered, just to welcome it in. Then the glow grew to the full brightness of day like a little knob was being turned with careful ease to "on."

Then, the sounds of Key West:

Birds, mostly.

And those crazy-ass roosters. Crowing and picking through the dirt, roaming every whichaway, standing on top of the tombstones, clicking along on people's porches, perched on fence posts, fancying down the street like they own the place. Maybe they do.

Justin feels like all the world exists beneath a conch shell and the sky is the pink of its insides. He knows his father will be up soon. He has to get moving.

He wishes he could have Evona and Bell and his father and Uncle Luke and Granny and his mother, all right here together, and they'd get along and everything would be fine. The light here makes you better and the water makes you happy and all the birds singing and all the flowers blooming and the trees greening and the sky pinking in morning and purpling in the evenings—they all remind you every waking minute that you're living and breathing.

It's a Sunday morning so Uncle Luke is bound to be at the church. It's not far; just a few blocks. Every little house Justin passes is shut up tightly for the night. On one porch there are several beer bottles that have been left lined up on the banister. There is a single orange flip-flop lying in the middle of the street. A rooster is strutting along the sidewalk on the other side of the street like he's on his way to church, too. Shady darts across, pulling the leash tight and causing Justin to almost lose his balance. Shady gives a deep *whuff!* which causes the rooster to jump in the air a little before flapping its wings and charging toward Shady, who retreats.

There is something about the morning quiet that reminds Justin of the day before the flood, the day before it rained so much. He and Roscoe had risen early and gone down to the water's edge. Roscoe had jumped right in the Cumberland, holding his head high out of the water as his small legs dog-paddled around in a circle, showing off. Then he had gotten out and shook off, so hard that he couldn't hardly stop wiggling. There had been nothing but the sound of the river, the occasional song of a bird. The hills green and full of leaves. High summer. Then they had lain on the grass and watched the clouds, which were already turning green, a full day before the storms came. If he could have any day back, it'd be that one. The day before everything changed. But then again, he'd have never met Bell, or Evona, or even Shady.

He walks along with the leash in his hand and watches the sky for a time. The sun latches its heat to his face. But mostly he feels the cool air that is soothing itself over the island, moving in from the ocean in that last moment before the day will heat up.

There are lots of bright-red fire hydrants down the street and Shady has to pause to mark each one of them. He lifts his leg in the air, spurts out an arc of pee, a very serious look of concentration on his face.

At the corner of Olivia and Duval he isn't completely sure which way to turn but he takes a chance on it and goes right. For a long while he is passing stores and restaurants—all closed this early on a Sunday—and then when he gets to the fancier shops he can see the white tower of the church up ahead. A man on a scooter zips by, then a couple of women who have been laughing as they approach him stop and spend a long time loving on Shady, who eats it up. The women have on party clothes—shiny, short dresses and big heels.

One of the women is leaned over so that her titties are plainly visible. Lately he has started to think that titties are about the best things in the world so Justin can't help but stare at them jiggling there right in front of him. When the woman looks up from Shady she caps her hand over her cleavage, but a little smile plays on her face.

"What a sweet doggie," the other woman says. She's letting Shady lick her entire face. Justin starts to tell her that Shady sometimes eats his own poop but he doesn't. He doesn't want to say much so he can move on. He's got something important to do.

"Are you *from* here?" the woman with the pretty titties says to him.

"Yes," he lies. It's easy. "I have to go."

He pulls at Shady with the leash and they trudge away. He hates to be rude but he knows he doesn't have much time before his father finds him.

Before long there is the church, which seems very big when he stands on the sidewalk and arches his neck back to look at the white cross at the top of the tower. There's nobody about but there is a sign with small white letters:

ST. PAUL'S EPISCOPAL CHURCH WELCOMES YOU

SUNDAY

7:30 A.M. EUCHARIST I

9:30 A.M. EUCHARIST II W/CHOIR AND INCENSE

So Justin tries the door to see if it is already open. Sure enough, it is. Shady doesn't want to go in, but Justin tugs at his leash and he obeys, padding lightly on the tiles like he doesn't like the feel of them.

There are voices back beyond the communion rails, people from the church getting everything ready. Shady eases alongside him as they move their way up front.

"Justin?" Luke is moving toward him with his white robe billowing. "What are you doing here?"

Luke stands before him and the robe settles around his legs.

Luke glances down at Shady like he's not supposed to be inside the sanctuary but as far as Justin is concerned the dog has the right to be there as much as anybody. "I need to talk to my granny," Justin tells him. "And then I need you to take me back home. That way Dad can stay here with Evona, and he won't get caught."

30

rectangle of sunlight settles on Asher's eyes and causes him to awake. A rooster crows. These last few days have worn him out and he can't seem to get caught up on his sleep. This morning he awakes feeling less rested than when he lay down. Still, he can't go back to sleep.

Asher doesn't panic at first, when he finds Justin's bed empty. His stomach drops a bit when he doesn't find him on the porch. And he's not in the courtyard or the pool, either. By the time he rushes back to pound on Evona's door, terror is rising through his torso, the same as when Justin disappeared during the flood and then that first day in Key West, when he awoke exhausted on the beach and thought the boy had run off. But this time he knows that Justin has left intentionally, that Justin is headed back to Tennessee. He should've listened to him last night when he said he needed to see Zelda and Lydia. Did he find a bus leaving in the middle of the night? He could've pocketed a dollar here and there over the last few weeks, saving up. Who knows what a clever boy like Justin could do. Asher's mind feels cloudy but he knows he last checked on Justin around one-thirty. Almost six hours ago. Who knows how far he could have gotten by now. He could be anywhere.

Evona questions him, sleepy-eyed but completely awake, while they look everywhere, even inside Bell's house. They look under Bell's house, where Shady likes to hide out. But of course he is not there. He is not anywhere.

If he is gone, then Asher deserves it. This is how he made Lydia and Zelda feel, after all.

Time slows. Asher feels like he is moving underwater by the time he decides there is nothing else to do but get on the Vespa and go looking the streets for him. And just as he is taking off, there is Luke, and Shady and Justin.

Later, on the porch, while Justin is eating breakfast with Evona, Luke tells him what he already knows.

"This is no life for him, Asher. You have to take him back."

Asher nods. So weary that this one motion of his body wears him out.

"You're going to have to face up to what you've done, brother."

I know it, Asher thinks, but he can't make his mouth move to say the words.

"You did what you thought was right, to stay with him. But you just have to pay for your mistakes and go forward," Luke says. He puts his hand on Asher's shoulder and shakes him. "Hey. Are you alright?"

After a moment Asher nods. "It's just that I'm so tired."

"He is, too, Asher. He wanted me to take him back. Mostly he wanted me to find a way to get him back so you wouldn't have to go to Tennessee. He just wants to protect you. And I know this is the hardest thing you'll ever have to do in your life, but you'll have to go back and face the consequences. It's all you can do. I just don't see any other way around it."

"There's not," Asher says. "That's the only way."

He's so bone-tired. But at the same time, he will be okay. When Lydia had taken Justin from him, the boy had been all Asher had in the world. But now Asher also has his brother and Evona. Luke may not be able to forgive him yet, but he'll stand by him. And so will Evona.

Asher might go to prison for years. He might go for life. But he has to do what is best for his son. He has to go back.

31

L uke prays with Asher before they leave.
Asher feels an immense sorrow, as if the ocean is inside his body, pushing and pulsing to escape.

While Luke is praying, Asher is thinking about God and he is thinking about the God that lives in this place, right here on Bell's little patch of land, and in Evona, and in the palm trees and the ocean and the sand and the particular light that exists here, and nowhere else. He doesn't want to leave Key West the way he had once never wanted to leave Tennessee.

"Maybe it won't be so bad," Justin had said. "Maybe Mom will forgive you and move on. Maybe she won't even call the police."

But Asher knows that is not the way it will go.

"You could just let me out somewhere close to home, and then run off," Justin had said, trying to think of every option. "You can come right back to Key West and nobody will ever know the difference. When I get eighteen I can come see you."

"I can't do that, honey," Asher had told him. "I can't go that long without seeing you." What he had not said was that it was time to stop running.

"It'd be better than going to jail," Justin had tears in his eyes by then, trying his best to figure out a way to help his father.

"I have to go and make things right," Asher had said. "A man can't run from his troubles. Remember that."

Asher and Luke are knelt down across from each other but Luke has his big hand wrapped around the back of Asher's neck and even though Luke is praying Asher can't keep his mind on what he's saying. He is too busy trying to keep from falling apart at what is about to happen. He keeps his eyes shut so tight he can feel his eyelids trembling to stay closed. Luke's words circle round and round their heads and he pauses and they say "Amen" in unison.

Evona's been watching them because just when they finish she comes from her side of the porch and stands near the Jeep, which they've already loaded. She stands there looking at Asher.

Justin hesitates in the doorway but eventually comes down into the yard.

"You'll write to me, won't you?" Evona asks Justin.

He nods.

"And call me whenever you're able. Won't you?"

"Yep."

"What if they put him in prison, Evona?" he whispers, as if Asher isn't standing right there.

"They won't," she says, but she's not a good liar.

"Will you come see me? In Tennessee?"

"If there's any way in the world for me to be there, I will." Evona holds out her hand and there are two silver chains coiled all around two small medals just like the one Asher found in the guestroom. Instead of Saint Francis surrounded by animals, this one has a picture of a man with a child on his back. ST CHRISTOPHER PROTECT US in written around the edges in tiny letters.

Justin turns his back to her while she latches the chain round his neck.

"If anything bad happens," she says, looking at Asher while she fastens the necklace onto Justin, "if the cops pull y'all over or anything." She is measuring out her words to steady them. "You put your hands up and think about Saint Christopher. Alright?"

Evona leans down and kisses Justin's forehead. She draws in a big breath.

"Get on in there, buddy," Asher says, motioning for Justin to get into the Jeep. Luke helps him get settled into the back seat and lifts Shady up to join him. "Get ye seat belt on, buddy," Luke says.

And the rest of it happens very fast.

"I'll be right here," she says to Asher. That's all she needs to say. He doesn't want an extravagant goodbye. He can't stand it. But he kisses her, his lips against hers, a real love that he can't have, not now, maybe not ever. He feels the bones and muscles of her back beneath his hands, memorizing her.

Then Luke's up front, Asher's in the driver's seat, glancing back to make sure Justin has on his seat belt—an unbreakable habit—and Evona is rolling back the driveway gate and then they're pulling out onto Olivia Street.

"Olivia Bougainvillea Iguana," Justin whispers in the back seat, Asher hearing him clearly while he thinks

> *Good-bye Good-bye Good-bye*
> *Olivia Olivia Olivia*
> *Good-bye, sweet Evona, dearest dear*

and the tires are carrying them away. Asher watches through the rearview mirror as Justin turns in his seat to see Evona standing in the street, watching them, waving, waving and then Evona isn't waving anymore. She drops her arm and stands watching until she becomes so small Asher can't see her anymore although he is seeing her face in his mind and she is not crying, she just looks determined. She looks like she's saying a prayer with her determination and nothing else.

Asher turns left at the graveyard, then left again, and right, and right, and they're on Roosevelt and the ocean is on their right side. All those people out on the beach, setting up umbrellas and volleyball nets and spreading out their towels and blankets. And he loves every one of them.

Good-bye Key West, goodbye.

PART FOUR

The Last Days

1

U p through the South in the dying breaths of summer.
Justin and Shady in the back seat. At least Luke
is with Asher now. Helping him drive. Helping him
to do this hardest thing of his life. And for miles and miles and
miles there are:

Cotton fields.

Soybean fields.

Tobacco fields.

Cornfields.

On the radio: country music (steel guitars, cheaters, drinkers)
and Holiness preachers (the blood of *Jay-sus*! Rapture! Abomination!).

Gas stations. Trucks stops. Cinder-block restaurants.

Thousands of churches.

A legion of church signs:

YOU THINK IT'S HOT OUT HERE? HELL WILL BE WORSE
READ THE BIBLE. IT WILL SCARE THE HELL OUT OF YOU
GAY IS NOT OKAY

Dogs in yards, on porches, on chains, running free near the side of the road.

Tractors crossing wide pastures.

Eighteen-wheelers and police cruisers and school buses.

Evona has given them some Joni Mitchell CDs but Asher can't stand to listen to them. They remind him too much of Bell, and of Key West, period.

Oh, Florida.

They drive all the way to Valdosta. Nine hours split between Asher and Luke. They collapse into the scratchy sheets of motel beds near the interstate, exhausted from driving, from grief, from fear.

Georgia.

And finally, Tennessee.

Bugs stick on the windshield. The wind whips in when Asher takes off the top. Luke sings along to Peter Paul and Mary's "Early in the Morning." Justin watches the trees, his eyes glazed over with sadness so that Asher can almost read his mind. Shady sits in the back seat, watching the road with his whitish-blue eyes, so good, such a peaceful presence traveling with them, like God resting his hand over their Jeep as they head into the unknown.

2

PUMFPH TA-THUMPH go the tires and they cross the bridge over the Cumberland River and they are back home again, just like that. The trees, bushy and dark green, lean in on either side of the road with their big old limbs. Asher has missed the trees most of all.

All at once he's shaking so hard he can't drive anymore and he pulls to the gravelly shoulder so he and Luke can switch seats. He looks down at his hands, which are trembling.

"Let's go back, right now," Justin says.

Asher fastens his seat belt and looks straight ahead as Luke pulls back onto the highway.

"Please don't do this!" Justin cries out, as if he has been wanting to say this all the way across Florida and Georgia and Tennessee. "You should've let Uncle Luke bring me back. They would
have never found you."

"It wouldn't work that way—"

"He could have just dropped me off at Granny's and driven
away and they would've never found you!" He is yelling to keep
from crying. "They would've never known."

"I have to own up to this, Justin," Asher says, turning to face
him. "I was wrong—"

"But she was, too. Why won't she get punished?"

"That's just not how it works," he says, feeling numb, feeling
as if he isn't in his own body. "She went by the books—"

"That's bullshit!" Justin cries out, causing Luke to look back
at him as if he might chastise the boy, but he doesn't. "Please go
back."

"Hush now," Asher says, twisted around in his seat so that
his seat belt is strangling at his neck. He puts his hand on top of
Justin's. "We're going to be okay. I promise you."

Luke doesn't say a word. He keeps his shoulders square and
drives. There has always been something about Luke that has
made Asher feel safe. Asher knows how hard this must be for him,
to come back after all these years of exile. Luke is holding on to
the gearshift and Asher caps his hand over his brother's.

They have been gone almost three months but it feels like
ages, like everything has changed, even though every single thing
is exactly the same. They pass the Dollar General where the parking lot is always full, and the Cumberland Valley Church of Life

with its short white steeple and blue door. A yellow sign sits on cinder blocks out front. The smaller letters at the bottom used to spell out ASHER SHARP, PASTOR but they have been replaced with the name Caleb Carey. The sign's message today is REPENT SINNER FOR LO THE LAST DAYS ARE NIGH.

They pass pastures and hills and little groves of oak trees where Asher knows the shade is the best kind of sweet-smelling cool. Cows stand in ponds with still, brown water.

There are old farmhouses and new brick houses and trailers with no underpinning. A woman hanging clothes out on the line, her skirt flapping around her legs. An old man picking tomatoes and holding them in a line on his other arm against his chest. An old woman sweeping her front porch, which is covered in that scratchy green indoor-outdoor carpet. Asher will remember all of this.

They pass people on the side of the road selling green beans and jars of honey and collards from the tailgates of their pickups or on folding tables. One woman has laid out a bunch of clothes to sell right on the shoulder of the road. She's sitting in the shade in a pink plastic chair, smoking a cigarette and staring with menace at every passing car.

Always there is the Cumberland River alongside the road, twisting and curving along with them. Asher recalls a time that he and Justin were walking along the river in the cool of the day and they saw a huge, straight beam of golden light falling from the trees and onto the water. Justin had asked him why the air always felt so much better down by the river. Asher had told him it was because of how the light filtered through the leaves and because water made everything better. "That's why people always go to it, any chance they get," he had said. He would give anything to have that day back.

"Why don't you just let me out up here at the store?" Justin asks, one more desperate attempt. Already Asher can see the tall sign, HOSKINS' GROCERY, above the trees, even though the building is still out of sight. "Cherry will probably be working," Justin says. "She'll watch me until Granny comes."

Luke and Asher keep their eyes on the road and don't reply, as if they haven't even heard him. Asher can't bear to speak. Not right now. Luke has left the radio on low and Asher can just barely hear Jason Isbell singing about not chopping wood. Shady eases up between the seats and puts his wet nose against Asher's hand like he's reminding him he's there.

Luke drives on by Hoskins' Grocery and Asher watches it go past, just a little rectangle made out of concrete blocks with a row of red buggies out front, a woman carrying her baby on her hip as she comes out the sliding glass doors, and it's just a flash but he is sure he sees Cherry and Kathi standing at the side door by the stockroom, smoking cigarettes.

There's a stoplight just past the grocery where they can go straight on into Ashland City or turn left and go back out into the country where Zelda lives. Luke slows and gets in the turning lane but they're stopped right beside a long golden Cadillac with two old women with wigged-up hair, sitting there jawing away. They are the kinds of old ladies who still go to the beauty salon once a week to get their hair done.

Then one of the ladies looks over. Asher sees the moment

on her face when she recognizes the Jeep. Asher knows that old women like this watch the news *all* the time. She leans against the window so she can see better, peering over her eyeglasses. Asher can tell when she recognizes him and she's hollering to her friend and searching all about for something, probably her cell phone. The old lady driving gets so excited she runs the red light.

"She's recognized you, Asher," Luke says, just like he's saying *It sure is a nice day today.*

"Don't matter now," Asher says. He sounds like a version of himself, like somebody else playing him in a movie.

Then they are in woods again and the trees are close, hunching down over the Jeep as they pass underneath. Shady is cocking his head to the side the way he does when he hears something far off in the distance before anyone else does. There's a hush, too. Even the radio seems to be going quieter.

The car sails down into the rolling hills and the Cumberland is so close he can smell the mossy logs and the old ferns on its banks. Asher is still holding his brother's hand.

Suddenly he realizes that Justin has unlatched his seat belt and is slipping between the seats so he can latch his arms around Asher's shoulders, his wet face pressed against his father's neck.

3

J ust before they reach Zelda's, Luke pulls over on the shoulder of the road in a thick shade of tulip poplars. He turns off the engine and they sit there in a world made of birdcall. Justin's holding on to Asher tight, his little arms squeezing around Asher's neck, his warm breathing right in the nape of his father's neck, not moving, not saying anything.

I can't do this, Asher thinks. *I can't.*

But he knows that he must. He has to. Justin didn't ask to be born into any of this mess, yet they've put him here.

Heat gathers in the cab of the Jeep even though they're sitting in a deep green shade. The birds are incredibly loud. Ironweed and goldenrod grow in clumps all down the side of the road, barely moving in the heat, their purple and yellow blossoms shining like lights.

Asher knows the police cruisers will be there any time now.

"Go on to Zelda's," he tells Luke. He doesn't say out loud that he doesn't want Justin to see him get arrested, but Luke knows.

Asher holds on to Justin as they drive down the hill. They pass over the crackling gravel to Zelda's house and Asher feels he is leaving his own body. He feels that he can look down and see his son, the most important thing that ever happened to him. He is looking down and telling him goodbye.

The long lace of the willow tree rests on the windshield—*shush,* it goes against the glass—and then Luke turns off the ignition and they sit there with the engine clicking and the breeze moving into the cab of the Jeep while Justin remains latched on.

Asher hears a redbird calling: *birdie birdie birdie.*

Asher climbs out and the boy scrambles out from behind the seat to stand close to him. Asher squats down there beside the Jeep beneath the shade of the willow tree with Zelda's house on the other side of the vehicle. He knows she'll be out soon. Soon as she sees Asher's Jeep she will rush out to get Justin, even if she fears Asher now, although he doesn't think she ever would. And any minute those police cruisers will be here. He can't let Justin see that. He has to hurry.

Asher takes hold of Justin's shoulders.

"It might not be as bad as we think, buddy," Asher says.

"I'll talk her out of charging you. She won't do it if I ask her to. I know she won't." His words are rat-a-tat-tat, the tears streaming down his face from his red eyes. "They can't do anything to you if she doesn't want them to."

Asher isn't so sure about that. He figures the state will do its own thing, no matter what. Maybe even the feds, for all he knows. Right now Asher has to tell his boy goodbye in case it's a long, long time before he lays eyes on him again.

"No matter what happens, don't ever hate. You hear me?" Asher says. "No matter what?"

Justin nods, hard. He's so little, too little for nine, too little for how big that mind is. Justin wears his bright orange *Key West* tee shirt he had insisted on buying, which makes him look even smaller since it's too big. Asher feels that sense of peace and goodness that radiates from him. He's like a balm.

"And always believe. Try your best to not lose that."

Asher is barely conscious of Luke standing near them. He may or may not be telling Asher that they have to go. Asher may or may not hear sirens in the distance. He can't be sure. He's outside himself.

He holds his son one moment longer, kisses his forehead. He knows that he has to go, right now. Over and over in his mind he tells Justin how much he loves him and he knows his son can hear him.

"Go on," Asher yells to him, pushing him toward Zelda's porch, and he jumps back into the Jeep, and then they are bumping back up the driveway in reverse. He watches as Zelda runs from the porch and collapses over Justin, covering him up in her body, kissing the top of his head.

The sirens.

Zelda takes Justin's arm and is trying to pull him into the house but he won't budge. He's trying to run toward the Jeep. She knows what's going to happen and she doesn't want him to see, either, so she grabs him up and although he is kicking and screaming in her arms like a catfish on the hook, she holds on. Good old Zelda. Asher knows Justin will be safe as long as she is in this world.

Thank you thank you thank you, he says to her in his mind.

And then Luke is jerked out of the driver's side first and then their hands are on Asher, two big old troopers at the same time, right there at the top of the driveway where the gravel meets the highway. They throw Asher to the ground, in the grass near the drive. He breathes in its green scent—*Tennessee*—and feels the sun on the back of his head and he is vaguely aware of a silver pain in his spine as the cop's knee digs into his back while he latches the cuffs too tightly around Asher's wrists. People are hollering: *He's unarmed. We got him!* And walkie-talkies are crackling and somewhere far off he can hear someone hollering his name.

Asher closes his eyes and all he can say is what saved him over and over all these years. "Justin," he says.

Epilogue: The Everything

Justin spends most of his time down here by the Cumberland River. It's the only place he can think straight, seems like. He lies back and watches the light coming through the lime-green leaves. He listens to the birds. Watches the water. Shady is always right beside him.

Sometimes he hears something scampering through the leaves and brush and he thinks it might be Roscoe coming back to him after all this time. Any day now he might dart out of those woods like nothing ever happened and they'll pick right back up where they left off the way Asher and Luke were able to do.

You never know. It might happen. Anything's possible.

When they lived in Key West Justin thought the Everything lived in the ocean. Sometimes he thought the ocean *was* God. But if the Everything lives anywhere, it's in a river. Because the river moves along and touches every little thing on its way. And he thinks the Everything would be quiet like a river. Even still sometimes. The ocean is always moving and noisy. The sky's always changing. But rivers are always there, even when the water has moved on. You've got to find the Everything wherever you are. That's what Justin believes. And that's why God is the Everything, because there is God in oceans and rivers and dogs and little boys. In Evonas and Lydias and Bells and Ashers and Lukes. In iguanas and frangipani and bougainvillea.

Justin writes things like this in his letters and postcards and emails to Evona and she doesn't seem to think he's crazy. He still hasn't said this sort of thing out loud, but if he ever sees her in person again, he'll be able to. Because she's read the words written down, and she keeps talking to him. She even says that she thinks he's right most of the time. When he calls her from his grandmother's house they don't talk about that kind of stuff. But maybe someday they will.

He might even try to say some of those things to his mother sometime. Maybe not the God stuff. She'd never get that. But the weird stuff he thinks sometimes, maybe that. She's getting better.

When his mother first saw him she wept like he had never seen her cry before and said she thought she had lost him forever. She's different now. Not all the way there, but changing, rolling along. Partly because she thought she lost him but also because his grandmother doesn't take her shit anymore. She stands up to his mother now. That's what Lydia needs, someone to look her in the eye and say, *That's enough now*. That's what his father did, he sees now, with the church, and with her. And that's what his grandmother has done now, too. All of this could have been different if both of his parents had taken a breath. That's what he does when he gets upset.

They're not going to keep his father in there forever. He knows this. His grandmother won't let that happen. And Evona says she will do everything in her power to get him out of there. Even his mother has said she will go testify for him, if that's what Justin wants. *Yes yes yes*, he says. *You have to*.

One night she came in and sat on the edge of his bed. Shady raised his head and perked his ears at her, thumped his tail against the mattress a couple times. She sat there without saying a word, her back to Justin, her eyes on his open window, but he felt like by being there she was telling him that she knew it wasn't all his father's fault, that she had had plenty to do with it, too, and that she was sorry, and that she hoped he could forgive her someday.

Forgiveness is the easiest thing in the world, Justin thinks. All you do is just decide to do it, and then it's done. Instantly you feel better, like pushing aside a quilt that is too heavy for sleeping. Forgetting is the hard part.

The thing Justin can never say to anybody is that he's glad it all happened the way it did. Otherwise he'd never have known Evona and Bell. He wouldn't have Shady. He'd never have known Key West and all of its special sounds and smells. His father would've never found his Uncle Luke. He never would have seen Olivia Street and the frangipani tree in Bell's courtyard. He would have never laid eyes on an iguana or a bougainvillea.

He still says those words in his head when he gets scared or sad or when he starts to think his father might never get out of that jail. *Olivia, bougainvillea, iguana.* He always says each of them three times and then he's calmed down:

Olivia Bougainvillea Iguana
Olivia Bougainvillea Iguana
Olivia Bougainvillea Iguana

That's how he prays.

ACKNOWLEDGMENTS

ON PAGE 59, the line "Sometimes the hurt is so deep deep deep" that Asher finds on the postcard is from the Patty Griffin song "Rain," which appears on the 2002 album *100 Kisses*.

On page 242, Bell says, "Everything that is, is holy," which is a phrase popularized by Thomas Merton and coined by James Agee, who was inspired by William Blake's adage that "everything that lives is holy."

On page 303, Bell borrows a line from the same-titled William Wordsworth sonnet when she says, "The world is too much with us."

I am thankful to early readers Alice Hale Adams, Kevin Gardner, Amy Greene, Karen Salyer McElmurray, Jennifer Reynolds, and Aimee Zaring. Kathi Whitley was a guiding force throughout the writing of this novel. This book could not have been written without Annie Dillard and Bob Richardson, who helped me to understand the spirit of Key West and connected me with the generosity of the Studios of Key West. I cannot thank Lee Smith enough, for everything. Michael Croley offered advice and support for which I am grateful. My thanks for research help goes to my dear friends Donavan Cain, Carla Gover, Donna Birney, and Martha Copeland. I am indebted to the kindness and artistry of Jim James and My Morning Jacket.

I could not keep writing without the support of all the independent booksellers, librarians, teachers, and readers who have been so good to me through the years. I appreciate the support of friends and colleagues within Berea College and Spalding University's MFA program. My agent, Joy Harris, believed in this book from the beginning and stuck by me all the way. Thanks to Adam Reed for his great work. The wonderful editing of Kathy Pories made this book shine; I am indebted to her and the hardworking team at Algonquin Books.

This book stands in memory of all the good dogs I have known, particularly Rufus. It would not exist without my family, both blood and chosen; you know who you are. Endless gratitude to my daughters, Olivia and Cheyenne, who taught me how to write this novel by teaching me how to be a father. Jason, every word is for you.